the pied piper's
poison

CHRISTOPHER WALLACE

the pied piper's
poison

Flamingo
An Imprint of HarperCollins*Publishers*

Flamingo
An Imprint of HarperCollins*Publishers*
77–85 Fulham Palace Road,
Hammersmith, London W6 8JB

Published by Flamingo 1998
3 5 7 9 8 6 4 2

A catalogue record for this book is
available from the British Library

ISBN 0 00 225627 4

Set in Sabon by
Rowland Phototypesetting Ltd,
Bury St Edmunds, Suffolk

Printed in England by Clays Ltd, St Ives plc

For everyone and Elvis

I HAVE NO choice but to return to those eyes watching me. Eyes that should have been on the road ahead but instead were fixed on the rear-view mirror as I sat in the back of the Soviet automobile concentrating equally hard, trying not to betray my growing unease. What a pair we must have made – fearful passenger and mute driver, travelling east towards the Tatras mountains of southern Poland, a journey which then seemed as if it would last forever though now long frozen in the time of its passing, the winter of 1946. Yes, we were truly an inseparable couple, bonded together as prisoner and jailer that afternoon, only now it seems so much less clear as to who was who. A cold afternoon, ominously darkening as evening approached, as cold as I had ever known. Those eyes were never off me even though the road ahead was treacherous and full of pot-holes. I pull up the collar of my army greatcoat and try to wrap it around my head to protect my freezing ears. But the garment is not up to the task, obviously fashioned to combat the gentler chill of a British winter rather than this uncivilised freeze. The collar folds like wet cardboard, chafing the back of my raw neck, the coat having all the warmth of a thin school blazer.

Another field goes by, the flatlands endless. Ragged women and children scrape bare-handed at the silvery frozen soil. I focus momentarily on a cart bearing a few tiny potatoes. Is this the time to plant? I realise with a shock that this is their pathetic harvest, turning away once I realise I am being watched again – my driver's fascination has not waned. Is it because I am as strange and alien to him as this terrain and surroundings are to me? Is he wondering if I have money, a concealed weapon? Perhaps his Red Army commander has warned him to look out for any sudden moves by his charge?

None of these. It was only much later I would realise the reason for his interest. He was fascinated by me, yes; but not because of any innate quality *I* might have. It was because he knew what I was being taken to see.

Would it be so inappropriate to talk of this? It would certainly not be what was expected. What does one normally hear at these occasions, where should one begin? With thanks, I suppose, gratitude to those colleagues whose support I am meant to have enjoyed through the years. Or perhaps an attempt at humour, to put the audience at ease; a medical school jape involving a display skeleton and a frightened caretaker, way back in the Thirties when it was all somehow less serious? Perhaps not. If I were to speak of the real starting point it would have to be the eyes, staring back at me in silence, squinting into the rear-view mirror, mile after mile. Not what they're expecting to hear, no; I've never spoken to anyone about those eyes. Dark eyes, slightly slanted, almost Chinese, Slavic eyes tucked under a flat forehead, as new to me then as I was to them, the world between us.

I stare at the page. How long am I expected to last, twenty minutes? I suppose it must be up to me. When would they start to shift uncomfortably, playing with the gift set, the engraved watch and all, anxiously craving for the old bugger to finish? There have been enough hints about what is required, not that I need them. I've had to sit through enough of these things myself, nobody likes them. Still, they need to be done, and I should keep mine short. Witty but humble. Warm farewell and best wishes for the future to all at the practice. And once that's been safely negotiated there's the photographs – me with the other doctors, with the nurse and receptionists, and then with my wife and daughter. My son won't be there of course, 'too busy', too involved in something more interesting. I expect his wife will send a card or telegram; she's good at that sort of thing. Imagine – twenty-nine years old and already 'too busy'. He's impressive, Stephen. Up-front, a thruster, and with a definite presence about him. I often wonder if he's ever had a moment of real doubt in his whole life. Not that there's anything wrong in that; that's what all the school fees were about, and the holidays, and the love his mother invested in him. All of it so that he could be as he is. So why do I feel so bitter, so jealous when I think of him now? Why would the speech I *want* to give be directed at those who will not be there?

I've given up fighting off the memories of the past, it's just been impossible to stop it crashing back into my life. Somehow events have conspired to revive the nightmares, an orchestrated campaign of coincidence.

An elderly patient sits before me in surgery. A quiet, unassuming man, embarrassed to be there, dragged in by a shrewish wife. I feign interest in the mumbled symptoms. Breathlessness? Anxiety? How long's it been going on for? Months? Is there anything else bothering you? He is still for a moment and then begins to unbutton his shirt. The vest is pulled up; underneath, an angry rash, a raw and scarlet attack on his pale skin. And this? How recent is this? Ever had anything like it before? You were in the war, weren't you? He nods. Paratrooper, seen action in the desert and Normandy. And you've been thinking about it recently, haven't you? Getting scared on the back of old memories, dreaming about it all, remembering those who died, and it's almost as if it's happening again, isn't it? The head stoops slightly, yes, how did you know, am I going mad, doctor? I roll up my sleeve. There, at the top of my left arm, the same colours, the same eczema. Snap. No more mad than me.

Arthur Lee's manuscript arrived out of the blue seven months ago. His brother had died and when they looked through Arthur's original papers they found my name for some reason. It took several weeks' contemplation – or do I mean hesitation – before I could bring myself to look at it, let alone start reading its yellowing pages. I thought back to those nights when I would watch him toil with it, seeing him grow progressively shaky as it drained him of energy, wondering why he would persevere when the effort obviously agonised him. He was convinced, of course, that amongst the ruin he'd found the truth, that something

4

positive could be gleaned from it all. Perhaps that's why he was so wretchedly protective of it, frantically covering up all his notes, locking the case away each night. Another of his eccentricities? No, having at last read it I can tell you all it is a fine work, every bit as haunting as the memories its sudden reappearance inspired, and I shall quote freely from it in the course of my speech. The method in his madness is at last apparent. The tragedy of Arthur Lee is our tragedy.

So please forgive me, ladies and gentlemen, if I spend longer than might have been anticipated, and if the content of my address is perhaps more sombre than one would normally encounter at such an occasion.

You see, I cannot talk of my 'career' in medicine because I am, and always have been, a fraud. I cannot heal. I have never been allowed to. Now I have to tell why.

Perhaps it might be appropriate to spend a little time detailing the background to the journey we begin with. What was going on in the mind of that nervous, self-conscious young man then under such unyielding scrutiny?

I was twenty-four.

A qualified doctor for less than a year, I had barely seen out my first six months of army service. It might seem a relatively mature age by today's standards but please try to imagine how innocent and green I would have been then, plucked from a comfortable childhood – yes, childhood – in the tranquillity of Helensburgh on the outskirts of Glasgow, to be sent on a mission to mop up one of the war's more unsavoury legacies. A virgin, ladies and gentlemen, in every sense.

When I travelled out to join A-M-U-4 – Army Medical

Expeditionary Unit 4 – it was the first time I had ever been overseas. I had never met an American before Vesey, the Unit's chief, held out his hand and welcomed me aboard with some inane platitudes in what seemed an absurdly deep voice – a parody, surely, of the stereotype I would have expected from the cinema? No, he was for real. And when I was billeted with Arthur Lee it would be the first time I had shared a bedroom, my initiation made all the more alarming when he sobbed himself, conspicuously, to sleep on that and every other night that followed. Having to pass judgement on the wretched creatures brought before me in the Berlin camps that winter was the first time my opinion had ever mattered to anyone other than myself, let alone been the basis of a life or death pronouncement; here was a sudden and near fatal overdose of responsibility.

An innocent, then. I was too naive to question why one so lacking in experience should have been selected for a unit especially formed, according to Vesey, to deal with 'delicate matters'. Anxious, for some preposterous reason, to create a favourable impression – serious, capable, I even saluted Vesey at the end of that first meeting, the only time I would ever make him feel awkward. He looked up from his desk, startled and irritated. '. . . There's ah . . . no need for all that . . .' he murmured, returning to the mound of files in front of him.

The unit was based in Berlin, or the point on the map where the once great city had stood before every brick and stone had been pulverised to dust. The fresh golden timber of the camp huts in which we sat stuck out in the grey land-scape like saplings bursting through a ground floor of ancient lava, lava that covered over a thousand terrible secrets.

The ruins of the Reich's capital had become a staging post for a great tide of migration that followed the end of the war, mostly Germans moving west from the Soviet-held east. Our work, Vesey explained, would be centred on these people, assessing them, ensuring they were fit to travel and, more importantly, screening them for any contagion which they might carry with them on their travels. It was sensitive work, he said; these people had been through a lot and their tolerance levels were low. I thought I was following his brief and that he was referring to their general resistance to disease and infection. However, as he continued I realised with a quiet jolt that he was talking of crowd control. The numbers travelling were now huge, and threatened to overwhelm the support services. Panic was liable to break out if the refugees thought they were to be denied access to their dream in the west. Already there had been a few 'regrettable' incidents at the Soviet-run refugee camps to the south-east of the city; a repetition in the American or British sectors would be both tragic *and* politically embarrassing. Did I understand?

He seemed to assume that I would, not even glancing up at my vigorously nodding head. '. . . And the *Russians*. Well . . .'

This time he did face me, rolling his eyes in mock panic, drawing a deep breath. Vesey was a large man, in his early forties, almost as broad as he was tall, his physical presence imposing. His voice sounded as if it had a Southern twang to it, and I imagined he must be a Texan, a country boy reared on a rich diet of beefsteaks, corn and buttermilk. I turned out to be wrong. He would later tell me, over a midnight whisky and with an illogical pride, just how hard his upbringing had been, in a steel-town, somewhere north, near Chicago. He was now nodding at me, I didn't have a clue what he was getting at.

'The Russians are suspicious about everything, and everything we do. So let's not give them anything to be suspicious about. Agreed?'

I agreed, still bewildered.

'Thanks, Rob. I knew you'd understand. Now, you're a young man, I know you'll want to get out and explore, and . . . heh heh . . . have your fun . . . heh heh . . .'. As he laughed I noticed his teeth, small for such a face but perfectly even. '. . . But I'm afraid all that will have to wait for later. From now on I want you to confine yourself to this base in the evenings and to make your way straight back if you're ever out at another camp. They watch everything. You might also keep an eye out for any situation where you might be . . . vulnerable . . . and remember to watch who you get friendly with. These are interesting times . . . Okay?'

He was smiling at me, his naturally tight and aggressive face trying to look amicable. Behind him, incongruously, in this barren wooden shed, hung an American flag, like a prop from a stage set.

'So where you from, Rob, Scotland?'

This was the second time he had called me Rob. I wondered whether to correct him. Was that what he had on the form or was this a friendly abbreviation?

'Yes. Helensburgh. On the west coast.'

'And that's where you did your medical training?'

'Well, Glasgow University; originally chemistry but I switched to medicine when the war broke out. They had an accelerated course . . .'

8

He cut me short. 'Best doctors in the world, Scots. Apart from American ones.'

The smile at his own joke waned as he studied the form now in his hand.

'Ever been a Communist, member of the Communist Party, or any group having associations with Communists?'

The notion made me start. Communism hadn't reached Helensburgh, the only association I'd ever been in was the Boys' Brigade – was that on his form?

'No.'

'I know you haven't, Rob. It says here on this damn paper that I've got to ask.'

Another unconvincing smile. 'And you speak German. It's just great to have you with us, sure could do with your help, but remember what I said. Hut 107.'

'Sorry?'

I was puzzled by his last remark. I had not studied German for nearly ten years – where did he get his information from? Again I held back the urge to correct him, somehow not wanting to disappoint.

'You're in Hut 107. Why don't you go get settled and we'll take it from there.'

It was then that I saluted, in between gathering up kitbag, coat and freshly-stamped papers, and tumbled out of the room with all the poise of a harassed schoolboy, already late for his next lesson.

It would take daylight to reveal how much of a prison my new surroundings really were. The base was in the Gershalt district, in what was to become East Berlin. The Russians had already laid claim to the area, but provision had been made for an Allied medical team to be stationed there because of its proximity to the nearby transit camps. Vesey was right, the Russians were suspicious of everything we did, and had erected a daunting perimeter fence around the compound, ostensibly to 'protect' us. For the next six months, I was to feel as securely in quarantine as my new charges.

Daylight, however, was still twelve hours away when I made my clumsy exit from Vesey's administrative cabin in search of Hut 107. A frustrating search lay ahead; the huts were numbered in the order they were erected, not by location. Not all huts were for accommodation, some had been supply holds which had been lifted lock, stock and barrel when required elsewhere, and so a base with less than forty buildings had an infuriating system whereby identifying numbers were random and went as high as 200. I eventually found 107 after half an hour.

I climbed the four stairs to the landing and edged in. The hut was a prefabricated type similar to Vesey's office; rectangular, maybe ten feet by twenty, wooden floor and whitewashed interior walls, with one small window by the door. A bare light bulb hung over a small table covered in books and papers which separated the two parallel single camp beds. A man was lying on one of them, propped up on his side, evidently engrossed in the book lying open on the bed. He looked up with a mixture of wariness and disdain.

I dropped my bags and offered him my hand.

'Robert Watt. Pleased to meet you.'

He was still for a second.

'Bugger.'

He sighed, unenthusiastically offering his hand. 'A jock. Arthur Lee.'

He returned to his book; he was a thin man, balding, with a ginger-brown moustache and pale complexion, the sort ready to erupt in freckles at the merest hint of sun. Older than me, maybe mid-forties, giving every sign of being both languidly sullen and highly strung. I thought that perhaps he was perturbed at the thought of sharing with someone half his age. Whatever, he seemed reluctant to initiate any conversation.

'So . . . how long have you been here, Arthur?' I scanned around for somewhere to house my belongings.

'Too bloody long.'

The only chest of drawers was on his side of the room. I dumped my kit-bag in front of the other bed, and sat down on it.

'I've just met Colonel Vesey, gave me my briefing. Seems alright. Nice man.'

His eye remained on his book.

'Really? I think he's a cunt. You know he's not even a bloody doctor? What does that tell you about our cosy little set-up then, eh? Asked if you could help out with his "special problem", did he? Mention any secret trips east?'

I was too shocked by his language to take notice of the questions. The only time I'd heard swearing like that it was delivered in a heavy Glaswegian accent – workmen and labourers arguing outside the rougher pubs on a Friday night. Arthur Lee didn't speak with any kind of accent at all; his was an educated, 'neutral' tone, one that would be described as 'middle class' nowadays.

'What do you mean?'

This time he did look up. 'What do I mean? What do you think I bloody mean? Why did you volunteer for this, what were you expecting to find when you came here?'

He had lost me again.

'I didn't volunteer . . . I was assigned straight from induction camp.'

He turned away, groaning.

'Oh bloody hell! They don't even want to pretend any more!'

He lifted his book to cover his face and lay motionless, arms folded across his chest. I hung my coat on the back of the door and pulled out some items from my bag – a hairbrush, razor and toiletry bag, pyjamas which I tucked underneath the lumpy pillow. All done in silence.

At last he stirred, getting to his feet and pulling out his coat from under mine. He opened the door, paused and turned round, the cold air blowing in as he spoke.

'You eaten? That hut over there, sixty-four, the large one. Canteen hut. Starts serving for us in five minutes. Five minutes, alright? Yank food, thank God. Only decent thing about them.'

He strolled off, banging the door behind him. I knew he was lying when I arrived there, five minutes later as briefed, and saw him finishing off his meal. He just hadn't wanted me anywhere near him. By the time I had queued up and been served my meal he was off again, and I sat down to eat alone.

There were about twenty others in the room, and about six tables. I placed myself at the end of a four-seat table where two other men were grunting monosyllabically as they progressed through their stew. I smiled politely, unable to hear if the conversation was in English or not. The gesture was ignored, and I felt my ears burn with embarrassment. The rest of the meal passed uneventfully, the stew a lumpy indistinguishable mix of browns and greys, but edible all the same. As I ate, steam billowed out of the large steel vat, making the air one breathed taste the same as the food itself.

As I contemplated my last remaining mouthful of coffee I heard a female voice mentioning my name, the sound distant, ethereal, as if I was dreaming. I lifted the cup and was startled to see the face of a young nursing auxiliary looming over me, close enough to kiss.

'Robert? Hello! I'm Joyce, Joyce Redford. We've all been looking forward to your arrival. Hope you play bridge!'

It wasn't a particularly pretty face. All the features were large and rather squeezed into the available space; teeth, lips, nose and eyes all jostling for prominence. I noticed that the glasses, through which she stared rather imploringly, had thick lenses. She wore no make up.

'Yes. Yes, of course.' I tried to cover my discomfort, hurriedly wiping away any remnants of gravy from my mouth. I felt embarrassed again. It might not have been beautiful, but it was the only friendly face I had seen all day. Somehow, I wanted to repay her interest with a more animated reply than the one I had given.

'Super! We've been dying to get a new set together for simply ages!'

'Well, I can't claim to be an expert, or even particularly good.'

'That's alright! None of the gang are too brilliant either.'

There was an excitable, gushy tone to her voice, the

words coming out in gallops followed by pauses as she contemplated the next jolly barrage.

'Geoff . . . Geoff Marlow, he played for his church, in leagues I mean, but the rest of us are pretty average, it'll be good to get some new blood. Penny's not bad though, all the trumps as they say! Do you play the same rules in Scotland?'

'I think so. I can't see why it would be different.'

'Well super . . . no problems there then!' she jumped back in, probably realising how inane the question was. It was the first time she mentioned anything related to my personal background, and it was the only time she would. It said it all about our future relationship that we then went on to discuss our respective understanding of the rules of bridge rather than anything connected to my arrival, or to our situation in that canteen and the work of the unit, or even to the war that had just ended.

Joyce eventually gave me another hut number, 51, where I would rejoin her later that night, together with other similar spirits, and sit through three hours of tedious card playing. I have nothing against the English but that night I began to understand how such an unprepossessing race had successfully colonised half the world. I imagined all the other bridge parties that had gone on and were going on at that moment in huts scattered wherever the English had roamed. From desert to jungle, tropics to ice-caps, they would be playing as we were. And as the natives looked on and listened to the good-natured yet stifling conversation that accompanied the cards, they would be too dumbfounded to offer anything but the most placid resistance.

Joyce's exaggerated yawn about half past ten was the cue to wrap the session up. The room was tidied, with tables and chairs stacked to the side and ashtrays emptied, and for a while everyone stood around wishing each other goodnight without actually making a move to leave. I was completely spent and ready for sleep but didn't want to be first to go. For one thing I wasn't sure I could find my way back to 107. It was Joyce who again led.

'Coming?' she said, opening the door on the outside world.

We walked in silence past the canteen, heading toward admin at the camp gate. It was very dark; the billet huts were lit either by candlelight or small gas lamps and neither had the strength to shed light onto the paths between them.

'You're 107, aren't you? It's down there.'

Joyce pointed down the slope to the left. She had stopped walking. We both looked to the hut with a faint orange glow in its tiny window.

'Looks like Arthur's still up. Bit of a shame being billeted with him, he's a bit on the strange side.'

She turned to face me as if waiting for confirmation, but I wasn't about to share my first experience of him with her.

Two orderlies appeared from around a bend and started to head towards us, young girls, giggling, lowering their voices as they neared. I thought Joyce was about to speak to them, introduce us, but as they passed I realised they were talking in German. I closed my ears to them and stopped myself from turning when they laughed out loud again a couple of paces behind. Joyce was still in contemplative mood, looking to me once more.

'Do you think there is such a thing as being too clever?'

I didn't know what she meant and wasn't really interested. I was tired and cold, and it was too late in the evening for me to enjoy this kind of conversation. I folded my arms and shook my head, watching my breath hang like thick smoke in the night cold. Part of me was still thinking about those girls, wondering where they were bedding down, letting myself dream about snuggling in between them.

'You know, too intelligent to . . . feel . . . emotions, and stuff.'

'I'm sorry, Joyce, I'm not with you.'

'We were at a clinic once, Arthur and me, and he never smiled, or joked . . . or even talked the whole day. He was staring at me and I thought he was annoyed, that perhaps he thought I was over-familiar with the people, the Germans. There was this old woman, she was so distraught, her husband had just gone and we were trying to calm her. And I asked him if he minded . . . you know the way he can look so cross? You know what he said? He said it was my choice but that I should be careful, that compassion is like quicksand, the more you give the more it pulls you under. I just think that's so horrible, to not let yourself care, don't you, Robert?'

The point was lost on me.

'I suppose it is. Not to . . . feel, I mean.'

She smiled, shaking herself back to life with a brisk little march on the spot.

'Right! Time for bed. Sorry to keep you up so late. Still,

I know I'm really going to enjoy having you here, Robert. The games will just be super!'

My first day out was a calamity from beginning to end.

After a fitful night's sleep, Arthur Lee was kind enough to direct me to the latrines. There, I waited for a free toilet cubicle, uncomfortably aware of the noise of flatulence emanating from the nearest one. When the latch door finally opened and the bulky figure of Vesey emerged, I was mortified.

'Morning, Rob. Could you call round to admin block once you done breakfast, say eight-thirty? I'll give you your duty rota then.'

Vesey was wearing a tartan dressing gown over his pyjamas. He had rolled up a sleeve and addressed his watch as he spoke. Even in this attire, he still managed to exude a natural authority, although this time I managed to stop myself from saluting him. I gave a nod of agreement and he held the door ajar for me to pass inside. He must have known that the smell lingering there made this a less than appealing prospect but showed no trace of shame.

'Catch you later, Rob,' he shouted, as I unbuttoned my fly.

Vesey's briefing was hurried and short. I was to travel eight miles south-west to a new camp at Reichstroem, my task to issue certification to those deemed fit to travel. Although the Russians usually provided transport, an American unit would take me and the team – a nurse and two orderlies – over to this camp since it was in an Allied-controlled zone.

I saw the nurse waiting outside the admin hut when I arrived, the grey-haired and humourless Matron Whiteside. Our transport waited whilst Vesey called me inside for a last private briefing.

The four of us travelled on the back of an open truck. The orderlies spoke no English and once my opening conversational gambits had been rebuffed by Matron the journey went ahead in silence, giving me a chance to take in my first view of the ruined heart of the Reich.

There were uniformed men everywhere, toiling like ants in the dusty landscape, ferrying materials on their backs or passing chunks of broken masonry down the line, their purposeful air perhaps masking an underlying melancholy. Many seemed to be soldiers, but were work brigades formed from the last living remnants of the defeated. The gangs pulling down or putting up the skeletal buildings wore a chaotic range of colours. There was hardly a structure that had been left unscathed by the Russian invasion and the Allied bombing that had preceded it, and it was impossible to imagine what once had stood in place of the wreckage.

As we moved further from the centre the damage appeared to be less concentrated, with only the occasional crater in a row of suburban housing a reminder of errant targeting from above. We arrived at Reichstroem after an hour's tortuously slow progress on the pock-marked road.

Our base was an old school. The others had been there before, and I followed them to the main hall, where the examinations would take place. Some women in white aprons with crude scarlet bands sewn on them were waiting for us. I took them to be Red Cross. They had set up a line of old desks which zig-zagged left and right to form a queuing path. It went right back to the end of the hall, and I tried not to contemplate how many people it would soon hold, familiarising myself instead with the forms which had to be filled for every refugee, trying to remember what Vesey had told me. Some forms were in German, some in English, some even in French. Thankfully, the refugees were out of sight, probably in the rest of the school buildings trying to keep warm. There was no heating or electricity, and it seemed colder inside than it had been on the back of the truck.

'Shall we begin?' asked Matron, impatiently.

I scanned around again. There was a set of scales over near the wall, and a wooden measuring stick beside it. Aside from that there were no medical facilities. I was glad I had brought my own stethoscope, the one my mother had bought me when I first transferred to medical school. I felt a sudden heart-rush, anxiety and homesickness rolled into one.

'Yes,' I said. 'Let's make a start then.'

The message was relayed to the pair of white-apronned helpers at the far side of the hall. The swing doors behind them opened, the floorspace was suddenly covered with a miserable tide of weary-looking travellers, the ragamuffin flotsam of war. Hundreds of them, bony old men, children, cowering old women supporting each other in pairs. Yes, this would be a long day, and nothing could have prepared me for it, not even my spell as an orderly at the Western Infirmary when the blitz had come to Clydeside five years previously.

Slowly, a form of order began to emerge from the chaos.

The first to make it through the maze of desks were checked by the orderlies for height and weight. A Red Cross worker would then interview them as their papers filled up with detail: name, place of birth, destination. The first of them was soon led to me. He was an elderly chap, somewhere in his sixties. Wiry and weatherbeaten, he obviously hadn't eaten properly for some time. I tried to offer a reassuring smile, but he stared back nervously; perhaps the gesture didn't translate. No matter, I looked into his eyes anyway; pupil dilation okay, and no signs of jaundice. Open the mouth, please; yes, okay, nothing swollen or infected, perhaps a little dry. Pull up the shirt now, thank you; belly slightly distended, obviously a hungry man. A check of the glands under the arms, fine; then the throat, right; now the groin, can you get him to drop the trousers. *Der Hose? Jawort*. He pulled down his pants in front of me. He was wearing no underwear but I carried on regardless, hoping to get it over with fast for his sake and mine. The glands were normal but his scrotum hung oddly. I cupped it in my right hand. He had lost a testicle – was this recent, was he aware of it, was he in pain and in need of treatment?

'*Es ist nur einer Hoden?*' I tried to frame it as a question; there is only one testicle? Did he understand? I looked round to the auxiliary for help with the translation but she was busy stacking the man's papers into different sets. I hoped my German was accurate enough for him to understand.

'*Sei Still!*' spat the man. Leave me alone! He snatched to pull up his trousers, cursing at me in his native tongue. The people waiting behind him started to snigger. I realised I had been heard, he had been humiliated.

I left him to pull his ragged clothes back together whilst I looked at his papers. My mind was buzzing and I found it hard to concentrate, some of the forms seemed to have no purpose at all. The man's weight to height ratio looked suspect but he was probably dehydrated, his natural weight would see him back into safe territory. I decided to pass him fit and began to tick the appropriate boxes. I was signing the bottom section when Matron Whiteside approached me.

'I hope you're not going to take as long with the rest of them, son. There's hundreds still outside, you know.'

She drifted off before I could reply. I looked up and saw the multitude in front of me. She was right, I would have to speed up somehow, to stick to the necessary.

The rest of the day passed in a blur. I lost count of the number of forms I signed, pushed under my pen by a succession of helpers. I rejected about one in ten patients. I didn't know what would happen to them or what the procedures were for these cases. I hoped they would get whatever treatment was required, and attempted to write down my initial diagnosis on their form, but as for proper examination, there simply wasn't time.

Somewhere along the line, Matron Whiteside dropped out of the picture. She came to me around noon – we didn't stop for lunch – and told me she had a terrible headache, a migraine attack, and that she was going for a lie down. I didn't mind her leaving because I couldn't see exactly what her contribution was anyway, other than to glower sternly at the queue from time to time. Good riddance.

Finally, as daylight faded, the Red Cross staff pushed

back the rest of those standing in line. They would have to wait until tomorrow.

The journey back to camp was less entertaining than the one out. I was exhausted and this time felt the cold seeping into my bones, an experience made all the more sour by the realisation that there would be no hot bath waiting for me when we returned. I began to scratch and wondered how many of those I had examined were verminous, a disturbing question I struggled to ignore.

I was glad to arrive back at headquarters and made straight for the latrines. All that nervous energy had been waiting to take its toll on my guts. I must have sat there a long time.

When I finally made it back to Hut 107 I found Arthur Lee lying on his bed in much the same manner as the night before and he didn't bother to greet me. I sank onto my bed and started to untie my boots. I hadn't realised how sore my feet had become.

'Well, Arthur, I'm bushed. Never worked so hard in all my life.'

'I'll say,' came the reply. 'I hear you passed the entire camp fit to travel.'

I looked to him. Was this his first attempt at friendly banter, or was he being serious?

He pensively chewed on his pencil. 'Vesey wants to see you, better go sharpish, old fruit.'

He was serious. I pulled my boots back on and set off wearily for admin, trying to work up a defence for whatever confrontation was ahead. Why should they be angry with me? I'd toiled flat-out all day, it wasn't me that asked to be swamped like that. What the hell else could they want?

I kicked at the muddy path in frustration as I walked over.

Vesey was behind his desk when I entered. He motioned me to sit down opposite, glancing at his watch as he did so. Dinner was about to be served so hopefully this wouldn't take long.

'How many people did you examine and pass today, Rob?'

He was reading something as he spoke. I had the distinct impression it was something relating to me.

'Hundreds. They never stopped.' I knew I must have sounded vague but was too tired to care.

Vesey looked displeased at my apparent lack of concern.

'Well, how many hundred then?' he snapped. 'One, two, three, more? Tell me for Chrissakes!'

'I don't know, I was so busy . . . Perhaps three hundred or so . . .'

'And were the orderlies passing you the documentation to sign off as you worked through them?'

'No, the Red Cross people did that.'

'Rob, there *are* no Red Cross at Reichstroem. Who the hell was in charge of your documentation? I told you . . .'

Vesey's voice was raised, he was almost shouting.

'But there were, I saw the uniforms . . .'

'And you checked their accreditations? Did you *read* what they were asking you to initial? You didn't, did you? You were *had*.'

He shook his head in disgust.

'Had? I'm sorry, what do you mean?'

He took a deep breath. 'According to this, which you signed, you passed off one thousand two hundred refugees. That's more than the damn camp holds, Rob – I *told you*

23

to watch out – More than any camp will see in a month. These are desperate times for some people, signed papers are worth a lot. There's a trade in them, for Chrissake. Didn't Matron say something about this?'

'She wasn't there really. Had a headache. Went for a lie down.'

'You examined three hundred people and let her go have a lie down? Jesus Christ! We sent you there to *take charge* of the situation, not to be overrun by it. What the hell did you think . . .'

I could tell he was struggling to hold back. Much as I wanted to explain everything I knew it was a time to keep quiet. Nothing could help my case.

He paused and took a deep breath. 'Next time, Rob, try not to be so . . .' He searched for the right word. '. . . just try not to be . . . okay?'

A pained smile came across him; again I kept silent, a tacit acknowledgement of guilt.

'It won't happen again.'

Vesey showed no sign of acknowledging my remark, and continued to shake his head as he studied the papers in front of him.

'I'm sorry, Rob, but I'm afraid I'm going to have to invalidate everything you signed today, including those you genuinely passed. I guess we'll just have to start again tomorrow.'

He gestured to show that I could leave. I pulled myself to my feet, relieved to be able to get outside. I was thinking of the old man I had examined first of all, of what I had put him through and how he would now have to go through it all again. I wanted to cry.

Hysteria-Mediated Psychosis
A Historical Perspective

Dr A.G. Lee MD, MRCP (Submitted by B. Lee)

January 1947

INTRODUCTION

It is an enduring irony of war that the anarchy and confusion generated by one conflict can directly facilitate an understanding of the motivations and history of an earlier one, even one which took place centuries ago.

This process is twofold. Firstly, the historian who directly experiences the culture, complexities, and paths to violent struggle that come with every war, as well as the chaos within it, will be granted a new empathy with those involved in previous wars, victims and antagonists.

Secondly, the same destructive forces which wreck lives, alliances and buildings will often serve to unearth archive materials which have hitherto escaped the historian's scrutiny. After the heavy Allied bombing of Nuremberg two years ago, the damage and disruption to the Cathedral's foundations revealed the previously hidden subterranean vaults of the Diocese. These in turn gave up the library of correspondence between the Cathedral court and surrounding Bishoprics from the early sixteenth century, together with the more surprising cache of the accounts and expenses ledger of the Swedish army of King Gustavus Adolphus of the same period.

Documentary evidence of this kind, formerly known only to select groups, currently abounds in central and eastern Europe, where the ravages of the recent war are still acutely felt. The war and its aftermath have served to open up many secret tombs to scrutiny, and have weakened the grip of the hands that might normally guard such materials (as well as, it must be admitted, providing needy survivors with a very welcome source of income).

This paper will make use of documents acquired in such a manner during the winter of 1946 in the Polish/German borderlands, to establish the truth behind one of the most disturbing myths in history, that of the so-called 'Pied Piper' whose musical charms conjured away first the rats, and then the children of Hamelin, according to legend.

The war that Gustavus Adolphus had led his army to Germany to participate in was the Thirty Years' War of 1618–48. It remains, despite the efforts earlier this century of Kaiser Wilhelm II, and more recently those of Adolf Hitler, the most devastating conflict to have taken place on European soil. Although those two world wars can claim more deaths in actual numbers, those who died as a result of the seventeenth-century struggle formed a larger percentage of Europe's then total population.

Notionally a conflict inspired by religious divisions – the struggle for ascendancy between the Roman Catholic Papacy and the early Protestant Churches – the Thirty Years' War had by the end of its third decade long lost any semblance of cause, reason or order. For its combatants in the field the war had simply become a ravenous beast which demanded to be fed, the penalty for non-compliance being death, the same being the only means of escape.

Three decades of fighting also left its indelible mark on European economic and cultural development. Over a third of all German towns in existence at the war's beginning were extinct by its end, having fallen by slaughter, pestilence or worse. The final horror of the times was that of disease, for these were the years of the Great Plague. The prevalent belief of the age was that those left living had sinned and had slipped without knowing into hell, a belief perhaps reflected in the actions of the war's soldiers, often cited as the most brutal and inhuman ever witnessed on the European stage.

Germany was the main theatre for the battles of this war. Over the years of the struggle men from almost every country in the known world were to enter her and fight on either the Protestant or Catholic side. From the north came the forces of Sweden, Denmark and Finland; from the west the French, English and Dutch; from the south, Czechs, Slavs, Italians and Spaniards; and from the east the Poles, the Hungars, even the Turks. Zealots and mercenaries from all of these lands and even from lands further afield such as Russia, Scotland and Ireland rushed to join the fray and share its bloody spoils. Germany, lacking any national unity or natural borders, was powerless to resist as one such intervention after another prolonged the war to its notorious thirty-year span.

It is no coincidence that the two world wars of this century were Germanic in origin. Both leaders mentioned earlier shamelessly exploited the legacy ingrained in the

German consciousness by the war – the fear of the return of the invaders, rising on the flat horizon and coming back to destroy all once more. The only permanent defence, they reasoned, was attack. So strong are the visions of these marauders, still lingering centuries on, that such sentiments found a receptive audience in the German people, with inevitably tragic consequences.

That the horrors of the Thirty Years' War had retained their place in the German national consciousness is no surprise; German children are reared on a potent mix of fables and fairy tales which, on examination, can be seen to be thinly-disguised war episodes. There is a tendency in history by which incidents which are too distressing to be readily assimilated into a common experience pass into legend instead, and myths evolve when the memory of an event is corrupted with retelling. Some can be the result of repeated exaggeration until a simple occurrence grows into an epic fable, whilst others make the reverse journey, sanitised to make gruesome facts more palatable. The thesis presented on this paper, supported by new evidence and analysis, is that the legend of the 'Pied Piper' falls into the latter category. The true facts of what really happened in the town of Hamelin, and how Hamelin came to lose its children and rushed to its own extinction will be presented for the first time. The paper will explain how these events, which were real enough, were so abhorrent, even to a population numbed by war, that the process of ascribing them to a far-off place and time began almost as soon as the first reports of the awful truth emerged.

For Hamelin was not a town of Brunswick, in northern Germany, as tradition has it, but of Lusatia, a Hapsburg province (later ceded to Saxony) on the Polish border. The Pied Piper himself arrived first to save, and then destroy, Hamelin not in the fourteenth century but much later, in 1649, at the end of the Thirty Years' War. And although Hamelin, a once prosperous and orderly town, had been reduced to unbearable squalor by an epidemic infestation of rats, it was not this scourge that the Pied Piper had volunteered to rid the town of.

For Hamelin was a town under siege.

VESEY ARRANGED IT so that I didn't carry out mass clinics alone again. For the next four months I would work in tandem with a succession of other doctors – Geoff Marlow, a chap from Bristol called Sneddon, a Welsh half-wit called Evans, and sometimes Arthur Lee.

A difficult man, Arthur, difficult to warm to. Sometimes we were spending almost the entire day and night in each other's company yet we would hardly pass two words to each other. Joyce would let slip snippets of camp gossip she'd heard about him after our card games, and this was the only way I would learn anything about him in those early days, before we went to Poland.

She told me one thing that I'd already guessed; he was a highly skilled doctor, a surgeon – a cancer specialist – whose expertise was far superior to ours. Other doctors came and went from the camp but Arthur was always retained, as I was, for some unknown reason. Perhaps this explained the impatient manner he displayed; knowing that his talents were being wasted on fairly low-grade activities. What made his retention more peculiar was the fact that he and Vesey didn't get on; Vesey had disciplined him several times before I arrived for buying artifacts and books from the locals. This had developed into something of an obsession for Arthur, and with Vesey's concern over feeding the Russians' suspicions regarding our activities it had become a constant flashpoint – one which could have been best solved by Arthur being sent to a more appropriate assignment away from the sensitivities of the east.

Ultimately, tragically, the opposite happened.

And myself? I suppose I too must have begun to change, some of Arthur's attitudes rubbing off on me. Faced with an endless queue of stumbling, broken refugees there was no choice but to get on with the process of screening them in the most pragmatic and mechanical way. Anyone who threatened the steady progress of the line – fumbling nurses, incompetent auxiliaries, renegades trying to con their way past – was liable to irritate me. I developed a sharp tongue barely recognisable in the young man signing counterfeit forms at Reichstroem only months ago. Worst of all, I began to lose sight of the human element of the cases brought before me; as people, they and their papers became one and the same, both needing to be signed, stamped and processed, and then passed along the line. Any honest doctor will admit to occasionally suffering from this condition; in my case though, such early exposure to it has probably meant a lifetime of never fully losing the symptoms.

In fact, this period marked the beginning of my spiritual decline. On Sunday mornings a bus would arrive to transport those of a religious inclination to a church service over at Hansa, a fifty-minute journey away. Of course, there were nearer churches, but none of them Anglican. I made this trip just once; Vesey had told me about it and had asked if I would go. I had said yes almost automatically and then felt compelled to be there in case some kind of attendance record was kept. In the event, I found it a depressing experience, one I vowed not to repeat. The problem wasn't the company of those with whom I was obliged to share the coach seats and then pews, although the excursion did seem popular amongst those I had found the most lacking in charity and Christian spirit, Matron Whiteside greeting me with an icy 'Good morning' as I mounted the bus. No, it was the mood of melancholy and maudlin reminiscence I fell into on our return. In my mind, Sunday morning meant a bracing walk at home along the sea front after the service, the salty iodine tang of the air sharpening the appetite for the roast already cooking in the oven. When would I smell either again? It meant reading each word of the hymn we were singing and judging at the end of every line how long to go, how long to suffer my brother's embarrassingly flat tenor booming in my ear. It meant hoping my parents didn't meet anyone on the way back so that we'd be home sooner to listen to the radio, and enjoy a final sibling squabble before lunch, father blind to the silent wrestling, head buried in the pages of the *Sunday Post*. Childhood is made up of such routines, none of them amounting to any significance on their own and most suffered at the time rather than enjoyed. Yet those are the days that are missed the most, having a sentimental gravity that pulls relentlessly at the heart. I could escape this only by denying myself Sundays, and weekends themselves, and from now on convinced myself the week was made up of seven Mondays.

My bridge improved. With night after night spent at the card table, it had no choice. Not that there was any pressure involved, those playing would never be so vulgar as to consider wagering cash stakes. The nights would pass by with an air of surreal tedium, silence during games, lighthearted analysis and congratulations afterward. Only occasionally would the games, or indeed the conversations, have any kind of edge.

There was one occasion though, and it set in motion the sequence of events that would ultimately test my judgement, and find it so desperately wanting.

James Clements arrived at our Berlin camp two months after me. I was aware of his imminent arrival because, like mine, it was so eagerly anticipated by Joyce, who seemed to enjoy inside information from Vesey's admin depot. Clements was five years older than me, but much more experienced in terms of both medical and military service, having been part of the field medical teams that followed the advance from Normandy to Berlin. Joyce obviously had it in mind that he would be some sort of hero, and she made this plain in her ever more excitable chatter as details from his file were fed to her. A real man of medicine – his father was a Senior Registrar at Guy's – what would he make of our ramshackle unit? Should a member of the medical aristocracy be expected to work for someone as uncouth as Vesey, an American?

Joyce brought him to the hut one icy Wednesday night, introducing him with a feverish gusto. Evans was good enough to drop out of the game to let the fresh recruit make up a pair with Joyce, myself and Sneddon the other. Right from the off I noticed an arrogance, a condescending air about him. Bridge, I could see him thinking, why how dull, how provincial, is this how these fools entertain themselves? I found myself wanting to explain that this wasn't by any means my idea of fun either, but one which seemed to mean a lot to the others, a game that one played for their sake, to be sociable. I suppose there was also, to be fair, a touch of jealousy in my mind. Clements had, with his five years and experience in the field, an attractive and mature bearing to him, not something that anyone would claim for me. Tall and handsome, blue-eyed and with cropped blonde hair, I suppose women would have described him as 'dashing', and he would have been used to hearing it.

But not only did he break convention by talking during the games, he also managed to add an adversarial, sniping quality to every aspect of his own conversation.

'Glasgow?' he purred, in his public school voice, '. . . of course. I'm a Guy's man myself. London . . .'

He slowly blew out the smoke from behind thin lips and looked down again at the cards he was left with. There was an expression of mild disgust on his face; it was left to us to decide whether this was at the idea of a medical degree from Glasgow or the quality of his hand.

'Robert's a bit of a scientist as well though, aren't you, Robert?' Clements' haughty manner had Joyce eager to throw him anything that might conceivably impress.

'Really?'

'I was three years into a chemistry degree, actually bio-chemistry, before I transferred to medicine, when the war broke out. I took an accelerated bridging course. One day I hope to complete my original degree.'

'But you'll stay a doctor, Robert, won't you?' Joyce seemed hurt by the prospect that I might not.

'Och aye.'

I meant it as a joke at my own expense, the only jock in the room, but I regretted it instantly when I saw Clements' smug smile emerging.

'So the medical facility at the university is a temporary one, for the war?'

He was being deliberately thick, trying to imply that medical degrees only came out of Glasgow in dire emergencies.

'No, James, in fact I think Glasgow has one of the longest established faculties of medicine in Britain.'

He nodded whilst staring at his cards; he had no interest at all in my answer.

'So where are you from then, Joyce, somewhere exotic?'

A shy smile flushed in response. 'Hardly. Guildford.'

He stared at her, unblinking. 'How nice. Know it well. What about you, Robert, ever been?'

'No. In fact I've never heard of it.'

I had meant this to sound like a rebuff to Clements, but as soon as I said it, Joyce seemed to take offence.

'But you must have . . . just outside London.'

'You *have* heard of London?'

It was now my turn to force a smile.

'Of course. Just outside Scotland, isn't it?'

I waited vainly for a reply; he'd turned his smug gaze back to Joyce.

'Family?'

36

'Dad's in insurance. Mum is . . . well, Mum! I'm the oldest, two sisters . . . one still at school, one just started medicine at Bart's. That's Jennifer, brains of the family. I just bustle along.'

'Oh, I'm sure you do a marvellous job, Joyce. A regular Florence Nightingale . . .'

He took a deep draw and smiled at the same time, a gesture that made his face transform itself into a kind of manic leer. I noticed the dandruff on his shoulder and the yellow nicotine stains on his fingers. It began to dawn on me that this might all be part of a play he was making for Joyce, the way he was seeking to put me, and the others, down. I wondered whether he could actually be interested in her, and studied her for a brief second. She was looking her normal self, slightly toothy, dark hair held in place by those ghastly grips, but there was a brightness and liveliness to her eyes that he might find attractive, and there was no knowing how long it had been since he had slept with a woman. Although the olive green nursing uniform she wore could not flatter any figure, her bust seemed compellingly large. As my eye lingered I saw how young Joyce really was, almost from a different generation, with none of his sophistication. What if he was a rake, after only one thing? I decided then and there not to let him have her, even if she was beginning to warm to his attention.

'James' father knows Arthur Lee. He's a Senior Registrar at Guy's as well. Says he's a bit of an oddball.'

'That's right. A pacifist. Member of some organisation, an agitator . . .'

'. . . and that his wife and son died in the Blitz. House came down on them.'

'No excuse to be a pacifist. None at all. He's not the only one to have suffered.'

To my surprise I found myself defending Arthur Lee.

'With all due respect, James, I think Arthur is a man of some intellect. I'm sure if he has a belief it's on the basis of a rational, rather than emotional, judgement.'

Clements shifted in his seat. 'Think so? No, he's just feeling sorry for himself, unwilling to think of the sacrifices others have made.'

'But would the fact that he lost his family not be liable to test his belief? Surely most of the war-bereaved are more anti-German and pro-war than the rest of us, if only out of a desire for revenge?'

Clements chose not to answer, starting up a different tack.

'Look, chum, they're a waste of time, pacifists. Who would have seen off Hitler if we had listened to them? They ought to put them all in jail. Our boys who died deserve better than bloody fools like that mocking them. They died for more than that.'

'Died defending the right to free speech, James. It was Hitler who put pacifists in jail – are you saying you agree with him?'

He shifted again and made as if to lay down his cards. A voice from afar interrupted us.

'Steady now, boys, I thought you had a game of bridge to concentrate on?'

It was Evans, looking up from his book. I realised we had an audience – Geoff Marlow was watching as well.

'You're right ... south bid!' said Joyce, betraying her sudden anxiousness. She must have thought we were going to come to blows. If we had, I can't say I would have given much for my chances; Clements was well built, and had probably boxed for Eton.

'Oh come on, we're alright, aren't we, Jock?' he murmured, studying his hand without interest.

'Och aye,' I replied, deadpan.

The game must have gone on for another hour, nobody saying much, Clements puffing his surly way through almost an entire pack of cigarettes. Joyce usually asked me to walk her back to her hut when we wound up. That night, I thought I would pre-empt any action by Clements and volunteer for the task first. I'm sure he smirked again as we left, and I felt stupid, standing by the door as she made her usual emotional farewell to all. Awkward enough to leave her to it and hang around outside on the stairs.

The air outdoors was fresh and bitingly cold, a shock to the lungs after the stuffy smoke, but welcome all the same. Joyce was down moments later and we began to make our way in silence, the frozen mud crunching beneath our boots.

'That seemed to go well.'

I studied her face for any trace of a wry smile, surely she was being sarcastic?

'Sorry?'

'I mean James . . . think he enjoyed the game?'

I stopped.

'Joyce, are you serious? He's an arrogant . . .' I tried to think of a word which could adequately describe him yet not offend her delicate ears. 'You must have noticed an atmosphere?'

'I saw you were becoming a bit agitated at one point.

You really shouldn't take it so seriously … it's only a game, Robert.'

She smiled benignly. I decided it wasn't worth correcting her, what was the point?

'And why did you get so worked up about Arthur Lee?'

'I just …' Again I struggled for something appropriate to say. 'I just don't think he has an easy time of it. I hear him … he cries himself to sleep every night, for hours.'

She was quiet again, locked in thought.

'You know what? I think you're quite a caring person. You try to hide it, but you are, aren't you, Robert?'

I couldn't disagree because I didn't want to disappoint her by admitting that when I'd mentioned Arthur I meant the lack of good sleep was making me grouchy.

We started moving again, and soon were at her hut. She shared a cabin like mine with older women. Somehow they squeezed into three beds.

'Listen,' she said, turning round. 'Unit 3 are having a dance next week at their camp. There's an airforce band playing. I think Vesey will let us go if I can get enough of us interested. I think he'll even lay on a truck. What do you think?'

'Where are they, how long would it take?'

'Hour and a bit, what do you say, don't you think it would be super?'

It had to be longer than an hour, but anything was better than another night of cards.

'Of course it would.'

And then I leant forward and kissed her. A light kiss, slow enough for her to see it coming and avoid if she wanted. She didn't, probably too surprised.

'Goodnight, Robert. I'll talk to Vesey.'

She hurried up the steps and disappeared into the cabin.

I turned and began to walk back through the huts over to 107, where Arthur would probably still be working, poring over his latest acquisitions, tawdry junk and dusty documents he seemed happy to pay a relative fortune for. I was full of regret; the kiss had done nothing for me and it had been done not because I wanted her, but to save her from anyone else. I could only hope she'd understand.

The Town of Hamelin

FROM A VARIETY OF RECORDS a virtually full list of those comprising the ruling council in office at the time of Hamelin's demise can be constructed. The name most often featured in municipal despatches is naturally that of the Mayor, Heinrich Ebber. Although the name of Mayor Ebber's predecessor, Kunze, is also present in certain documents it is not clear whether this was actually the former mayor himself, or his brother. He is noted as an older man than the mayor, as having sixty years to the other's thirty-five, and it may have been that the two operated some sort of dual leadership, a steadying hand available to balance a youthful drive. Whilst it may appear that Ebber was surprisingly young to be shouldering such a responsibility (having held office for four years or more, Ebber must have first been appointed at around thirty-one), it must also be appreciated that the average life expectancy of these times was short. Disease, poor diet, and an abundance of untreatable (and therefore fatal) accidents meant that any man who reached middle age was considered to be exceptionally lucky.

Other names registered as being part of the council include the treasurer, Wolfricht, the priest, Seicle, and some whose precise role is difficult to ascertain – Schmidt, Strauss, Mannau, Unger (who seems to have held some kind of responsibility for defence), and Weiss, the key landowner.

Between them, these men would have exercised powers of considerable autonomy from the Imperial authorities, and their decisions would have had the most direct influence on the quality – and ultimately, the security – of the lives of Hamelin's four hundred citizens. Indeed, as the war years rolled on, the Imperial court steadily withdrew its presence from peripheral towns like Hamelin, and would have only been concerned with due payment of taxes and the occasional supply of men for its army ranks. These matters aside, Hamelin would have lived its last years in a state of virtual independence.

What can we tell then of the capabilities and policies of the presiding council, and more importantly, how did they contribute to their own undoing?

Any reader searching this paper for a confirmation of the vile and corrupt Hamelin chamber of legend will be disappointed; all available evidence suggests that these were diligent and honourable men, agonizing to the last over the events which would overwhelm them. This is particularly true of Mayor Ebber, to whose abilities and foresight the fact that Hamelin evaded the war's ravages for so long can be attributed. As this paper will demonstrate, the cause of his downfall and that of his beloved town was a combination of cruel circumstance and the manifestation of an evil which had been brewing for thirty years.

No archaeological remains of Hamelin have yet been found, although this author has repeatedly been offered artifacts which are supposedly relics from the town. Sadly, it is highly unlikely that they could be, as this paper will prove.

Any attempt to depict how the town might have appeared to a traveller of the time must therefore be conjecture, but some basic facts can be stated. Various correspondence speaks of the pleasant and attractive aspect of the town, and particularly its very centre, which was built on a natural mound. The town itself was probably not far from the east bank of the River Treuwe. It can be assumed that either its church, or its town hall, both of which were located on the cobbled main square, dominated the landscape of the Treuwe valley. Hamelin is not noted as suffering from the problems which would have been rife in neighbouring towns, those of overcrowding, insanitary conditions and lawlessness. Land registers show that the growth of the town area kept pace with population growth, even in the years where this showed a rapid climb (1585–1605). This indicates that the new prosperity behind this growth was both planned and wisely invested, a tribute to the efficiencies of Mayor Ebber's predecessors. It was only during the latter war years that the town began to retract, with ever increasing numbers seeking sanctuary behind the old town walls, and so Hamelin duly assumed the squalor prevalent elsewhere.

Agriculture would have been the source of the town's original wealth; the surrounding valley was noted for its rich and fertile soil. Mayor Ebber and his colleagues would all have been associated with this land in some way, either as farmers or as landlords. The richest (and most astute) would have developed further careers as private bankers and merchants, buying up harvest for resale, lending capital. Indeed Mayor Ebber's first mention in the municipal records is as the originator of the town's own bank, a semi-co-operative, investing tax surplus into council projects such as the sinking of two new wells in 1637, and the development of new grazing lands.

Other projects which are recorded however, for example the upgrading of the town wall in 1643, or the building of the grain silo and the re-arming of the Hamelin arsenal in 1644, could be said to be symptomatic of a town that had stopped looking to the future and had instead turned its gaze inward, fearful that events outside would soon overtake them.

As the war entered its final phase, this fear of its imminent intrusion stifled all town development, physical and spiritual. Old jealousies and suspicions amongst citizens resurfaced, the atmosphere became tense and ripe for intrigue. The townsfolk would have heard from the few passing traders that the Swedish army was at large in Upper Saxony, and that the Imperial forces would be regrouping to face them. Who amongst the townspeople was already in secret collusion with Gustavus' men? Who was planning to lure them to Hamelin, and for what personal gain? Or was the devious Mayor pinning Hamelin's colours to the dying Imperialist banner? Was the council stupid enough to court both opposing sides, were they all to die for this treachery?

It would undoubtedly have saddened a man of Ebber's intellect and integrity to have faced such questions. He would have known more than anyone that the appearance of soldiers would have meant ruin. Whilst the Swedish forces would strip the town of provisions and destroy what remained to deny the enemy any sanctuary, any 'friendly' Imperial unit would threaten in a different way. They would seek lodgings and food, and in return bring to the town the spoils they had accumulated elsewhere in their campaigns: lawlessness, syphilis, typhus, plague. Either way, Hamelin had to be protected, and it was worth paying any price.

A MORE EXPERIENCED MAN would no doubt have noticed that Joyce had developed her fondness for me long before I did. Certainly, in retrospect, the signs were all there – the way she would engineer it so that we sat together at the card table, the new questions about my family and background, the crosses suddenly sprouting at the foot of her notes to me. Perhaps a more experienced man would also have spotted the way the Unit 3 dance was being set up as a triumphant 'coming out' party for our 'relationship' rather than the group outing originally proposed.

My actions that night were despicable. I have no pleasure in recalling them. I do so not out of any spurious sense of pride but as part of the quest for truth and understanding we have embarked on. These details remain a source of pain, but they must be aired. I have long seen them as significant.

In the event only seven of us made the two-hour trip over to Unit 3 at Freiburg, James Clements dropping out, preferring to hitch a lift towards the British sector, a night of boozing with some old school chums ahead of him. He was quiet all the way through his part of the journey, and turned his back on us as soon as he was off the bus. Joyce didn't seem too perturbed though, and it bothered me that he didn't either. I could already sense my victory was a hollow one – Joyce had preferred me because I was somehow the safer bet, the one with less devil in him. Was he ever keen on her anyway?

Geoff Marlow had purloined a bottle of whisky somewhere and brought it along to liven up the trip. My first taste of it was none too pleasant, but as the grey evening chill seeped through the bus the bottle was passed around with increasing frequency, even Joyce swigging down a few fiery drams.

We were all merry when we eventually arrived, high with drink and a sense of anticipation. I think we all imagined the dance would have a much greater sense of occasion than it actually did. Unit 3 camp was housed in what used to be a public park, and was a haphazard collection of tents and huts, even in comparison with our ramshackle base. By virtue of being in the free American sector it had no fence to guard it, and therefore no coherent feel as to where its buildings stopped and other departments started. The dance was held in a large marquee to the rear of the main block, next to a boating pond, now drained. The band were playing as we arrived. The place was still half empty. It wouldn't be until after midnight that it would fill up with airmen and the rest, and there was no problem in finding a table to accommodate us all.

Two impressions of the set-up. Firstly, how intimidating it all was. I suppose we all expected some kind of instant rapport with our colleagues in the other unit, even some sort of welcome. There was none of that and I don't think I recognised a fellow medic all night. Instead, the place was swarming with American servicemen, loud and brash and aggressive, leering at the women, occasionally throwing a drunken punch at one another before collapsing into a brotherly embrace. Perhaps it was a result of my four months of relative isolation at Gershalt, or maybe because I just didn't know them, but either way I felt threatened, and conspicuous in my British uniform. That was why I drank so much, a cheap American beer that sounded like a German one, Budweiser I think.

Secondly, the shortage of women. With the heavy ratio of men to women, the few women actually there found themselves feted and fought over like queen bees, kept on their feet all night with a perpetual chain of dance partners cutting in over and over. The way Joyce clung to my space however, meant that I was somewhat removed from this competition, and that I could afford to be more sanguine as I smoked and drank my way through the proceedings.

This was a situation I was familiar with in many ways. Marlow had begun to drone on about his time at Cambridge, boasting about drinking exploits and his capacity to hold a skinful, the connection to student days seemed oddly appropriate. I thought back to my arrival at Glasgow University five years before, unpacking my books in my digs, leaving the picture of mother and father in the case squeezed under the bed, trying to convince myself that this was the liberation I had dreamed of, not a punishing exile from the comforts of home. I struggled to banish these thoughts, to put them away like childish things; it was time now to be a man, to find new friends with whom I could reinvent myself. Trouble was, although I gravitated quickly enough towards those with similar aspirations, these were young men cast in an image of myself, all of us amiable in a shy and slightly shallow sort of way, all of us aware that there was now a different game to be played, yet none of us possessing even a basic understanding of the art of seduction. The alcoholic culture then endemic in student life was founded on such frustrations, a compensation for other out of reach pursuits. An image flashed through my mind – a 'boat race' in the Halt Bar, two weeks into my first term. A drinking relay, seven-a-side, three teams. Full up before we begin, I watch in horror as the first pints are downed in impossibly fast swallows. It will be my turn soon, the whole bar is cheering, I look at the full glass swaying in my hand, utterly unappealing; it will be my ninth of the night. In front, Hamish, a stocky chemist's son from Oban who shares my landing. Normally a picture of health, now pale and unsteady. If he can do it so must I. The pint ahead has gone and the crowd turns to us. Hamish does well, half his drink has gone with two huge gulps when suddenly he stops. His glass is filling up again as he retches back into it. He collapses, spinning toward me, knocking my drink, both our glasses fall. A cheer in the far corner, another team has completed and won and I turn to see but there's a punch on my shoulder, the landlord, shouting aggressively. I can't hear him but realise I'm being thrown out, together with poor Hamish. Another cheer as we leave and I wave uncertainly in salute. Is this an honourable exit or are we being mocked for our juvenile level of performance? I remember leading Hamish to the kerbside, and wrapping his arm around a lamppost before leaving him to vomit his way through to daybreak.

The memory was enough to slow me down for a while, but Marlow forced a rapid pace, commandeering the kitty and ensuring a constant flow of orders to the bar whether the rest of us were ready or not, then clearing the table and insisting we all start again on whisky.

We left just before one o'clock, our driver searching us out and telling us time was up. Geoff and the boys were soon slouched in sleep once the bus was moving again, whilst I was sandwiched in at the back between Penny and Joyce, occasionally puncturing their girlish chatter with what passed for droll remarks. I was already thinking about what would happen when we arrived back.

So what exactly were these thoughts? It's hard to remember. Alcoholic thoughts, meandering thoughts: would we get a chance to be alone, and did I want to be alone with her; was she more of a beauty than I had given her credit for? She was leaning into me and I could feel her warmth and smell her perfume. I would try to find some neutral ground and see what happened; maybe the canteen would be unlocked.

We dispersed quickly once we had drawn up inside the camp gates. Evans led off Geoff Marlow, propping him up on his shoulder. He looked a sorry state. The others made their own lurching paths back to the huts, and then only Joyce and I were left. We went for a walk 'to clear our heads'; as I recall, we might have been holding hands. Everything might have been different if the canteen door had been locked, but it wasn't. How I would wish later that it had been.

It happened, then. A kiss in the darkness, once inside, with her back against the door. A kiss that developed into a longer one, a breathless one down on the floor among the chairs, where the smell of boiled cabbage was stronger. In my mind the kiss becomes an urgent, panting, undignified scramble. There is saliva on my chin and I can taste her lipstick. We are fumbling, clutching, squeezing. I'm pawing at the buttons on her blouse and she's not stopping me, it's too late to stop. There's an imperative rush to all of this that's so new to me, no sooner are her breasts exposed than my hands are below, testing her silent compliance. Then I'm on top, and my focus is tightening ever closer until it withdraws inside, concentrating on me and then on narrowing down to only a part of me. The urge pushing my actions is irresistible, everything around is suddenly superfluous and unimportant, unnecessary to the acute pleasure surging through my groin. A surge that comes from the deep, and then, it is over; rationality, composure, awareness, all flooding back.

My virginity gone. Hers too. I'm saddened, surprised to find the same sense of guilt and inadequacy that I have learned to associate with the solo act here too but stronger. A realisation of what I've made happen, what I've perpetrated, clarifies through the muggy haze in my brain. I must look ridiculous, trousers and pants at my ankles, shirt riding up my back. Joyce is the same – I catch sight of a nipple, an auburn pubis, both having suddenly lost their power to excite. I wish she'd cover up, hide her shame, and mine.

'Are you alright?' A crass question. I curse my stupidity. She doesn't answer, lying still.

I try to help her dress but she shudders as my hand gets near her. She is crying softly.

'Joyce . . . I'm sorry . . . I shouldn't have . . .'

I stop, my words are making her worse, her sobbing more audible. What if somebody hears?

'Do you want to be left alone?'

No answer. I take it as another yes.

I panicked when Vesey asked to see me first thing that morning, my duties for that day suddenly cancelled; I could only suspect the worst.

From the earliest hours I had wrestled with an over-whelming urge to confess all and have done with it. I watched Arthur Lee rise, stiff and cantankerous, and found myself full of envy at his clear conscience. Why hadn't I stayed in and read books and papers, why had I gone to that damn ball?

Vesey was pouring himself a fresh coffee as I entered, a shiny metal flask in his hand. I thought of the dressing down he'd given me months earlier, the one I'd thought so unfair. I could have retched when I thought how much more serious this was, and this time I deserved everything I would get.

'Morning, Rob! Take a seat. Like a coffee?'

'Sorry? . . . Sure. Thank you.'

I had been distracted by the sound of voices outside. I had tried to tune in, were they talking about me? How many people knew apart from Vesey?

'You look . . . heh heh . . . as if you could use some . . . heh heh . . . Good night, last night?'

'Yes.'

'Yes? That all you gonna tell me? How much did you have to drink? What about dames? I hate to think I sent you all that way for nothing ... heh heh ... What was the action?'

He bared his tiny teeth, a reptile smile.

'Too much ... Too much, I'm afraid.'

He grinned again. Either he was the greatest actor I'd yet seen and was trying to put me off my guard, or he knew nothing. I suspected the latter, and wondered where Joyce was. I'd managed to get to the latrines, through breakfast, and over to admin without seeing her, but how long could it go on for?

'Suffering, yeah?'

I grimaced. My head was pounding. It had to be the worst hangover possible.

'Well, I guess there's no harm in you boys having your fun every while. You work hard enough.'

My spirits rose, this had to be something new, nobody could be so callous if they really knew what had gone on. The smile slowly faded as Vesey's face took on a more serious expression.

'Listen, Rob, I got a real problem and I'm wondering if you could sort it for me. You think you'd like to do that?'

My heart sank again. He was about to ask me to confess, or resign, or both.

'If I can.'

'Good.' He blew out the word softly, in his bass baritone, 'gooooooood'. I felt it wash gently over me, and again felt the urge to confess.

'Rob, you were picked for this unit because it was known that you had certain talents that we might use for a particu-

lar task. I'm referring to the scientific studies you undertook before the war. You understand?'

I did not. I could not. Never in my life have I met anyone
else with such a peculiar habit of throwing unanswerable
questions and following them up with a 'You understand?'
To have me down as a scientist after three years of a
chemistry degree course was as rational as calling me a
German linguist because of two years' school study.

'As you are aware, this is the only unit with access to
Soviet-held territory. Now you've been in most of the local
camps and you know the kind of pressures we operate
under. What I have to tell you, Rob, is that there are other
camps, further east, that we don't want to get involved
in but from time to time have to. You don't like your
coffee?'

He pointed at the untouched cup I'd been holding in an
ever tighter grip. I'd been too absorbed with the questions
in my mind to even notice it. I sipped hurriedly, and he
started again.

'The Russians are holding a small number of people in
a compound at Tatras, in Poland. Germans, well, what
they call 'ethnic' Germans. You know what that means?'

I shook my head.

'It means their ancestors came from Germany, emigrated
hundreds of years ago. Now they want to go back, and I
guess it's none too safe calling yourself a German in Soviet
territory. Anyway, Germany's willing to have them, the
Russians will let them go, but neither of us want to let them
move because these people have got a habit of breaking out
in strange illnesses. We don't want them until we know
for sure what it is. How do you feel about that?'

'It would seem to make sense. Surely it's in these people's own interest to get . . . whatever . . . treated.'

'I mean, have you got any idea of what it might be? Think you could supply a diagnosis?'

I remembered Arthur Lee's first comment to me about Vesey, that the man wasn't even a doctor. Questions like this last one showed up his real ignorance. How could I commit to diagnosing an illness I knew absolutely nothing about? Why did he think my earlier background in bio-chemistry had any relevance? Surely it was an experienced doctor they needed?

'See, Rob, we're hoping you might explore the . . . scientific angles on this, not just the obvious things we've already looked at.'

'Of course. How many patients are there, what are the symptoms? Perhaps . . .'

'Symptoms? Ulcers . . . Strange kinds of ulcers, no more than half a dozen go down with it at any one time. Now don't you go thinking you've gotta examine a roomful of them in half an hour. This is different and I want you to take your time, experiment, establish a cause.'

'How long will it take?'

Vesey shrugged. 'You're the expert, Rob. How long does it take to diagnose anything?'

'I'm sorry, of course. I mean how long will I be out there, is there a deadline, are we talking days, weeks?'

'I just can't say. This is a different challenge. Others have had their shot at it, if you can't crack it we'll try something else. Interested?'

'Look, I am, of course I am, but I think that perhaps you've over-estimated my science credentials, you see . . .'

'Relax, Rob, you're the best we've got, that's all there is to it. Thing is, I need you to go right away. Russians are impatient for action from us. I'd like you to go today. I'd really value someone of your background giving a view on just what it is that's going on with these damn people.'

Right away. Alone. It was the dream escape I'd prayed for, the Gods were smiling.

I agreed right then, and Vesey was handing me my travel authorisation an hour later, my very own ticket to oblivion.

The Soldiers

IN THE SUMMER OF 1633, an army of 20,000 men set out from Spanish-controlled Lombardy in northern Italy under the command of the Duke of Feria to intervene in the Thirty Years' War on behalf of the then beleaguered Catholic cause. Crossing into the Rhineland over the Alps, this force was charged by Philip IV himself with restoring the initiative to the Imperialists following a series of disastrous and near-fatal defeats at the hands of the marauding (Lutheran) Swedes.

Disciplined and ably led, this was one of the finest fighting forces ever assembled in Italy, its ranks containing hardened battle corps from as far afield as Sicily and Sardinia, and its impact in the field was immediate. Feria's men reversed the losing tide with stunning victories at Konstanz, Breisach, Bregenz and Rheinfelden, successes that so alarmed the Protestant league that a new French army (then fighting on the Protestant side) was raised to counter them. Before the two armies could meet however, the bitter winter of 1633 set in, causing a temporary halt to the campaign season, and both sides withdrew to shelter from its excesses. The victorious Italians therefore arrived at the apparent safety of the Alpine foothills in good spirits, eager for their commander to contemplate their next move.

But the Duke of Feria's men were never to fight again. All summer the Black Death had been waiting in these same foothills, and that winter it finally caught up with them. The plague duly succeeded where their opponents had failed, and by the spring of 1634 the Duke and most of his men were dead, their achievements swiftly forgotten or assigned to an irrelevant past as the war progressed without them.

The valleys and flat-lands of the Rhineland are littered with the ghosts of such men, as is the history of the war itself. There are many more examples of such initially promising yet ultimately futile initiatives; and of vain efforts, vain suffering, and vain death. It is not out of the question that the fighting men themselves, although from largely simple and uneducated peasant stock, had an insight into the realities of their situation, that they knew how expendable they were, how their hard-fought victories could be traded at the negotiating table, how allies could be turned suddenly into enemies with the payment of a tempting enough bribe. Perhaps such an insight could help explain their actions, for while the Thirty Years' War was a conflict of staggering diplomatic complexity, the routine barbarity of its combat was stark and simple enough.

A popular battle anthem of the time (on both sides) included the refrain that 'every soldier needs but three peasants to sustain him; one to give up his lodgings, one to provide his wife, and one to take his place in hell'. From such anecdotal evidence an image can be drawn, not only of the economic hardship caused by the war, but of the savage mentality of its participants. Yet if this was an especially brutal war, the question of what it was that determined it should be so must be asked.

The most basic of reasons concerns the nature of the battles fought, and in particular the weaponry and tactics which were employed for the first time. Two weapons made their debut during this conflict, both bringing a carnage and destructive force to the battlefield that could scarcely have been imagined before – the musket and the small-bore cannon. Although neither was strictly speaking a 'new' weapon, the battle strategies now built around them during the war meant that both wielded a formidable new power. In the case of the musket, the Swedes under Gustavus Adolphus were first to master the art of synchronised loading, re-arming and firing of continuous salvos in three lines of advancing infantry. This technique, though often appearing comic in its effete choreography, meant in practice that the opposing numbers (initially, pike-carrying infantrymen) were cut down in a ceaseless hail of lead. It would not be until the Great War three centuries later, when machine-gun fire was used to similar effect on advancing lines in the trenches, that men would fall in comparable quantities. Where the latter victims were at an advantage however, was in the nature of their death. Primitive weapons such as the musket rarely killed outright, instead they left their crippled targets to die from gruesome wounds at their leisure, unless an enemy (or colleague) saw fit to finish them off with a bayonet blade. Advances in gun-barrel calibration meant that light and mobile cannons could be brought to the battleground in the same way as the musket, and fired onto the same massed ranks of unprotected limbs, torsos, heads, all of which would fall in the wake. It is recorded that often there would be too many dead and dying left for victors to bury, and the bodies would simply be left to rot for months on end.

Perhaps the aspirations of those actually fighting should be questioned too. Though the war was religious in origin and doubtless attracted those embarking on a spiritual crusade, the evidence suggests that such enthusiasms waned during its thirty-year duration, that sponsoring sovereigns and governments did so with an increasingly resentful sense of obligation, emptying their jails to fill up troop quotas. Thus convicted criminals found themselves fighting for the 'True Faith' rather than hanging from the gallows, and the widespread adoption of the notion of salvation via service in penal battalions meant that German lands were soon filled with Europe's reprieved criminal classes.

Such men made dangerous deserters, and desertion, though nominally a capital offence, was rife in the conflict's latter years, when the elegant diplomatic manoeuvres of the key states led to widespread anarchy in the field. Again, it was entirely predictable that the main protagonists would seek to disentangle themselves from this disastrously costly fray – by the end of the second decade of fighting most of them were virtually bankrupt. However, the cost of running the war was by then sustained by those noblemen and merchants wealthy enough to fund armies in their own right under the authority of the relevant Imperial and League chiefs, such men hoping to call in the debts incurred once outright victory was achieved. This system of 'sub-contracting' the financing of the struggle can be directly blamed for fanning the flames of chaos since it is clear that many of the war's patrons took this process a logical step further, raising forces under the guise of one cause or the other, then auctioning off their services to the highest bidder. There are recorded instances of entire brigades as well as individual unit commanders changing sides up to six times during the war, sometimes even mid-battle.

Mercenaries, of course, had long been an established component of European warfare, but nevertheless, the Thirty Years' War saw a new breed of soldier of fortune emerge: the deranged, the desperate, and the lawless all took up arms and headed for the German plains, eager to claim their share of spoils. Moreover, the astute amongst them (such as the Castilian, Armando D'Ortez, whom this paper will examine in detail shortly) would have realised that their market value rose in direct proportion to the amount of blood on their hands. For the men of Germany itself, it was often *safer* to be inside an army than out of one, even if the inevitable consequence was the pillage and plunder of one's own kinsmen and country.

D'Ortez is a figure of interest since his recorded exploits epitomise the murderous pragmatism of such men paid to champion the noble Catholic and Protestant causes. Certain assumptions can safely be made about this man: that he would have been an experienced campaigner and would have been involved in the war for several years before the first reference to him found by this author; that he would be an athletic, imposing individual, a skilled horseman, duellist and shootist; and that he would have been a cunning and resourceful man, possessor of a considerable war booty, hoping for the promise of more to come. However, it is for other historians to trace his activities and precise whereabouts prior to 1643, when the state treasury of the Imperial Court first records payments and promissory notes made out to D'Ortez.

This archive lists his force as being over 400 strong, containing cavalry, pikemen and musketmen. The same source also provides a useful breakdown of the nationalities of those under his command; mainly Spaniards like himself with lesser numbers of Bavarians and Irish and some Flemish gunsmiths (who almost certainly provided cannon and salvo-firing expertise). To have amassed such a force is testimony to his battle-hardened experience; to sustain it with sufficient munitions, lodgings and food on the increasingly barren plain through 1646 and 1647 would have required great mental acumen. Other contemporary sources describe him as a 'swarthy, bearded and bestial villain', with a 'savage contemplation' to him. Nonetheless, such claims have a faint air of falsehood to them, as it would have been in D'Ortez' own interest to promote such a reputation in order to ensure prompt payment from his masters as well as to intimidate future opponents. Again, perhaps such statements reinforce impressions of him as a creation of his times – immoral, cynical, but also shrewd.

Yet by the winter of 1648, when he led his men south to Lusatia, D'Ortez may have been a troubled man. Rumours abounded that, at last, a permanent peace might be found, the great powers having been in secret conference for months, and he doubtless wondered what such a new environment might bring. He would certainly be owed ransoms and past levies from previous deeds, and would have concluded that his debtors may soon therefore wish him dead, to wipe out their debts now that he had outlived his usefulness. He may also have been troubled by the prospect of his own men's imminent demands for payment at the campaign end, irrespective of his own problems in gathering in funds to meet them. And on a more immediate note, the recent conversion of Saxony from the League to the Imperialist (Catholic) banner (in return for the Imperial territory of Lusatia) whilst theoretically granting his force the benefit of a new ally against the Swedes, would have raised the spectre in his mind of secret deals and negotiations being concluded to exorcise forces like his from the diplomatic equation, to destroy the obscene and now obsolete tools of war.

So the Saxons were now supposedly his allies, yet would they really fight against their brothers and fellow Lutherans the Swedes? Would any invitation to join forces with them be sincere, or might it not be a trap, drawn to rid the Imperial Court of an embarrassing echo of the past?

It would have been for reasons like these that D'Ortez would have led his men south into Lusatia rather than north into Saxony to join in the planned decisive battle with the Swedes. It would have been for reasons like these that he sought to evade the war for that moment, until a clearer pattern emerged once more. And it would have been for these reasons that he summoned the Germans amongst them, seeking local knowledge on where they could find a ready source of shelter and winter supplies.

'We must rest and clean our weapons,' he would have

told them, 'for this war has many a turn left to make and we must be ready for them. We need somewhere to take off our boots, someone to cook us our food, women to be with. Somewhere where we can enjoy the respect we are due for serving the Empire.'

He would have smiled as he relayed this, and the men would have understood what he meant, appreciating the underlying irony. They were used to the challenges of securing lodging, which usually meant storming a lightly guarded town or hamlet by night. Villagers seldom made for willing hosts; 'respect' was usually gained only after use of the bludgeon and the flaming torch. The problem was that after so many years of pillage there were few places of refuge left standing. Where could they go in search of their comforts? Was anywhere left unspoiled by the fighting?

'Sir, I have heard of such a place . . . my cousin told me last summer . . . he had spoken to some natives . . . good troopers, sir . . . of Heidelberg.'

D'Ortez cannot make out what the stooping figure in tattered leather jerkin and knee-breeches is shouting. Although his command of German is normally adequate the man's accent is impenetrable, a sonorous Bavarian drawl that coming from his toothless mouth has a tendency to dissolve into a peasant yodel. D'Ortez steadies his horse and gestures for the man to come forward, the beast snorting instinctively as the reins are flexed. A warm cloud of vapour rises from its mouth, and D'Ortez watches it disappear into the cold air above him. It is time to move on, winter is falling fast. He is lost in concentration for a moment, failing to notice the other man's progress through the mud below. The horse twitches again and he looks down, fixing him in the eye.

'Speak.'

'To the east . . . follow the River Treuwe . . . about forty miles.'

'And what is this place, what is it called?'

'Hamelin, sir . . . the town of Hamelin . . .'

You WILL HAVE TO take my word for it that the camp at Tarutz ever existed, or for that matter, that the incidents I will speak of actually took place. Before I set out in the car that would take me on to meet my Russian driver, Vesey pulled me aside one final time. 'Don't take too many notes,' he'd said, somewhat cryptically. 'Try to keep as much of it as you can in your head.' I suppose I should have known then that this was to be no ordinary mission, that given Vesey's gift for euphemism, this 'different challenge' was likely to be as harrowing and fraught as it would eventually prove itself to be. But I'd already had experience of what could happen if one ignored such snippets of friendly, almost casual advice, so I took him at his word. No notes then, only what has remained for these years in my head.

Tarutz was a makeshift refugee camp on the plains north of the Tatras mountains, the range that traditionally has marked Poland's border with the Ukraine. Quite why the camp was established there and not closer to Germany, where the refugees were meant to be heading, was never made clear. Neither was the precise location of the camp. Bizarre as it undoubtedly sounds, I was to spend the next six months out there without ever knowing exactly where I was. You won't find Tarutz on any map; either it is too small and insignificant to merit inclusion or Tarutz is a Ukrainian name, one rendered obsolete when the territory was passed back to Poland at the end of '47.

The drive there took eleven hours, an inordinate amount of time when one examines the distance between Berlin and southern Poland, even considering the state of the roads. There are two possible reasons for this – the prolonged tour was either a calculated attempt to disorientate me, to discourage me from any thought of escape, or my driver simply got lost, not once but over and over, disconcerted by the infinite flat horizon. This is an area not known for heavy snowfalls; nevertheless what comes down tends to stay, freezing over into a pale grey glaze, thicker and more uniform as we went further south. As the car ploughed on after yet another barren crossroads it was hard not to believe that we had strayed far off course, onto the very ice cap on top of the world, home a long way away, far below.

It was dark by the time we arrived and, deliberate or not, the combination of so much travel, growing hunger, unfamiliar territory and the memories of recent events had left me feeling profoundly unsettled, with an anxious longing for the familiar, even Gershalt.

The car stopped at what looked like a gatehouse. We were about to enter some kind of estate. The driver got out and chatted to the man on duty, passing over my papers. They spoke briefly in Russian, a strange tongue, its patterns sounding at once both primitive and complex. They began to laugh and my driver returned to start up the rasping engine, the barrier across the path leading beyond was raised and we were through it, weaving through the trees and bushes on both sides. Looking back, I think the despair hit me as soon as we entered, seeping in silently through the windows, through the leather soles of my boots, the wretched earth laden with poisonous seed. If hell has a garden, an underworld equivalent of Eden, we were now there. It wasn't just the fact that it was cold, unwelcoming, alien; no, Tarutz had an aura that struck you as soon as you entered. Something terrible was happening there, or had happened. It was as if haunted by both past and present. Even a twenty-four-year-old innocent from Helensburgh couldn't fail to pick up on it, to feel it grating against the soul. I peered into the darkness ahead – tents, a dwindling bonfire, derelict stone sheds. No colours. It was like being in a film. The sentry post through which we had passed was attached to the remains of what had presumably once been a gatehouse, illuminated by the car lights which threw it into a harsh contrast with its sur-roundings, speckled silvery greys of frozen evening dew standing out against the darkness all around, the shadows of the trees nearby throwing alien silhouettes. I caught the reflection of the driver; this time he didn't look away, nodding and smiling, taking a delight in my obvious con-cern. So you feel it too?

The car was moving at walking pace and then it slowed even further until the engine was cut. The driver got out and then was round at my door, gesturing for me to get out and follow. My legs were stiff after such a long journey,

it had been hours ago that we had stopped to excuse ourselves by the roadside, and I staggered like a drunk man
behind him. We were walking on an incline, on a stone
path, heading toward what seemed like another ruin,
although much larger. In the gloom it was impossible to
tell, but I thought I could discern in the moonlight the
remains of the estate's main building, perhaps once a
stately home, and I realised that the rubble all around
would have once been part of its courtyard. On its own it
might have reached up to four storeys at one time, it was
rectangular and sat astern the small hill we were climbing,
roof and upper floors blown away. I recognised the random
formations left behind by mortar shell and explosive, so
familiar from Berlin.

I was so absorbed in them I lost sight of the driver
for a moment before I caught him again. He had moved
downhill, and was talking to two armed guards at my left.
They shared a quick embrace and guffaw, shuffling in the
cold and then they were up at me, pulling me back down
where they had been, under the once ornate stairs that led
up to the reception hall. The driver pointed to the guards
and walked back to the car. I had been passed on. One of
the guards jangled a huge set of keys and I realised I was
to be locked up in some sort of cellar underneath. A surge
of adrenalin went through me. All that travelling for this?
To be a prisoner, a hostage? Did Vesey know this would
be how it would end, or was this one of those situations
he would expect me to take charge of? I stood still.

'Who's in charge here? *Wer übernehmen?*'

They looked to each other, then to me. I realised it was
probably a mistake to speak German to them, they might

74

recognise it but would never understand it, and if they mistook me for one it would be a disaster.

'Me, British! British! Where . . . is . . . your commander?'

My attempts to explain myself were futile. They stared back with disgust and growing irritation. The one with the keys moved briskly toward me.

'. . . *niet* . . . *niet*,' he mumbled, grabbing me by the arm, and pulling me down to the cellar entrance. I tripped and jerked forward, punching him in the side as I instinctively tried to raise my arms as I fell toward him. He swore furiously.

It would be an exaggeration to suggest that his companion had raised his gun behind us, yet at that moment it felt as if events were spiralling out of control and that the rifle butts were about to come down on me. I tried not to cower or to show weakness, but my resistance was at an end. The jangling sound of the keys covered my heavy breaths, an iron door was opened and I followed them in.

The guard behind shone a torch ahead of us – we were in a stone-walled corridor underneath the former mansion. There was a disgusting dank smell permeating the air, the torch occasionally lingering on the moss- and mould-covered brickwork. The passageway was narrow, about three feet, and seemed to halt in a dead end. The guard in front disappeared from view for a second and I paused long enough for the one behind to walk into me, shoving me round the hidden corner I had failed to notice. The keys were ringing again, the torch followed the sound and I saw we had arrived at the entrance to a cell, whose barred door was being unlocked. The guard shouted inside as he pushed it open with his boot. Then he took a step back and turned to me, nodding and gesturing with his head to show that I should go in. My heart sank. Why did it have to end this way, what had I done wrong, couldn't they let me go back to Scotland? But for some reason I was resigned to it all; as I said, my resistance was over. It is strange the inertia which can seize you in moments of real danger. Somehow I assumed that I deserved this.

I walked in. It was totally dark inside, but the smell was even worse. I could feel that there was straw or some kind of matting underfoot and wondered if I would ever get tired enough to lie down on it. To my surprise, the door behind me was not immediately shut or relocked, instead the cell filled with light as the torch was shone in. The room was longer than I would have thought, about fifteen feet. The light flickered ahead, picking out the shape of a bundle of rags in the far corner. Both guards stood in the doorway, shouting at me. The one with the torch kept pointing it into the corner, they wanted me to do something with the heap lying there. I was so drained I was finding it difficult to stay awake on my feet. It was so dark I could no longer discern when my eyes were closed, and found myself trying to peer through my own eyelids in confusion.

Suddenly, a commotion. There were raised voices outside. Another light was now darting around the doorway; others had followed us. My two guards turned behind to argue, a figure appeared between them, squeezing its way through to join me, not a guard but a white-coated being, also carrying a torch.

'English? . . . You are English?'

I was drifting off again, and took this to be part of a

dream. For a second I could not answer, all concentration required to prevent myself rocking on my feet.

'Yes . . . British . . .'

The man moved forward. 'They say you are German . . . Idiots!'

He shrugged and held out his hand.

'Igor Geigy. I am pleased to meet you, Dr . . . ?'

'Robert Watt.'

'They were meant to tell me when you arrived.'

He shrugged again and shouted back at the other two in Russian. It must have been something derogatory, they waved their arms angrily in response.

'. . . and have you had chance to examine patient, Doctor?'

I didn't understand what he could be getting at, was he confusing something in his translation from Russian? I shook my head. He then shone his torch into the corner and moved toward the bundle lying there, going down on his knees to touch it and pull it toward him.

'This one. We notice first symptoms two days ago. Put in here for quarantine. What do you think?'

He pointed the light straight at his hands and then I saw it. This was no pile of rags, it was a man. I inched forward. It was a desperately sick man, unconscious, feverish, wrapped up against the cold. My Russian colleague was parting the ragged shirt covering the man's stomach. Again, he held the light to it.

'What you think, Dr Watt?'

The man looked as if he had some kind of surface wound, a fresh cut about three inches long, with signs of tissue damage under the skin, possibly extending wider

77

than the area of cut flesh on the surface. The longer I studied it however, the more I began to change my mind.

'An ulceration . . . an ulcer of some sort that's connected to a cyst or fissure inside. Shouldn't it be cleaned up?'

My companion shook his head. He seemed rueful.

'Better to leave open. Ulceration? We call this condition five. Tomorrow, when we come and look again, condition six. You will see.'

I would see, see what? What sense did it make to leave a sick man in this crawling environment. Were they trying to kill him, break his will?

Geigy stood up and turned. I was surprised to feel his arm around my back, resting on my shoulder, gently guiding me through the shadows back to the door.

'Come, friend. You must be tired. I will take you to your quarters. Welcome to Tarutz.'

Mayor Ebber

ANY FAIR JUDGEMENT of the role of Heinrich Ebber and his leadership in Hamelin's demise can arguably only take place once certain conditions of our own culture are acknowledged. For, as Mayor, Heinrich Ebber sought not only to provide control and direction regarding the practicalities of the town's life but also to offer a moral lead, and there are those reading this paper who will feel a revulsion at the notion of the latter. The danger is that in doing so, the prejudices of a modern age are being unfairly used to assess events of another, completely different, time. For example, the requirements of the recent war will have temporarily forced many readers of this paper into subservient relationships where they endured experience of notably poor command, similarly there will be a broad spectrum of subjective opinion regarding the 'class system' which will flavour any British view on authority.

Whereas we live in a society increasingly less deferential to authority, leaders of previous centuries were routinely viewed as having arrived at their position through Divine choice, and whereas modern leaders achieve their positions because of their functional skills it is certain that Mayor Ebber's moral ambitions for Hamelin would have been a major factor in his endorsement by his predecessor. His mandate to provide such a lead would have been entirely legitimate.

What then, would have been his goals? Fundamentally, it was to let Hamelin grow, to flourish economically, and to liberate all its citizens from a self-limiting peasant-class mentality.

The peasant class of Europe lived (and live) off the land in an agriculture-based economy, but never as landowners. By reason of birthright, their opportunities for advancement were negligible (consider the conditions of virtual slavery endured by the serfs of Russia prior to the communist revolution of 1917), and further limited by a complete lack of expectations and aspirations amongst the peasants themselves. For the peasant had a low regard for the value of his individual life; to him the family, and preservation of its blood-line, was the overwhelming focus, and individual members' sufferings were not even of secondary importance.

Heinrich Ebber's aspiration was to eliminate such suffocating ties and to replace them with a broader allegiance between citizens and their town authorities, to allow all such citizens to lead more fulfilling lives, each reaching his or her potential, with security and safety guaranteed by the larger body fit to provide it in a consistent and objective manner – the municipal state. His vision was one of each citizen enjoying a mutually beneficial relationship with the state, and what drove him to pursue this vision was not a pious conceit but a sincere 'Christian' conscience. The tragedy of Hamelin was consequently a deeply personal one for him, his having tried to lead the town and its underclass into an age of enlightenment despite the hostility this would have generated from some of those protecting their privileged station. Yet when all citizens finally did unite it was not in pursuit of Mayor Ebber's utopian goals, but to indulge in the grotesque and bestial rites that annihilated the town's humanity. The irony would not have been lost on the Mayor, nor would he have been unaware that many would regard his constant striving for the best of human values as a weakness. Indeed, it can be imagined that at times he would ultimately feel jealous of those in possession of more selfish and ruthless personal traits; but as this paper will detail, Mayor Ebber consistently responded to the catastrophic events of the winter of 1647 in a manner never compromising his beliefs, and this despite the realisation that his dream was dying long before the Pied Piper cast his evil spell on Hamelin.

Certain private correspondence, now in the possession of this author, contains descriptions of Mayor Ebber as a 'furtive and secretive fellow' whose closed sessions with the treasurer Wolfricht aroused suspicion amongst their council colleagues. From the remaining Imperial (and Saxon) correspondence of the period, an understanding of the thought-processes and strategies employed by the town council immediately prior to the town's demise can be surmised. The key evidence is the flurry of dispatches in the aftermath of the transfer of the Lusatian territory to the province of Saxony at the tail-end of the Thirty Years' War. There is a seemingly endless stream of requests for clarification on status and sovereignty and interpretation

of past Imperial edicts and laws from Hamelin; and a progressively terse series of replies from Vienna. Eventually,
an ultimatum was sent. In response, the Hamelin treasurer,
Wolfricht, promised to raise the issues in question at the
next full council session, on 1 November 1647. These fiscal
matters can only be resolved by the unanimous agreement
of all councillors, he explains, adding (perhaps disin-
genuously) that all councillors concerned will act in the
'appropriate manner', and that the resolution will be a
matter of 'non-contentious debate'. It is likely that the
meeting took place in a very different atmosphere, Ebber
and Wolfricht knowing that recriminations would flow
once they finally broke the news to their colleagues in the
council chamber.

'What is this?'

Lothar Kunze recognises the Imperial seal at the head
of the scroll Ebber has just handed to him. He checks the
date by its wax stamp and sees that this is a recent dispatch,
21 October. He had not been aware of any recent visitors
to Hamelin.

'A formal . . . and final, warning. We are to pay fifteen
thousand Thalers in levy of outstanding taxes to the Saxons
by December or "face the consequences" of our illegal
contempt of court.'

A troubled murmur reverberates around the council
table. Kunze puts down the scroll: it is too gloomy inside
the room to begin a painstaking study of the paper's elab-
orately calligraphed menace. In any case, the Mayor's last
comment is of a more alarming concern.

'Have you lost your wits, man? The Saxons? What is
the meaning of this . . . a joke?'

The scroll is snapped up by the occupant of the neighbouring chair, Strauss, who begins to pore over its detail, Councillor Mannau peering over his shoulder as he does so. All other eyes are on Mayor Ebber, the youngest man in the small panelled room. Mayor Ebber speaks with a weariness and bearing that could be mistaken by those not familiar with him for disdain. He takes deep breaths between statements, his eyes are fixed on the oak ceiling above, only occasionally does he glance down to search for momentary support from his treasurer at the opposite end of the table.

'Lusatia – the entire province – has been traded to Saxony in return for their allegiance to the Imperial cause. We are therefore subject to Saxon authority and tax levies. Past debts and tax liabilities which the Imperial Court deemed were still due from us at the time of the territory transfer have also been passed to the Saxons, who have been pressing for payments they deem overdue. The notice in Councillor Strauss' hands is the final stage of that process.'

There is a silence. Mayor Ebber appreciates the sense of shock his announcement will have inspired, how it will take more than a passing moment before the full gravity of the situation is appreciated, and how an angry backlash will be an inevitable part of the process. The decision to continue full payment of taxes even when the Empire's very existence seemed under threat had been unanimously agreed, the plan being that recognition of Hamelin as a diligent and consistent tax provider might counter any danger of the town being bargained away to enemy powers at the negotiating table. This policy had now obviously floundered disastrously, Hamelin's schemes being dwarfed by much larger concerns. More distressing was the fact that the Imperial Court had denied receipt of the latest payments, and in effect had passed on demands, for the Saxons to claim, of double instalments from an increasingly impoverished treasury fund. They had obviously been an expensive ally to buy.

'How long have you known of this, Heinrich?'

Kunze's tone holds both despondency and lament, but there is no sign that any of the others are sensitive to it, only the Mayor grimacing slightly as he continues to stare upwards.

'Six months . . . seven now . . .' He brings his head down directly to address the older man. 'Please . . . please be assured that my failure to involve any other members of the council, or to inform them of this correspondence has not been a calculated exercise in deceit or born out of contempt for any councillor's duties or responsibilities. The decision was mine alone, and taken out of the highest concern for the town and well-being of its people. I have, perhaps misguidedly, tried to protect you all from unnecessary anguish and from living with the terrible secret which may have forced you to be similarly closed with your friends and loved ones.'

'And please be assured, sir, that your words are no comfort to me at all, and that I would have you grant me enough respect to make my own judgements rather than have you spare my sensibilities!'

Mayor Ebber searches for the words with which to apologise to his former mentor but his thoughts are interrupted, firstly by the stamping of approval which has greeted

Kunze's outburst and then by a new question raised at the far end of the table.

'Why would we choose not to tell the people? Why do you assume we would have chosen to maintain your silence over a matter that affects the entire town?'

Ebber and Wolfricht exchange glances. The latter indicates his readiness to answer, anxious lest Ebber's concentration is still distracted by his concern for his relationship with old Kunze. Ebber nods to him and he begins to speak, his voice higher in pitch, almost effeminate, in comparison with the Mayor's, despite his seniority. Once renowned as one of Hamelin's most eligible bachelors, although such sentiments have long given way to rumour and gossip over his failure to marry, he now cuts a faintly ludicrous figure at the table, buckled hat and wig sitting astride a plump and ruddy-cheeked face. His accounting skills are still well enough respected to ensure his words are greeted with quiet.

'Over the past four years we have received numerous threats and demands for support and payment of war levies. We have received requisitions from at least four different states and newly assembled regional authorities, all claiming jurisdiction over our land. Had we entertained these at face value we would have exhausted all funds many years ago, and would have let ourselves be accused of treason by our true masters. It has long been an established procedure to keep any such contact secret, until the legitimacy of such contact is ascertained. You would agree, surely, that the potential for unrest amongst our citizens which could be caused by such dealings makes any other practice unwise?'

'And how is the validity of such claims achieved?'

'We have used different policies. Whilst we have never refused to pay any claimant outright, we have usually sought to prolong the courtship as long as possible by entering into a lengthy discourse over conditions and terms. By this method, we have often outlasted the period of ascendancy of such powers that would seek to gain from us, or at least, outlasted their patience.'

'What then of Saxony – can we not treat them in a similar fashion?'

'We have tried. The paper in Councillor Mannau's hand is the latest in a series of communications.'

'Are there any pretexts left for us to question?'

'There are many . . .' He stretches, gesturing for the Imperial notice to be returned to him. '. . . many.'

'If I may . . .'

Wolfricht turns to face the Mayor who has interrupted his reply. Another nod and he falls mute.

'That is a choice open to us,' continues the Mayor, 'and we must select a new policy from those available. Before we address that, however, there are a number of other issues worthy of our attention.'

Mayor Ebber pauses and seeks out eye contact with each member of his fellow councillors, one by one. It is important he carries them with him. Almost instantly, however, he finds his head tilting back of its own accord, or as if under direct instruction from his nose. The stench inside is unbearable, odours of excrement, urine and animal carcasses permeating the chamber from the alleyway out below. Normally this room, like the town itself, would be immune, clean and hospitable. But the town is overcrowded, the population swollen by those now fearful of the brigands roaming the countryside, and the lack of rain and rationing of water has meant there is nothing to flush the streets of their vile debris. Hamelin's inhabitants are now wary of touching any stinking offal for fear of being bitten by the rats likely to be feasting on it. The rats are inescapable now, their numbers silently growing by the day, having long since overtaken the townspeople as the largest group within the walls.

Ebber leans forward and concentrates anew. 'Firstly, the Saxons. Are they are true masters, or are they imposters like the rest? I'm afraid we can have no doubt over that, they have been granted full Imperial control over all Lusatia, therefore we are in a somewhat new situation. Secondly, are they in a position to exercise their authority over us? I suspect they are. They have fresh armies recruited across the north, and may choose to tour their newly acquired lands before the next campaign season begins. It is unlikely that an army would be dispatched on our behalf alone, but if our neighbours are in a similar predicament to ourselves, which we must assume to be the case, then our fate may be sealed regardless of what we decide.'

'What do you mean, Mayor?'

'That it has been decided to extort whatever monies can be raised from all towns and cities regardless of their previous payments to the Imperial Court. That these charges are fabricated in that they bear no relation to our record.'

'Are you suggesting that we should challenge the honesty of the claim against us?'

Mayor Ebber grimaces again and scratches his head. The

point he is trying to make is surely simple enough, why are the others failing to understand? Is it his choice of words or do they choose not to hear him?

He looks to his fingernails, a crushed louse curls on an arched back. Another surge of despair sweeps through him; he has lived for two years without lice and now they were back, swarming in hives with the rats. Perhaps his daughters had picked them up whilst playing with the others, or then it could have been Anna, whilst taking her reading class. Should he tell her, would she not already know? If she didn't, would the news upset her when she had no means of changing the situation? The same dilemma over and over.

'What I mean is . . .' He stops for a moment, the rest of the table have begun to scratch, prompted by his own outbreak, and he feels his concentration waver once more, thoughts passing back to his family, infestation.

'. . . that the Saxons and their allies will probably dispatch an army to this area in any case. There is no point in paying, or even paying what we can, as they will simply demand more. They have deliberately asked for what they know we cannot afford to provide an excuse to strip the town of whatever assets they desire.'

'What assets would they choose?'

'They will let the soldiers decide when they visit.'

'And we should not pay because of this?'

'Payment is an irrelevant issue. We should prepare for an invasion.'

'Nonsense. This is the counsel of despair. We must organise reparations immediately. Hamelin must be spared!'

Councillor Unger's strident exclamation meets with

another round of noisy approval, hands thumping the table surface, heads vigorously nodding. Three men out of the twelve remain still; Kunze, treasurer Wolfricht, and Mayor Ebber himself.

Unger speaks softly, making no effort to raise his voice over the others' chorus. 'Gentlemen. We cannot pay. If Hamelin is to be spared we must defend it.'

The noise subsides as his words register.

'What is the balance of our treasury fund?'

Wolfricht glances at the scroll in front of him. 'Four hundred Thalers.'

'Then we must offer that and a balance in grain, livestock and promissory notes,' suggests Mannau.

It is Kunze who snaps a reply, seizing the chance to rekindle a once extinct enmity. He now finds himself despising the thin-lipped merchant's lack of resolve and strength. What has he got to offer the council? 'We can write as many damned notes as we choose, nobody in their right mind would accept them when Hamelin itself might vanish along with those that signed them. We have barely enough grain to feed the town through the winter if the rats don't devour it first, and the rats are the only livestock you will find within our walls this winter. The Mayor is correct, the time has come. We must prepare to defend what we have.'

There is a shaking of heads, an audible consensus of disagreement slowly rises. Kunze continues, voice straining to lift itself above the commotion. 'And we should include those who would destroy us from within. Anyone found looting the grain store should be expelled from the walls of the town!'

Mannau smiles, a pained, condescending smile.

'But Councillor, many of our citizens no longer view this as stealing, merely taking their share of grain now before the rats eat it all. The store is overrun with them, is this such a crime?'

It is the Mayor who once again makes himself heard above the rabble. 'Can't you see? It is because so many have broken into the silo that we have this problem with rats. Every night a new trail of grain is laid from the store to his home by someone whose greed outweighs his ability to carry. All our harvests under one roof, protected by one ratcatcher rather than an army of ratcatchers, is that so insane? Tell me where I've gone wrong! Give me the benefit of your damn wisdom!'

Ebber stops and looks to his hands clenched tight on the tabletop. He had been addressing them all but his gaze had been fixed on Mannau. He studies his own white knuckles and realises that for a moment, however fleeting, he had wished the man real harm. His hands are brought together, palm to palm, and he clasps them in a moment of silent prayer. Forgive me, Lord. Forgive us all for failing this test you have sent us.

The room is in uproar, walls reverberating with the sound of accusations and insults. Ebber's instinct is to curtail the disputes with a call to vote, but no motions have been set or even outlined. He watches on, distanced from the fray, the arguments now too starved to draw his contribution, and he silently continues his petition to God. He must see Seicle, the priest, before he returns home when this brawl finally ends. Meanwhile, questions are being raised over old spending decisions, policies attacked; some insisting on viewing the past meeting minutes and budget statements. There is no sign of any resolution, only new divides opening up like wounds splitting over a skin stretched too tight.

Moments later, a knock on the chamber door. The door opens and a figure, head bowed, walks solemnly to the Mayor's side. It is the town aldermaster, apologising for disturbing the meeting, there is news the Mayor should hear. Ebber tells him to address all of them, there are no secrets in the chamber. The remark draws a number of wry smiles from the assembly; however, these vanish as the aldermaster speaks.

'Soldiers, Sirs, eight miles to the west moving this way. A force of five hundred heading for our town. An Imperial army, led by a Spaniard. They say they are on orders to take Hamelin.'

I AWOKE WITH A START and that ghastly feeling of not knowing where on earth I was. It seemed to take an age for my heartbeat to settle down as the realisation set in that the never-ending journey and dark visitations in that cell had not been a dream after all, and my sense of panic was gradually replaced by one of weariness as I took in the scene around me. I was in a camp bed, but this one made my usual one at Gershalt seem the height of luxury. The mattress could only have been an inch thick, and the base itself was barely off the floor. When I hung my head over the side during the night it must have been only inches from the dust, earth and mouse droppings lying there. The bed linen consisted of about four blankets, all different colours and weights. They didn't seem to be any kind of army-issue, and I shuddered to think who or what had been sleeping on them before. I immediately made to get up.

Finding a space to do this was my next problem. I was in a tiny hut, with walls of corrugated iron, crammed high with boxes, tools and cabinets. There was no heating, and the cold attacked as soon as I stood up and scrambled over towards my clothes, lying on top of a crate with Russian lettering stamped on its side. I cursed and scratched my head as I hurriedly dressed. I felt disgusting, stiff and clammy from the night's restless sleep but also exhausted. I'd had enough stress and yet knew that another day of fumbling lay ahead, of struggling to understand and make myself understood. What I craved more than anything, aside from a long hot soak, was for someone to take it all out of my hands, to tell me where to go, what to do, and what to think. But I knew it would be just me again on my own, Robert Watt, out there facing the unknown, representing Vesey, Unit 4, and the whole free world. There had to be a joke in this somewhere, perhaps I was too tired or just too plain stupid to appreciate it.

I checked my watch: five past nine, it seemed much later. Outside, the bustle and clamour seemed well established, the rest of the camp must have been up for a while. I hauled on my boots and stepped out to join the fray, following a worn path through the mire leading up to the main ruin. To be honest, I didn't have any plan or notion of how to start the day, I simply wanted to start walking, and let myself be directed to wherever it was deemed I should be. On reflection, I think I must have been in a state of shock, perhaps depression; I had lost my way. Later, I would ponder on the strange countenance and manner of the refugees milling around me, for these were a very different set from those I had been used to dealing with in Berlin. Broken, hollow, completely resigned . . . these were empty souls with none of the pride or sense of affront of a people trying to reconnect to a world that had tried to shed them.

Had they committed some crime for which they knew there was no redemption, or had they looked too long inside the war's abyss? These were questions for later, right then I watched these people pass me by, shuffling up to join the various queues at the corners of the camp at which food, water and medications were being dispensed.

I began to drift toward the ruin itself, retracing my steps from the night before up to the stairs under which was the entrance to the basement cellars. Although the building had suffered extensive fire and explosive damage I could see that there was more of it left standing than I would have guessed in the shadows of the previous night. Indeed, almost the entire ground floor and parts of the first were being used by the Russians as their administration base for the camp. There were soldiers everywhere, still clumsily wielding their heavy guns, but I didn't feel the same sense of menace or threat I'd experienced the night before. Most of them were young boys, seventeen or eighteen, cold and bored, slouching on a stair as they lit up their cheap, wood-smelling cigarettes, killing time. Around them, a few of the residents of the camp below, pleading in an unknown tongue, wringing their hands in begging gestures, probably anxious to see relatives held in the basement underneath. The soldiers would wave them off with an embarrassed shrug, occasionally making as if to sweep them away with a swing of a rifle. I wandered past, their confused bickering humming in my ears. I was looking for the man who had introduced himself but I couldn't remember his name. No one seemed to notice me, although I must have been a conspicuous presence in my khaki British uniform amongst the Red Army greatcoats and rags of the refugees. In fact, this was another thing that struck me later, the costumes of the herds all around. They wore clothes that I had never seen before: women in headscarves, long overdresses with many layers of petticoats underneath. So many layers of clothing everywhere in fact, shirts under waistcoats, themselves under embroidered over-shirts, tatty boots pulled on top of smaller shoes, buckles cutting into wet leather which had been stretched over them. Many of the men I would notice wore knee-length boots, as one might associate with horse-riding, and would have fittings tied over the top of each boot to keep them closed tight to their thighs, to keep out the dirt. Almost everyone's garments, although obviously once brightly coloured and clean, were heavily soiled and muddy, collars and cuffs ingrained with dirt. I wondered how long these people had been on the move. This was not a simple case of overdue laundry, what was on view was a relic of what I had assumed was a long-dead lifestyle. These people hadn't changed clothes for years. Watching them about the ruins of the estate was like wandering into the landscape of an Old Master painting, a Dürer or a Brueghel, the emaciated, grubby faces hauntingly familiar.

'*Da?*'

It was a fatter face staring at me now. My hovering presence had drawn the attention of a rather portly army officer sitting at a desk in the room just off the main entrance on the ground floor. There were two others in with him, but I could tell he was the most important by the pips on his shoulder braids and the way he was barking indignantly at me. Behind him, in between two huge faultline cracks in the wall, hung a sepia portrait of Stalin.

'*Da!*' he bawled, louder, presumably in case I had failed to hear him the first time.

'British ... Doctor, do you speak English? Arrived last ...'

'*Da!*' he cut in again, and started to shout at the others, something in Russian. They started to answer back, mumbled excuses and thrown hands countering the insults and accusations coming from the other direction.

'That's right. I am a British spy, sent here in this cunning disguise to learn your most important secrets. I'm looking for the doctor I met last night who spoke English, well, any bugger actually who can tell me what is meant to be going on and where I might get some bloody breakfast, unless you buggers want to bloody starve me.'

'My dear Dr Watt, I can assure you we do not wish to do that.'

I turned around. Standing behind me was the very same doctor I had been asking for. My cheeks must have flushed with embarrassment, I had only spoken to remind myself I had a tongue, the rest had just spiralled from there.

'I'm sorry ... you must think ...'

'It is fine. These fools would not have been able to understand a word. So, you are hungry?'

'Yes ... rather, I haven't eaten since yesterday morning. I'm sorry, I can't remember your name.'

He laughed again. A warm, good natured laugh. I tried to connect him to the man in my mind from the night before. He was about forty, dark-skinned with astonishingly pale grey eyes. One might have thought him blind, or troubled with an opaque glaucoma. He held out his hand, thin and wiry like the rest of him, the back of it covered with jet black hairs.

'I am Igor, Igor Geigy. Doctor of camp.'

He seemed more harmless, more approachable than I remembered.

'Of course, Dr Geigy. I remember now.'

'You must call me Igor. And you, Robert?'

'Rob.'

'Come then, Rob. We try to find food.'

He led me out of the building and back down the hill toward the tents and huts of the main camp itself. We veered off to the left, however, and walked along the path that marked the inner perimeter, and as he talked I saw how heavily guarded Tarutz was. Dr Geigy spoke in an animated, chattering sort of way. Several times he paused to tell me what a pleasure it was for him to be using his English once more, how it had been so long since he had been able to converse with anyone outside his immediate circle of colleagues and family. Tarutz, he said, had indeed been a country seat of a member of the Polish aristocracy, but he didn't know for sure who, or what had happened to him. Did I have any interest in horticulture?

I confessed I did not.

But surely I had noticed the garden, the unusual variety and mixture of bush, tree and shrub? No matter, from the castle you could see the apparent lack of plan was in fact highly patterned; the path cutting off selections of shape and texture, a square of silver birch to our left, and triangle of yew, oak and pine to our right. Then there were those he could not name. It was an eccentric collection, unusual for the East, unheard of in Poland, possibly inspired by the great Victorian collection at Kew. Had I been there? A pity, I might have been able to help identify some of the more extraordinary growths. Were these tropical species that had adapted to the climate, mutations, or the real thing? Perhaps they had been grafted onto coniferous stock and slowly taken over the host? What kind of mind had thought this all up, genius or fool? Would he return to check progress before the whole creation became overgrown?

Anyway, it was too late now for anyone to reclaim these grounds since the new Polish government authorities had ceded the land back to the people. As to whether they would restore the once magnificent baronial mansion was for them to decide once everyone here had cleared out. But when might that be?

His face took on a more solemn expression as he explained the background to the medical mission we had been charged with. Dr Geigy would bring his hands together as if to cup the air whenever he sought to make a serious point, which was often. Everyone was frustrated, he said, doctors, soldiers, cooks, the refugees themselves. Everyone wanted to be moving on, they could think of nothing else. The fighting was over, thank God, and nobody wanted another war. It was time to be home, enough sacrifices had been made. But nothing could be done until the cause of the illness – Condition Six – had been found. There were obvious reasons for this – nobody wanted an epidemic on their hands, much of Europe was still in ruins and basic services and sanitary conditions had yet to be re-established. If Europe was a patient, it was ripe for any opportunistic infection. That was why the compound was heavily guarded and passage in and out so tightly controlled. Once inside nobody could leave until it had been confirmed the condition was not contagious. The other factor, he said, lowering his voice momentarily, was the generals. 'You know how suspicious they are, never happy unless they have a battle?' Anyway, I would have my own chance to solve this mystery, I may not have seen the best of my Russian colleagues so far, but if I could crack this and let everyone get home I would be hailed as a hero, the toast of the Soviet people.

Geigy paused, he was looking to see if I was smiling. I wasn't. I had just realised that I was now trapped here along with the others. I'd been a fool to agree to come. What chance did I have of solving this? Vesey had sent me here as a sop.

'What about the refugees, where are they from? Have all the cases so far just involved them?'

'Yes. First case was one year ago. Many more after that. We hear about this disease from the Polish authorities, they were concerned that these people would be . . . eradicated by the local people, out of fear of their illness. Again this is why we must guard them. The refugees? Another mystery. They say they come from Moldavia and Crimea, but originally Germany. We have no trace of these people being in these places. So where are they coming from? Rumania? Hungary? Bohemia? We don't know, what else have they to hide?

He paused again, this time halting his stride too.

'There are . . . certain people, Rob, I'm sure you have met them too . . . in Germany . . . England. People who have more interest in information than truth . . . in how facts can be . . . *used* rather than what facts tell. It takes courage to be honest. You must feel that you have my . . . sincere . . . trust, in everything we will do together, and I too must trust you to behave as a doctor. I am not a general, Rob, and I do not wish to be.'

He stood still, eyes fixing mine with an intense stare. I had only the vaguest notion as to what he was inferring, but knew that this was his way of reaching out to me. Whether this was part of my welcome or something more profound, I couldn't tell. Either way, he was waiting for a gesture from me. I held out my hand, and he shook it once more.

We made our way back to the huts and sheds containing my billet. Geigy apologised for the mess mine had been in and promised to try to organise a clearout. In the meantime I was to feel free to arrange it however I liked.

I could smell what passed for coffee, and realised we were nearing the canteen, although I was surprised to see how small it was. It wasn't like the one at Gershalt: there was no room to actually sit down and eat, instead you were expected to take your plate back to your own billet, and return it clean, for them to dish out your next feast on it.

I have never tasted food so bad: boiled meats of indistinguishable animal origin, stale bread, onions and an endless supply of pickled cabbage. By my own estimate, my weight must have dropped by at least a stone and a half during my spell there, and I had already thinned out at Berlin. I suppose it is tempting to link some kind of symbolism to this change, but I must have been carrying too much fat to start with. I look back at photographs taken before

I left Helensburgh and find it hard to recognise the chubby, earnest-looking youth smiling back at me. That Robert Watt disappeared somewhere between Gershalt and Tarutz, I'm still trying to find out just who replaced him.

I collected a few of the available remnants of the earlier breakfast offering, together with a cup filled with the last dregs inside the steel urn on the counter. We walked over to Dr Geigy's consulting room where he waited politely for me to chew on the bite of rye bread I'd taken. It was stone dry. I took a mouthful of chicory and acorn coffee to wash it down with, I couldn't decide which tasted worse.

'So, Robert. Tell me. Are you named after the poet?'

'Poet? Which poet?'

'Burns! Famous Scottish poet. Robert Burns, no?'

'Of course . . . I mean no, I'm not named after him. At least not that I know of anyway.'

'But you are admirer of Burns?'

'Yes.'

'In Russia, Burns is very popular poet. People's poet. He speaks for the oppressed workers, against capitalist landowner, English imperialists. Approved by Communist Party.'

Igor seemed sincere and eager for me to share his enthusiasm, but my own recollections of any of Burns' verses were scarce. I thought back to junior school, forty of us led on a class chant of 'Tae a Mouse' by Miss Kerr, a lash of the strap if you got it wrong – perhaps that was why I associated verse with pain. 'Wee, sleekit, coo'ring beastie . . .': the subversive socialist element to it had escaped me.

'. . . and what other poets do you admire, Rob? Do you know any Russian ones?'

I swallowed down another gulp of the leathery-tasting mulch. 'No . . . I'm afraid I've never read any of your country's . . . stuff in that manner.'

'Literature!'

'Sorry?'

'What of literature then, Rob? You must love Sir Walter Scott, Robert Louis Stevenson . . . great Scottish writers, yes?'

His features held such a child-like animation that I was left feeling vaguely guilty about letting him down with my ignorance.

'Look I'm sorry . . . I've never really read that much, apart from textbooks, never had the time . . . Couldn't even tell you the last novel I read.'

He shook his head. 'No, no. Please do not apologise. It is I . . . I did not mean to be so . . .'

His voice gradually faded as he gave up the search for an appropriate word, and a silence hung over us. I forced down my last bite and pushed my plate to one side. I was still hungry, but not enough to overcome my growing revulsion at what was on offer.

'Chess?'

'Sorry?'

'You play chess? There are many players here in the camp. Perhaps we have a game?'

'Of course. That would be fine.'

'Excuse me then. I will find board, and pieces. They are in the next door. I will bring them to here if you wait.'

He made to get up from the table, pushing his chair back across the floor. I remember a feeling of resignation rather than exasperation at this behaviour, although when

I made to speak something seemed to alter between thought and expression.

'Look . . . Igor . . . Dr Geigy, I don't know if you think this is the best time to begin a game of bloody chess. When I said yes I thought you meant later, not now. Just what is it you think I've come to do? I'm very much aware that there is a patient we saw last night whose condition you expected to deteriorate. Shouldn't we examine him? For God's sake, isn't that why we're all here, can't the chess wait until later?'

It was like my earlier outburst in the admin office. Once I started the words created their own momentum, all of them sounding more spiteful and belligerent than I had ever heard myself. Bridge at Gershalt, chess at Tarutz, what was it with these damn camps? To my surprise I found myself gripping Geigy's sleeve, holding him down to the table. He froze, staring at it. I let him go.

He rubbed his arm where my hand had held onto him. 'I thought perhaps you might like a chance to digest your first food for such a long time. No matter. We go now if you want.'

His manner had changed; he was looking at me with some hurt, suddenly downbeat. My fault, why had I thrown it all back at him, my only ally in this place? I didn't know, maybe I suspected he was trying to stall my examination of the suspected case but that thought only occurred to me as we walked over to the holding cells. No, something else was changing inside me and I didn't feel inclined to fight it.

No explanations then, and the atmosphere was suddenly different. Geigy walked over to a cupboard by the door and pulled out two grubby white housecoats, a stethoscope and a magnifying glass. His actions were slow and deliberate, the opening and shutting of the door carried out with a pedant's precision. He handed me one of the coats and unlocked a filing cabinet, drawing out a clipboard with a sheaf of documentation attached. A curt nod to the main door and we were out, marching in silence back towards the cells at the top of the hill.

It took us about three minutes of brisk walking to reach the ruin, and another five before Geigy could persuade the guards there to open up. There seemed to be an animosity between him and them, he must have upset them in his earlier dealings, for their discussions were a snapped, barely civil affair, and the guards took an obvious delight in keeping us waiting. Once inside, we had another delay whilst a key to the patient's cell was found. It would have been early afternoon by now, already the light outside was fading from a wispy to a darker grey, not that it mattered much what was happening outside once the main cellar door was slammed behind us and we were plunged into a state of darkness. Geigy started to argue again with the principal warden. It seemed he was reluctant to come along with us to the chamber round the corner of the passage, preferring simply to hand over the key. Geigy would have none of this, eventually resorting to pushing the man, jostling him along to the room in question. The guard stopped and braced himself for a moment, pulling out a handkerchief from his trouser pocket and holding it close to his mouth and nose before moving again. I noticed Geigy had done the same.

All day I had been reappraising my view of the camp

after the nightmare experience of my arrival, but here, in the gloom of the underground tunnels of Tarutz mansion, I found the conditions even more eerie than I had remembered them, and was gripped by the same sense of foreboding I'd had when first entering the camp gates. My throat was dry, neck beginning to wilt under the strain of supporting a head which itself was aching with tension. Something terrible had happened here, what had these walls and rooms been witness to? Why had I insisted on being brought here?

A shake of the keys preceded the creaking sound of the chamber door being opened. The guard immediately backed away from it, bent double, almost bowing as he brushed by me, thrusting his torch into my hand. Geigy entered, and then waved me in with a sweep of his arm. I walked past him, purposefully, partly as if to show him I could maintain my composure, partly because I was some-how being pulled toward the ghastly apparition at the end of the room.

He was lying in the same spot as he had the night before, but had cast aside many of the ragged blankets which had covered him and this time seemed much more recognisable as a human form. I stood over him and shone the light onto his face. Thin and fevered, it was impossible to put an age to it. His head was split from the temple to his right cheekbone with a wound that was open enough to expose his skull at all points in between. This cut had stopped bleeding though, and he was completely still, prob-ably dead. I should have tried to feel for a pulse to establish this most basic of medical facts, but somehow it was as if I was looking at a museum exhibit, or a side-show freak one knew to be false, and my hands remained tightly around the torch. I pointed to the part where the cut was deepest, immediately under his eye. What could have done this? The cut was so perfect it had to have been a monstrous blow with a sledgehammer. I studied for a second with a detached fascination until I realised I had overlooked the key question: why had I not seen this before? Was this the same patient I had looked at last night? I scanned down to examine where the stomach wound had been previously. The vision revealed by the torchlight was enough to make me so giddy I felt I was going to pass out. Something told me this was the same man; I recognised the undergarments and leather knee breeches which had been torn back to expose his midriff, yet this man had now had his very skin torn back in the same manner, and his stomach, intestines and lower gut had spilled out on either side of him. He had been disembowelled, impaled with some instrument, organs then wrenched from inside him. It was then that the smell hit me. I had been aware of a putrid stench permeating the entire lower corridor once we had entered, but it was only now that I realised I was standing right over its source, and the full intensity of it struck. I reeled backwards, light scanning back up the man's body as I did so. I thrust a hand instinctively to my face, as if this might in some way protect me, and then found myself carried forward by a sudden convulsion, the taste of the morning's rye bread rising fast in my throat. I was falling directly onto the body below, and slammed down my hand to stop myself. For a second I thought I was going to bring it down onto his head but I managed to snatch it to the side at the last minute, and I felt it land in a pool of congealed blood just below the man's ear, cold and syrupy. My face must have been just above his; he blinked, and I screamed out loud.

Geigy stepped forward and pulled me away, but I couldn't stop myself lashing out at him as he did so, elbowing him aside as I made for the door. I threw up in the corridor immediately outside. Down the passageway the guard looked on impassively. Geigy emerged some time later, fumbling with the keys in the lock once more, shouting to the guard to come and help him lock up. Between them, they sorted it out, and then led me back out to the cold early evening outside. Geigy tried several times to start explaining but I kept breaking off to be sick again in the bushes. Eventually he relented, and left me to make my own way back down to the camp huts. He had wanted to play chess, discuss poetry, the plant life of the compound whilst all the time he knew what was lurking down there. Were the attempts at a delay for my benefit or was he trying to hide the camp's secrets?

I was glad to be alone, and out in the open – claustrophobia, a fear of confined spaces, how I had it right then. It would be hours before I would force myself to venture inside my cramped little hut, hours before I would recognise any small room as anything other than a medieval torture chamber.

Father Seicle

HISTORY has not been kind to the reputation of the pre-Reformation Catholic Church which still dominated towns like Hamelin at the time of the Thirty Years' War. Our impressions of this institution are likely to be dominated by its faults – insensitive, dogmatic, spiritually bankrupt; a church whose pursuit and jealous protection of its material wealth both prolonged the war and fuelled the success of its Lutheran and Calvinist opponents. Historians would note that the Thirty Years' War marked the end of the Papacy's influence on the European political and military stage; no longer would the cannon roar and armies march into battle at the behest of the Vatican. Indeed, this colossal struggle itself would end only when those governments of the day finally ignored Rome's demand for a continuation of hostilities until outright victory had been achieved (a triumph the Vatican presumably believed God was still waiting patiently to deliver) and began the tentative negotiations with similarly weary and realistic League adversaries that would lead to the Treaty of Westphalia. Thus peace arrived, in spite of, rather than because of the folly of the Catholic prerogative, and with it Europe's appetite for 'holy' war was satisfied for good.

Yet this reading of events, although superficially accurate, is perhaps unduly harsh on the proponents of the Catholic faith of this period. Before condemning them on the basis of such a deceptively simple analysis two potentially mitigating factors should be considered in their defence: firstly, that the actions of the Church's highest echelons did not fully reflect the full body of its members; and secondly, that those documented excesses and inequities in practice which had prompted the Protestant Reformation to begin with were reflective of the deficiencies within *society* as a whole rather than the Catholic Church which, as the principal religious faith prior to the Reformation, could but *mirror* the aspirations of its flock. It is in search of an insight into these considerations that the role of the Church in the demise of Hamelin should be studied, an inquiry that brings the intriguing figure of Father Seicle into view.

Andreas Seicle was the parish priest at the time and the place concerned. Though cited frequently as a signatory of municipal documents it is by no means certain that he was a member of the council; many towns of the region at the time had abandoned the automatic award of chamber seats to God's representatives, and it is possible that his inclusion in local government affairs would have been at the discretion of the Mayor and other senior council officials. Were this the case, it may not have been entirely to his dissatisfaction; again, the more progressive elements within the Church of his time had long argued that its position and standing could best be served by a return of attention to strictly pastoral matters, although there is no evidence to suggest where Seicle stood on these and the other vital issues of his day. In fact there is little to enable a picture to be drawn of this man as an individual at all, other than the fact that he was buried outside the perimeter of Hamelin, in the parish of Kulhun, over twenty miles east. This is a curious footnote worthy of some consideration and judicious interpretation. Was he an outsider in his own community, did he die an outcast? How could it have been that a God-fearing populace expelled its priest?

As a member of Hamelin council, Seicle would have been present at the emergency meeting which followed the first confirmed sighting of D'Ortez' army, on the 3rd of January 1648:

'Gentlemen, your suppositions are all hypothetical . . . it is pointless wasting our energy and council time passing motions on hypothetical situations. Should we not wait until we have made contact and found out what this force's intentions are? We must send a party out to meet this man, the Spanish general. They can report back to this chamber and we can decide then. Would anybody disagree with this course of action? Hands up those who do . . .'

The Mayor's words are measured, considered, calculated. Under the guise of reasoned progress he has intimidated those who might oppose him and forced the dissenters to show themselves. Seicle knows that those who do not concur will be asked for their alternative proposal. Experience also tells him it is unlikely anybody has one, hence the silence that greets Ebber's declaration. For a brief moment the two men's eyes meet, the Mayor throwing the briefest of grimaces to indicate his frustration. The Priest responds, a smile – gentle and restrained, but warm.

'Might be too late by then . . . by the time this "party" returns.'

Councillor Mannau glances furtively around the chamber for support. The Mayor intervenes before he has completed the circuit.

'Are you saying you disagree with my proposal?'

'I am pointing out that it might be too late for us to act if we wait for . . . whoever . . .' Mannau throws his gaze around once more, this time more aggressively. Clearly he feels let down by those he might have assumed would support him.

The Mayor leans forward to address him directly, blocking his view of those further down the table, a manoeuvre which, deliberate or not, elegantly starves rebellion's fire of air.

'Then you would agree with the policy if that party was to leave immediately, with strict orders to return by noon tomorrow?'

Father Seicle's mouth slowly divides into another smile, this time though he is more discreet, hiding his chin behind the sleeve of his robe. Mannau has been effortlessly out-manoeuvred. The arrogance of the young Mayor is almost justified.

'Well?'

'Yes.' Mannau's assent comes grudgingly.

'Then I take it the motion is passed unanimously. May I also submit the proposal to the council that Councillor Mannau is awarded the temporary post of Deputy Mayor until this crisis is resolved and that he assumes this office with immediate effect. I would further propose that as

Deputy Mayor he accompanies myself and Councillor Schmidt on our meeting with this D'Ortez. A show of hands please.'

Mannau's look of rage turns to one of astonishment as the arms around him are raised. He continues. 'Deputy Mayor, as you requested we shall leave immediately. Can you organise horses and seconds? I would suggest no more than four of us make the journey, it is important we pose no threat to this force.'

A nod. Ebber continues. 'This meeting is then adjourned. We will report back by noon tomorrow.'

As the room empties, Ebber indicates to Seicle to remain, aa downward sweep of the arm as he moves towards Mannau. Seicle waits as the Mayor tells Mannau to bring the horses to the town square; he will join him once he has said farewell to his family. Mannau scurries off, obviously preoccupied, at once both excited at his sudden promotion and rueful that he has somehow allowed himself to be coerced into a dangerous mission.

The door closes after him. Only the Priest, the Chancellor and the Mayor remain. The latter has his arm around Wolfricht, he is speaking to him in a resigned and hushed voice.

'I am sorry, I know how it may have appeared, but it is vital that there are no splits at this time. I had to pull any potential enemy factions within closer ... to pull him in with us. Do you understand?'

Wolfricht nods, head cast down, avoiding Ebber's eye.

'... and do you forgive me? ... Have I still your respect?'

A final nod, this time head aloft.

'Thank you, dear colleague, thank you. Will you excuse us?'

Wolfricht departs in silence. The panelled door closes once more, the two men are alone. Ebber sinks into a chair at the head of the table, he looks exhausted, mood changing now the chamber has dispersed. Seicle edges closer, pulling up a chair alongside. Only now does he feel relaxed about his own presence in the chamber, now that those he knows to despise him have left, and that the Mayor will turn his undivided attention to him. Mannau, old Kunze, even Wolfricht – they all made little effort to disguise their growing irritation and distaste at his participation in these meetings. Able men, sane men, he had known them for many years, why would they turn so against him? Did he drag the standard of debate down to a lower level, or was he guilty of insisting that his Church's view hold sway on every issue? He hoped not, indeed he made every effort to suppress his own opinion on the matters before council, seeing his role more as that of observer. Was it this that they did not understand? Only Mayor Ebber seemed attuned to the nature of his position, not an emissary of God's word, able to dispense Divine blessing on council edicts, but an interpreter of God's word, there to shed whatever light he could to help others find their own way. The resentment seemed to stem from his insistence that each make their own path.

'Will you hear my confession, Father? I doubt there is time to visit the chapel before I leave.'

'There is time.'

'Perhaps. The truth is . . . please do not be offended . . . I do not wish to be seen to emerge from the church before

I leave. I say that with the well-being of the Church in mind, not my own.'

'But your conscience is still troubled?'

'Hear my confession, Father . . . it is all I ask.'

'Then I must ask something of you in return. That you take me with you on your journey.'

'Father, I cannot . . . there may be danger. We must be seen to pose no threat.'

'Threat? A priest, unarmed, with four others. This is a Catholic army. Why should they feel threatened by me? No, I see your unease, Heinrich, it is obvious enough. It is noble of you to shoulder this responsibility but you must see that I would be neglecting mine were I not by your side.'

'You do not feel your place is here, amongst your people?'

Father Seicle holds still. 'Your people' – who were 'his people'? The detractors were by no means confined to the council chamber. Was it really his theology that was so repulsive, or something simpler? Was it he himself who was so unappealing? He studied the face questioning him for a moment; compassionate, handsome, blue eyes radiating a keen intelligence, a man in his prime. It was difficult to imagine his own countenance would prompt a similar appraisal; thin and drawn, the profile of a weasel, lank dark hair rather than the blonde locks shared by the Mayor and his daughters. It was as well he had chosen the priesthood, for surely no woman would ever have chosen him.

'I might serve the people better by being with you.'

'I'm sorry, Father, I cannot allow it.'

'Then I will not hear your confession, not until you

return, for hearing it now might weaken your resolution to return to us.'

Ebber sighs, breaking his gaze from Seicle, rapping the wooden table top with his knuckles. Seicle frowns benignly.

'You should go and bid farewell to your family, Heinrich, time is running short. May God protect you.'

The Mayor pulls himself up out of the chair, turning to shake Seicle's hand in silence, clasping it between his own as he summons the strength to say goodbye and commence the journey. It is dusk outside; they would travel through the night and the snow that was beginning to fall. Still Seicle envied them. For him, a shorter crossing awaits, across the square to the church on the other side of the chamber. A building once raised by the hands of the people as a mark of hope for their future. Where had that optimism gone to, should he be doing more to bring it back, was that the role they wanted him to undertake?

Seicle ambled slowly across the cobbled square, arriving at the church some minutes later. The streets had already begun to fill with those wanting to witness the Mayor's departure, but Seicle himself did not emerge to watch them leave, preferring instead to light candles at the altar and offer a prayer and reflection on their perils, half-listening to the gathering crowd outside. They would not want him there. Christ looked down on him from the cross in the stained-glass window above him, wretched and in pain. He had thought God to have forsaken him too, but for Christ during the crucifixion there was only the one God on whom to call, not a choice between a Catholic one or a Protestant one, or a German, Swedish or Spanish. No,

Christ had been spared these uncertainties. And if Christ had been approached by a citizen wishing to pay a tithe to eliminate the period his soul would spend in purgatory before admittance to heaven, would he have accepted? It was unlikely, but then he would not have faced the wrath of his Church for refusing it, nor indeed the wrath of his congregation for forcing them to travel to a neighbouring parish to secure the deal for their soul's direct passage to paradise. Interpretation, light so that they may find their own way? It was certainty and direction the flock bayed for now, 'Spiritual Leadership' as Mannau would put it, the same guidance that saw the Jesuit fanatics goad men on the battlefield to draw more enemy blood until the Almighty was satisfied. Seicle contemplated the glass collage hanging over him, Jesus sacrificing himself so that others might have their sins redeemed, searching for His faith in that moment of darkness and being rewarded. Seicle closes his eyes tightly, Jesus help me, guide me as you would deem fit . . . I fear am not worthy of your name . . . I . . .

It is a meditation that seldom leaves Seicle feeling enriched yet one he is drawn into, losing himself in the machinations between heart, mind and soul. The noise outside is dying, he is glad to be alone. Suddenly, however, a searing pain rises from his left foot tucked behind him, he jerks the leg fiercely, scraping his knee on the floor and almost toppling to one side in shock. A rat darts by up the altar, dark and large, the size of the cats that had been brought to control them, its coat wet and oily. Seicle clutches hold of his instep where the rat has bitten him. There is a tear in his stocking, beneath it he can see the deep cut its teeth have gouged together with other razor-like scratches. A scraping noise to his left, Seicle peers through the half-light toward the pews on the east wing of the church. He can see nothing. Then, as his eyes focus on the floor immediately on either side of him he realises he has been encircled by these creatures, now excited by the scent of his blood. Seicle rushes to his feet and makes for the communion table, jumps onto it and throws down a candle to the ground where the rats have congregated. This, together with the anguished shriek which has accompanied it, is enough to disperse them.

Father Seicle attempts to compose himself, taking deep breaths, pushing the fear of another bite to the back of his mind. He tries once more to pray, but his hands are shaking as he joins them together. Another glance up at the figure in the window. Jesus, why could they not let me go with them? Next time, I beg you, Father, please let it be me.

It was some time after noon two days later that the party returned; Seicle had been sweeping the steps to the vestry when he became aware of the growing commotion in the square. The town gates were being opened, someone was arriving; it had to be the Mayor. Sure enough, the voices of those nearer the portals welcomed the council party back from their journey, greetings that soon turned to questions. How many of them were there, were they as fearsome as they believed, why were they here, was there to be a battle nearby or were they marching on Hamelin? Louder and more urgent, but still unanswered. Eventually the returning party and the mob following it made their way to the square, the latter parting to allow Seicle a view of the dishevelled and travel-weary foursome at its hub. The Mayor looked drawn, troubled, and when he looked ahead to see the Priest studying him from the steps there was a disturbing lack of relief or joy in his salutation to his friend. Instead, he pointed to the council chamber; a meeting, immediately. Seicle acknowledges the gesture, and turns to limp inside the church. If the others are being called to the emergency session it will probably escape them that the Mayor and his Deputy will not have eaten for some time. There is bread and water in his quarters, he will take it over. Progress is slow however and with his foot so swollen Seicle hobbles painfully, spilling much of the water as he does so. Although his is the shortest trip to chambers of them all he is last to arrive, and the only chair left for him is at the far end of the table. His sufferings go unnoticed as he struggles along to his seat, all eyes being on the two arrivals. The pain in his foot makes it hard to concentrate, and Seicle's constant shifting and stretching in vain attempts to alleviate it were an immediate distraction to the session's progress. Nevertheless, he tries to hold as still as he can in order to satisfy the duties that God would have asked of him.

'We met with their leader ... the Spaniard ... formidable ... his force is strong ... four hundred or more, battle-hardened ... philistine. If he means us harm there may be little we can do about it. He himself seemed a composed individual. He was guarded as to his true intentions ... there was little sign of what these might be.'

'He must have made some impression. What did he want?'

'As he says, he simply wants to secure safe winter quarters for his army.'

'But a force of that size would overwhelm our town . . . we could not sustain . . . he could not . . .'

'That is ground already covered in previous debates, Councillor Schmidt. We are still unanimous that Hamelin must be protected?'

A murmur of assent passes round the chamber. Seicle is not alone in realising the more salient issue that has been overlooked. Schmidt continues to search for the truth. 'Then he did not mention the matter of the reclaimed taxes to the Saxons or Vienna?'

'He seemed unaware of that. You will understand, councillors, why we chose not to inform him of the recent correspondence.'

Seicle brings his hand down to his ankle, the slightest touch of the skin and it explodes in agony. He bites his lip and draws in sharply as the rest of the room digests the Mayor's remark in silence.

Schmidt draws a conclusion he knows to be false. 'Why then we surely have little to worry about?'

'Unfortunately that is not the case. They still demand that they exercise their right to take up refuge in our town.'

'And you refused?'

'We are in no position to refuse. They are on their way here.'

Silence again, a stillness followed by private mutterings of grief. For the first time, Seicle hears despair enter the chamber.

Mannau's voice is raised to fill the void.

'We have no problem in the immediate future. This force

will camp in the woods to the east for protection from the winds. We have agreed to supply bread, dried meats and brandy. They will not enter Hamelin.'

Seicle understands immediately that some foul scheme is afoot, Mannau's last words following an exchange of veiled glances with the Mayor.

'But why would they hold off from taking the town?'

The Deputy and Mayor's eyes cross again, the latter steeling himself as if in as much pain as the priest watching them. The room waits as he sips from his cup of water.

'Because we told them that we are a plague town.'

Seicle can only make out the distant forms of a few figures on the edge of the woodland, not the teeming, barbarous army that had been talked about. As the cart tries to carve its path through the snow toward them they almost become harder rather than easier to see. The fact that they had buried themselves in amongst the trees said something about them according to Ebber, something about their mentality, their condition and the Spaniard's plans. Was he alone in thinking that there was an air of falsehood to this, something disturbingly fraudulent about an army that chooses to hide itself away? Who were they trying to avoid, or were they trying to intimidate the citizens of Hamelin by this tactic, allowing them to conjure up a vision of them that was more terrifying than reality?

Seicle ignores the Mayor's endless quizzical reflections, turning to look back on the fading view of Hamelin behind them. The whole town had watched this second party depart, were they still watching now?

'We might tell them that their efforts are wasted, we can

see them clearly from inside the town walls. It might disturb him . . . give us an advantage.'

Seicle again ignores the remark, in any case it is as if Ebber is talking to himself, his growing nervousness forcing a rapid meditation. The Mayor was ever the politician, ever seeking motives, ever searching for base demands lurking underneath any straightforward request or remark. A good man, but his success stemmed from his ability to adopt this mentality. Was it a talent or a curse?

The cart jolts violently, its left wheel jarring on a boulder covered by snow. Seicle's hideously swollen lower leg falls from the restplate, colliding heavily against the undercarriage, and he cannot hold himself from crying out under his breath. The Mayor looks on anxiously, grimacing in sympathy. Seicle inhales deeply and gestures with his arm, the pain is passing. Up ahead, a growing clamour and bustle of armoury on the move as some of the soldiers of D'Ortez' army finally emerge to greet them.

'Which one is he, can you see him?'

Seicle's voice offers no hint of the disquiet that is stirring within. For seventeen years he had climbed to the top of the church bell-tower and peered out towards these same woods, always feeling a vague and irrational sense that a malevolence was lurking amongst the trees. Now, a spectacle matched that premonition as the men of war materialised like insects crawling out from under a stone.

'No . . . not yet . . . why?'

'How did he react when you told him Hamelin was under plague?'

'I could not tell. He has a strange demeanour . . . like his eyes are smiling, laughing, whilst the rest of him is still.

He said there were many excellent physicians in his ranks. That he would be happy to let them come and treat any injured citizens. I was sure he was lying.'

The Mayor's voice had become quieter before finally tailing off, yet it is not fear of being overheard that has forced this change, for the fringe of the wooded hillside is still half a mile away. Heinrich Ebber's head is in his hands as if the impossibility of the situation has caught up with him having followed relentlessly from the town behind. Seicle can offer a consoling arm over the younger man's shoulder, but fights his inclination to give other support. The impossibility of the situation; they have already cursed themselves with the lie over the plague, now there were two treacherous participants in this episode, how might God judge both?

'Heinrich, can I ask you something? I thought to raise this in chamber but there never seemed the grounds to do so.'

The Mayor draws a breath, turning toward the embrace. 'Of course, Father.'

'What part does *truth* play in all this. Where does it feature in our strategy?'

Mayor Ebber stares wistfully into the priest's eyes, letting his hurt reveal itself.

'Father, I have tried . . . always tried, to put those interests of our town and our people before any other considerations. I do not understand . . . always Hamelin first, always!'

'Yet we distrust those we deem to be lying and speak of plague ravaging our homes? You never considered disclosing our true fears of what this force might represent to us?'

The Mayor shakes his head in frustration, cheeks reddening with indignation.

'I'm afraid we will have to adjourn this discussion until a more appropriate time.' He nods toward the approaching figures a hundred yards ahead. 'Let me say however that the path that I – we – have followed is that which we have concluded to be the best in the interest of *our* people. Those we are about to meet are not of our world, and any naivety as to their nature could cost us dear. My conscience is clear that I have been true to the duties imparted to me by the Mayor's office.'

'I'm talking of *truth*, man, *truth*! God made truth the weapon of the just against the unjust, He did not mean it to be rationed out by those . . .'

'*Enough!*'

The Mayor's bellow has those travelling behind in the carts containing the rest of the meats and grain turning to each other in disbelief.

'Enough.'

He repeats it once more, under his breath as Seicle withdraws his arm. They have arrived at the forest perimeter and the horses are halted, there being no clear path into it for them to follow. Suddenly, however, men are swarming around them, pouring out of the shadows to engulf the four carts. These are the men the Mayor has been speaking of, and Seicle begins to silently concede that he was correct when he stated that they were not of their world; filthy, even by comparison with the citizens of the rat-infested squalor from which they had travelled, and reeking with the bloody scent of war. A throng had attached themselves to the rear of the cart the priest shared with Mayor Ebber, tearing into the sacks and kegs which had been so carefully packed, wilfully oblivious of the pair seated at the cart's head. Ferocious men, animals, with a naked and savage appetite. Seicle finds himself thinking back to the rats that had surrounded him in his moment of prayer. What would it take to scatter this horde?

His ruminations are shattered by a noise that has roared suddenly in his ear; searing, shaking the very air around them as if God himself has raised His voice in anger, the Priest has never heard anything like it. Those around though obviously have, and in an instant they are subdued, turning as one to face the source. Seicle follows their gaze to the mounted figure in black steadying his horse, tugging the reins in one hand, still clutching the smoking musket in the other. A second horseman draws up close to him, handing over another gun in exchange for the discharged one. The bearded man in black gives the briefest nod of acknowledgement.

When he shouts Seicle recognises the language as Spanish but cannot understand. Some of the men around the neighbouring wagons start to withdraw, and then the tongue changes, and becomes immediately familiar although heavily accented.

'The next man to help himself to these provisions will taste lead before a single morsel passes his lips. We will accept these . . . *gifts*. . . in an orderly manner.'

D'Ortez stops for a moment, content to let the silence amplify the depth of his resolve. '*Gifts*.' He had sought out the eyes of the Mayor as he said this, stooping slightly, almost taunting him with his derisive bow of gratitude; and his face, of course, Ebber had been accurate in his description of this individual's unsettling demeanour – he could smile from *within* without any outward manifestation of the scorn felt inside, yet leaving no doubt as to who is being mocked.

All is quiet until it is clear the men have understood the warning. D'Ortez then turns to his second. 'Untether the horses from each cart first, we shall keep the carts and send these fellows back on their own miserable beasts.'

Seicle tries to listen as the instructions continue but the language has changed again, presumably to repeat the same command. Within a short time teams of men have begun the task of unharnessing the horses, the rest of their number watching on. The Mayor had climbed down and was trying to approach the Spanish commander who feigned ignorance of his awkward presence below him, still engrossed in conference with his lieutenants. Seicle studies those busying themselves around him and those waiting impatiently in the foreground. What kind of an army was this where no two men shared the same uniform, where every instruction was relayed in three or more differing tongues? Ramshackle, desperate, and all the more threatening for it. There seemed to be a hierarchy – those on horseback less filthy than those on foot, and marginally better dressed. Some were shrouded in rags, wearing four or five shirts, gloves and breeches in the same manner – dead men's breeches. Of those on the ground, those wearing the crested helmets of pikemen gather together, aloof from the fray, setting themselves apart from the savages who had attacked the carts on their arrival. However, all shared the same sunken and menacing countenance, a permanent scowl etched in with the scars and lines on their faces.

'Our priest, Father Seicle . . . he has come to tender to your men's spiritual needs.'

The two of them were now looking at him, having come to wait at the cart's side; the Mayor, earnest, uncertain, in contrast to the steadfast bearing of the figure next to him, still astride his mount. The introduction over, Seicle seeks out the Spaniard's eyes, a new wave of misgiving sweeping over his heart as they locked with his, the same sensation he had felt those years ago when looking out to this forest from the safety of the church. Eyes set deep within a dark, olive-skinned complexion, incongruous with the wintry landscape, olive skin, brown mahogany eyes, as dead and reflective as a piece of varnished wood. As they stared across the freezing air through to the depths of his soul Seicle realised he could see nothing in return. What kind of man could close his heart so completely? 'These are not men of our world,' what if the Mayor had been right about that too? And still he stared, ever deeper, until Seicle could feel himself pulled by a malevolent current towards the very whirlpool of hell.

'Spiritual needs?' At last the spell is broken, the other throwing his head back as his entire body shakes with laughter. 'How kind! Although I fear it is too late for some of them to start hoping for redemption.' D'Ortez flexes the reins, as much as if to steady himself as the creature beneath.

'What else have you brought?' The change in tone is abrupt, an impatient snap of words, almost implying that it is the others who have enjoyed the comical distraction.

'Wheat, rye, bread and meats as we discussed. We have a small quantity of beer, and some grape brandy.'

'Women?'

The Mayor looks to the Spaniard in some astonishment. 'Women?'

'My men have informed me of their desire to enjoy some female company.' It is Seicle's eyes that are addressed as the new demand is issued, 'I would be grateful if you would oblige.'

D'Ortez turns to face the Mayor, thick eyebrows raised in anticipation of an answer.

'I'm sorry . . . I cannot . . . I will have to discuss this matter with my colleagues in the town chamber before . . . surely the risk of disease.'

Another loud cackle of laughter cuts the Mayor short.

'I'm sure if you can supply us with enough fine, healthy Hamelin women my men will be happy enough to take their own chance.'

Seicle's sense of dread rises anew as he watches the Spaniard fix Ebber with a dispassionate stare.

'See what you can do, Herr Mayor. I'm sure you appreciate the urgency of the situation.'

The urgency – what does this devil mean, what is he proposing? Seicle can only watch as the Mayor flounders under the Spaniard's menacing scrutiny. It is as well D'Ortez' attention is demanded by the appearance of another aide, informing him that the visitors' mounts are now free and ready, for Ebber is lost for a response. Evidently, he too is struggling to control an inner fear of these desperate portents. He leans forward, one eye remaining on D'Ortez, lowering his voice.

'Father, I cannot let you stay here.'

Seicle shakes his head, affecting whatever impression of courageous indifference he can muster.

'It is God's will, my son. He will protect me.'

'But I must . . .'

'Your horses are waiting, gentlemen. You should go now before dusk falls. I cannot guarantee your safety once it is dark.'

The close voice of the Spaniard shakes Ebber, he had not noticed that his disquiet had been overheard. It is Seicle who now shows the more composure.

'I shall stay, commander, if that is acceptable. I should like to offer God's word to your men.'

Another smile, callous and as cold as the biting wind over their heads.

'Of course,' he shouts, before again switching to an unfamiliar tongue. A horse is brought to the Mayor, two dragoons arrive at the other side of the truck and haul the Priest unceremoniously from his carriage. They laugh as he tumbles headfirst into the snowdrifts, jesting at his lack of balance and athleticism, failing to notice the distended leg making him wince with each and every movement. Seicle is pulled back to his feet, the soldiers grabbing an arm apiece, jerking him forward and then twisting each arm around their necks as if hoisting an animal carcass. Obviously, this is some kind of show to entertain the ranks and Seicle tries to laugh, to feign enjoyment and participation in this brutal comedy as the others look on, although D'Ortez himself is whispering asides to his aides. Another glance catches the ashen face of the Mayor, wringing his hands in unspoken concern. Seicle attempts one final smile before Ebber is reluctantly led away by the others in the party. The two men face each other one final time, the love between them a fleeting ray of warmth across this icy plain. It is alright, Heinrich, you must return to Hamelin. God will be my protector.

It had been late afternoon when Wolfricht's messenger arrived at the Ebber household to say that some soldiers had arrived at the town gates, the Spaniard himself included. At first he had thought this to be a delegation come to claim more foods, wine, and God forbid, the women. Yet when he had passed through the portals to see who was there on the outside there was only D'Ortez and a single dragoon waiting.

'Can we come in?' The Spaniard had spoken in a whisper.

'No.'

'Very well. Your priest, he is ready for you to have back.'

Mannau had been standing beside him as the exchange had taken place, and immediately began to mutter in a strange way, a whispery kind of wail, either through grief, anger, or fright. Ebber had remained silent, the noise of his colleague being the only acknowledgement of the declaration.

'Now?'

'If you want. There is no rush.' Did a black smile flash across the stranger's face for the briefest of instants? The evidently diminishing composure of his colleague made him the more determined to maintain his; the life of his friend could be at stake.

'Where is he?'

'We have him.'

'Then we shall have him back.'

'You must come and take him.'

'Then we shall do that!'

Ebber immediately realised that in rising to the challenge he had given himself no option but to enter into a potential trap.

The journey had begun a short while after, once a mount had been saddled for the Mayor and his two volunteer seconds. They travelled in silence behind the Spaniard and arrived at the forest edge within two hours.

D'Ortez had asked them to remain outside the woods, sending his rider back into the camp to retrieve the Priest. The four had then waited in the bitter cold for him to be brought out.

Eventually, when a figure wrapped in a shroud had been dragged forward on a makeshift cart, the Mayor had then dismounted, and pulled the rags back to reveal his friend. The Mayor's seconds shivered, far enough away not to hear the anguished gasp that had escaped from Ebber's mouth as he whispered to his friend, far enough away not to see the tears that quickly filled his eyes.

'Father, I begged you to return with us. I prayed for the strength to fight this battle with truth ... prayed that it would not come to this.' Ebber's words halted sporadically as his eyes took in the horrific extent of his friend's wounds, ruptured from throat to belly, gaping open from side to side. 'Dear God, please take our dear friend and servant to be one of yours. Please reward a life of piety in your kingdom.'

They watched in silence, too fearful to make any inter-ruption, as the Mayor then covered the body, tying it tight inside the shroud, and supervised its attachment to the sturdier of their horses. He had turned and studied the onlooking figure of D'Ortez for some considerable time before finally departing without any word.

They were a mile out from the woods when he halted.

'Here,' he said, turning to his companions.

'Fifteen Thalers. Take Father Seicle's remains to Kulhun. Make sure he is properly buried. Your journey may be arduous but I would ask you to make it out of respect for our dear Priest. You must not return.'

He waved down the confused pleas that immediately followed. 'Go . . . please go, and do not be ashamed to say you come from the town once known as Hamelin.'

T ARUTZ. EVERY MEMORY carrying its own baggage of regret.

Everything futile, everything defiled.

I spent the next three days or so in bed, drifting in and out of consciousness between bouts of diarrhoea and vomiting. Food poisoning, ladies and gentlemen, or so it was said, although if I weren't a medical man I'd have thought my whole nervous system had been overloaded, one way or the other, and had gone into some kind of shutdown. A withdrawal.

With Dr Geigy keeping his distance it would be almost a week before I would speak again; not that I minded, I needed the time to think. Geigy did go ahead with the promised clean-up of my hut though, and every time I came round it seemed as if another piece of junk had vanished, spirited away by magical benefactors like the shoemaker's elves. The cabin took on a more homely and ordered appearance, the floor swept, my clothes hung, a makeshift curtain suddenly covering the frosty window pane. Around the fourth day I awoke to find a rusting bathrub at the foot of the bed, filled with lukewarm water. I had just enough energy to avail myself of it before clambering back under the blankets, and then woke up later to find it gone.

The first mail from Gershalt arrived a short while after this – circulated memos from A.M.U. 4 about the usual stuff, a letter from my brother which had found its way to me from his base at Singapore via Helensburgh and Berlin, written before I had begun my induction training, imploring me to 'keep my pecker up' in the cheery yet impersonal style that was his way, the same letter a lonely schoolteacher might send a former pupil. There were also three letters from Joyce.

I held off from reading these until the boredom and curiosity finally overcame my mordant fear; for some strange reason I felt as if the Russians were watching me, waiting for me to read these so that they might share my grisly secret – if they hadn't found a way into my brain already. I propped myself against the bedhead and drew the blankets up around me, over my knees and up to my chest. Once comfortable I couldn't put it off any longer.

'Darling Robert . . .' it began, enough on its own to make my heart sink. There were six pages of air-mail writing paper filled with her dense neat handwriting. Mostly these talked of bridge schools and canteen gossip, all the inanities of the camp-life at Gershalt that now seemed so far away. Only on the last page did she stray from this babble, when she wrote of arranging our next leave together, of how much she was looking forward to seeing me again, to seeing Scotland, and meeting my parents. This was it then, she hadn't realised that it had all been a ghastly mistake, a black comedy, a farce. Her second letter was even more disturbing. 'More and more people are asking about us,' she'd happily reported. Could she tell them, or would I be annoyed if she didn't wait until I got back? The emotional stuff started just three pages in, there were rumours about what was going on at Tarutz and she couldn't bear to think of me in danger. Could I reassure her everything was alright? I never did read the third letter, too angry then, too ashamed later. I raised myself from bed and dressed to re-enter the world outside. Somehow, with these letters, she had invaded my privacy in a room that had just started to feel like my own, and I couldn't find it within myself to forgive her.

I also had it in mind that this was a period when I would require all the clarity of thought I could muster if I was to combat or help resolve the sufferings of the so-called 'Condition Six' outbreak. It was obvious enough what kind of practices were being carried out on the captives in the camp but I realised that on my own I had no chance of stopping it. All kinds of heroic visions had visited my mind, like leading a camp revolt and mass break-out, or capturing the unit radio and sending out an SOS message back west; delusions, every one. I would have to find a more subtle way of halting the torture or I'd end up a prisoner in the catacombs with the rest of them. Aside from that, the main issue was surely to find out what it was that made the Russians choose to carry out these acts, and how they sought to gain from such bizarre and inhuman treatment. Perhaps it was the recognition of the enormity of it all that had led to this minor breakdown.

So, what could I do? My first decision was to carry on as if nothing had happened, to pretend that I had never witnessed anything out of the ordinary in the holding cell. Dr Geigy had approached me as soon as I had re-emerged from my hut after the days of sickness, and after showing an appropriate concern for my health he had informed me that the patient we had examined that afternoon had died only hours later after my visit. The cold had preserved his corpse well enough for Geigy to hold off the post-mortem until I was strong enough to attend. Was I fit now?

My immediate thought was to refuse. What would a post-mortem prove when we both already knew the cause of death? Then it dawned on me that this was the kind of charade I would have to indulge in were I to keep myself safe and sane until I could get a message out. The examination went ahead then, Geigy and I standing over the rotting body as his assistants hacked out those organs that hadn't been excised when alive.

I was even given the opportunity to lead the examination, Geigy handing me his scalpel – was this a test of nerve? I steadied myself and peered at the gangrenous carcass below, a horrific sight. This man had endured sufferings I would barely have believed possible – bulbous swellings at the gut, thigh and calves. He had been bitten, probably by rats both before and after death, the more recent teeth marks had drawn less of a reaction as the fight had gone out of him. I had never seen rats in the cells – had they been introduced later, part of the torture? I kept my questions to myself. The findings were duly noted – 'overwhelming sepsis...', 'a profusion of necrotic tissue...' and 'ulcerations of unknown origin' were all recorded, even if no specific cause of death was entered on the victim's death certificate.

Geigy offered to copy the paper to Gershalt. I added my signature to it, more to show Vesey I was still alive and active in this mission than to display any degree of agreement with the official case summary.

Over the following weeks I became more comfortable with this facade, and better at concealing my true thoughts from everyone watching me. To them I hoped I appeared as troubled as one fully taken in by the spurious talk of disease and mystery symptoms, and as committed to helping my new colleagues find its source as any fool would be. Dr Geigy may never have had the conversations he craved about art and literature, but I made sure this was compensated for in other ways, and so we did have our games of chess, the contests taking place every second or third night when a knock on my door would invite me to stagger through the rubbish and the snowdrifts to the cramped shack he shared with two orderlies. He was a far superior player to me, and I cannot imagine what kind of challenge or gratification he would have gained from such contests. I can picture him now, chin resting on delicate hands, smiling ruefully as he shakes his head and begins to explain the weakness of my move. He would offer to coach me, set exercises, the same ones he would tell me he was writing for his son in Kiev. And me, I was smiling too, thanking him for his interest whilst inwardly vowing to expose this monster and his regime for all of their crimes.

My contribution to the investigation then? Initially it was to do with the autopsies. There was usually a morning one, until the rate of infection and subsequent death necessitated afternoon shifts as well. Four bodies a day were being carted off for outside incineration by the time I dropped out of attending the gruesome inquests. By then I had a new contribution to make – screening clinics. A systematic programme to cover the entire camp, refugees and guards. It took me three days to work out a system, based on what I'd learned at Gershalt about scanning impossible numbers of cases within a constrained time frame. Not only did I load the scheme so that only I could carry out the check-ups, but I managed to present the plan to Geigy and the military chiefs as a means of safeguarding the health of all camp inmates, thereby granting me access to every corner of Tarutz. Using the experience I'd gained so painfully earlier, I set up a monitor of every single camp member's weight, temperature, pulse and skin condition. The workload was punishing, eighty patients in a day to cover the entire population in a continuous eleven-day cycle. However, lying in my room at night it was hard not to feel self-satisfied, knowing that with this exhausting schedule of examinations and record keeping I was making it extremely hard for the Russians to conjure up the next outbreak of 'Condition Six'. Every patient was given his or her own index card which detailed their current status, details entered in a code known only to me so that no-one else could tamper with the data. I used dozens of different methods to ensure interference would be immediately noticeable, many of the tabulations and data matrixes dating back to my days as a chemistry student, Vesey being proved right after all about the value of my 'scientific' background.

The clinics I would perform by day, the transcribing of

records into my own personal codes would go on later, deep into the night, by candlelight. Where I found the energy I don't know, ladies and gentlemen, but I kept this up for three months, sustained by a belief that whilst I wasn't necessarily saving lives I was at least preserving them for the moment, and then I became incapable of looking any further forward as the personal importance of this responsibility intensified – I was in love.

Perhaps it might help if I were to outline the usual routine of these days, the tasks and the challenges, the actions and the thought processes. Perhaps through such a detailed recollection the riddle of the times might begin to be deconstructed, perhaps amongst the pieces the truth might still be found. How on earth did I find happiness amongst the suffering and deceit? Can I be sure this was not another symptom of the hysteria of the times?

Of course I'm aware of how crass this is likely to sound; an attempted logical analysis of an irrational condition – love. Preposterous? Again, perhaps. But there are also previously neglected elements worthy of consideration here when I look back, like how much of this was truly circumstance and how much was a set-up. And other more disquieting possibilities, that it was I who was insane, I who first lost grip on reality whilst the others kept their senses; and for that, everything that followed was my fault.

Then as I try to relay the sordid facts of this 'great love' in my life there's the cliche that I fall into, that of a western introvert succumbing to a smouldering gypsy-like passion of the east. Obvious but wrong, it wasn't like that, ladies and gentlemen, not like that at all.

Her name was Katryn. She was about twenty, could

have been even younger. Blonde hair with traces of a darker brown running through, some days it could look mousy. She had bad teeth. The left canine was missing, its absence gave her smile an odd, lop-sided quality, and could turn the expression into a cruel one. Her eyes were blue, and had dark shadows underneath, like many of the Poles. Small frame, about eight stone. Thin pale limbs with skeletal hands and feet. A fine downy hair covering areas of her skin, concentrated under her arms and the rest, also at the nape of her neck. Hardly voluptuous, flat-chested, almost the body of a pre-pubescent. Years of bad diet, bad breeding, not the daughter of the Aryan master race she might once have been called to rejoin.

I remember these facts so readily because I have retained them, running through her faults like a mantra, trying to hold myself back from falling. To me she was so beautiful. Katryn. How did she come to claim that part of me, how much can I blame on her?

In those freezing months the day would begin with an ache and a realisation that the cold had crept further inside my bones during the night, that the chill was that fraction nearer to my core. Slowly out of bed, pulling back the blankets to hang over the metal rail at its foot, to let the air, such as it was, freshen them.

Immediately, clumsily, I would drag on some clothes. I only had two pairs of trousers and shirts with me, Geigy had told me to place anything I wanted washing in the camp laundry. I did once, the shirt coming back dirtier than when it set out. My underwear I preferred to launder myself, over at the wash-house. Even this had no running water, you had to fill your own bucket from the tank outside and then carry it up to one of the free-standing basins grouped in a circle over an open drainpipe. Most mornings, I would never feel like washing, introducing another kind of chill to my body, but I would anyway, and gradually came to feel less conspicuous about standing naked in a roomful of Russians, joking and grunting in their indecipherable tongue. My clothes go back on in that room – underpants, socks, two vests, shirt, trousers, boots, jacket and overcoat. Then over to the food hut to queue up for the bread being rationed out – flat, oily and dark, the consistency of linoleum. I'd take it anyway but ignore the gruel-like porridge on offer, safe in the knowledge that some other offering would be waiting for me at the hut door when I returned, for my efforts amongst the refugees had won some form of approval. Through Geigy, I had insisted on a better system of refuse disposal. Each family's debris of bones, skins and rotten bread could now be gathered to be taken outside rather than left as a festering invitation for the rats to make themselves at home. Any enemy of the rats could be these people's friend but this was me at my youthful peak, a medicine man to the masses.

Given the abysmal quality, it was no surprise that the fare provided for the camp's inhabitants should prove unappealing to them. What was extraordinary was the ingenuity with which they supplemented these meagre provisions. The total area of Tarutz can only have been seven or eight square miles but the land seemed to house a never-ending supply of game. Rabbit, pigeon, vole, crow; all of these and more, including creatures of unidentifiable species would find their way into the stews and soups left by my door, a token of comradeship with the young British doctor. Generally, it tasted as foul as anything else out there although I was glad enough to eat it, deluded as I was with the notion of bonding with my charges.

Morning then, and the multitude of cooking aromas would lift with the early haze from the ground, mixing with the smells of the wood burning to fire the stoves and the acrid scent of drying animal pelts. This stink would be at its strongest around now; by evening the fires would be a mere glow, and the noise around them would have dwindled too, tones hushed in conversation by the tents and shacks. I never ventured amongst them at night, not because I felt in any way afraid, more that it seemed inappropriate, an intrusion in a way that would not be the case by daylight.

Once I'd finished eating breakfast and cleaned up again it would be time to head over to Geigy's administration pound where I stored my records. Here, in this damp and draughty lean-to, I selected the files of those whom I had designated for inspection, collecting a bundle of index cards and slipping them into my dayfile. I had a canvas bag that Geigy had given me – I think it originally held a camera or some such equipment (I had it until recently, a nondescript memento, yet one that could bring this whole thing back to me in an instant) – and into this would go stethoscope, flask of water, magnifying glass, spare pens, cloths and bandages. It didn't take much to pack these away, then I'd be off to face the day.

Over to my left, the wind usually blowing me down toward it, a grassy knoll where the men would tend to congregate before midday; jabbing, laughing, shouting, dividing into smaller groups nursing whatever resentments of the moment, playing cards. Sometimes I went in amongst them, performing an elaborate mime to show my intentions, for although these were people of German origin and my fluency in the language had improved since my arrival in Berlin, I was never able to communicate verbally with them, dialects and idiom too different, another language. All seemed illiterate.

Despite this, there was never any display of the animosity or suspicion towards me that was so evident between them and the guards. If today I headed for the northern perimeter of the camp, then there would be waves and shouts as I passed, a friendly punch in the back if I went close enough. Tolerance, even affection; not because they understood how my system of data collection and calculations protected their families but because a spin-off from my inspection activities was a provision of the most basic medical care. Thus dressing wounds, lancing boils, assessing sores and bunions became my key specialities. I'm sure my tutors back at university might have held higher hopes for me, but then they would never have imagined a more grateful clientele.

Nevertheless, every morning, the same sense of doubt, the same apprehension. Were they really my new constituents, innocent and trusting, or were they hyenas, laughing at me until my stamina gave out and the kill would be that much easier?

She was in a shack in the heart of the main encampment when I first saw her. There must have been about fifteen others in it with her at the time, mostly older women, shrieking and wailing. Relatives? Aunts? I couldn't really tell, and it didn't seem appropriate to ask right then. She sat at the epicentre of this commotion, a brooding and truculent presence, arms resolutely folded. I was pushed toward her, tripping as I squeezed through the crush. I tried to smile.

'*Was ist los?* What's the matter?'

Maybe she didn't hear, the question drew no response. All around her the rest were still poking, prodding, pulling at her blouse. '*Ist doktor! Doktor!*'

She raised her hands to her ears to shut their screeching out.

'*Katryn. Ich bin Katryn.*'

She was looking at me. Our eyes met. I felt an immediate flash of contempt being thrown at me, the ineffectual fop pretending to help, and at the same time felt a sudden and desperate urge to counter it. I had to impress her.

'*Rob. Ich bin Rob.*'

Her eyes were still locked on mine as she nodded. A hand drifted toward the buttons on her chest, pale and slender fingers slipped under the cotton cloth and then parted the blouse. She stood and thrust her bare chest towards me. A new wave of frenzied squawks assailed my ears as I focused on the ugly sore festering on the underside of her left breast. '*Das . . .*' she muttered softly, cupping the area around it, '*was ist das?*'

And then I could understand the reasons for all of this frenzy; they thought she had it, this disease that was keeping them all prisoner here. They loved her, cherished her, but wanted the infection to be excised from within them.

The noise and actions of the rabble were making it diffi-cult for me to concentrate, couldn't they see it was time

144

to leave, wouldn't they grant this poor young woman some privacy? They were also blocking out what little light had fought its way into this squalid hole. I decided to fix my attention on the case in hand rather than try to clear the room, to get this over as quickly as possible. I moved my hand towards the inflammation, gently stretching the skin next to the infected tissue, peering into the wound. One of the hags seemed to take this as confirmation that something was terribly wrong and set off another high-pitched whine which in turn set the others off again. Enough.

'*Ruhe!*' I snapped, turning on her. Be quiet!

I glanced up at Katryn. 'Alright. It's alright. Just a cyst ... *zyste, ja?*'

It had only taken this brief examination to see that this wasn't the kind of infection I'd witnessed earlier, or that the rest of them feared it was. The cyst in question had formed underneath the skin, forming a small deposit of fluid and pus which, because it too was trapped, had given the breast its ugly and swollen appearance. An incision was required to drain it, and then the inflammation itself, if cleaned up, would heal. I motioned for Katryn to dress again. She could come with me to the medical huts. I would treat her there.

'*Kommen?*'

She didn't budge. Again I wondered if she hadn't heard or if she somehow didn't understand. Either way, my patience had gone and I wasn't going to wait any longer.

'*Kommen!*' I offered her my hand and she took it. I led her out and didn't let it go until we reached my hut five minutes later.

*　　*　　*

Apologies; I digress. It must appear as if I'm avoiding the very issues I had promised to discuss. It is not inconceivable that that may be so, even if it's not intentional. I suppose I've lived with this so long I must have found a way of coping with it – does that involve denial? Perhaps it's just a reflex that has been developed along the way.

I'm on my rounds. Where to? Today, let's say the eastern perimeter. Tents filling with the smoke from fires simmering outside, women hanging out washing, older ones crying the dry tears of bewilderment I'd try not to notice out of courtesy. Some of the temporary dwellings had been fashioned out of the remains of the wreckage still standing – a three-sided outbuilding has a heavy tarpaulin curtain slung over a rafter to fill the gap of the missing wall, rafts of wood bound together to patch the makeshift roof. It must be colder in here than in my own hut. How can they survive?

I hover outside. '*Hallo? Sei bitte, Herr Doktor.*' Eventually a lined old crone will come to the wall, staring at me silently, unknowingly. I smile. '*Guten tag!*' and roll up my sleeve to show her to do the same. '*Puls?*' She scrutinises the floor before lifting her arm. '*Ratte,*' she mutters; rats. They were always complaining about rats but I can't recall ever seeing one, I think they came out more at night. They would say the word with a curious mixture of fear and contempt, as if these animals were more to them than ordinary vermin.

Again, on reflection, I think of the endless effort, the energy I would have expended on just one visit, as if I were teaching them their own language. Inside the shack everything is strange, rugs and clothes lie on chairs and the floor, a shambles. There doesn't seem to be any space for these people to store those things that are truly personal, the things they would seek to keep from eyes like mine, judging them with every glance. From the walls, ancestors caught in stern portraits look down; some captured in photographs, a sepia-toned husband and wife from fifty years ago, others painted in oils, profiles from a distant age. It took some weeks for me to realise their significance. Naturally, at first I thought that these were the images of loved ones, revered ancestors, founders of the family name, and that their display owed everything to notions of duty and honour. Then it came to me, a growing appreciation that those living in the present had an absolute need of these portraits as points of reference in an otherwise terrifyingly transient world. Reminders of previous struggles, markers of time, like maps with a cross marked on to show where you stood in that moment, and a revelation of how much journey remained. Somehow I had unconsciously acquired an empathy for how important this would be to someone born in an age of violent change, how one might cling to such comforts. No one had had to explain, the sentiment had been absorbed under its own impulse, like a seed blown in the wind. The faces became more and more prevalent, until they merged into a common visage, eyes all the same, moving with me from hut to hut; Katryn's eyes.

Which brings me to another issue. I know I have spoken of my methods and procedures, how proud I was of them, their integrity. Now I have to consider that from early on these designs were out of control, and that my readings weren't factual at all. Let us stay with the old woman in the eastern perimeter, let us assume she has understood my promptings and gestures and has given me her arm. I'm feeling around her wrist. The skin is cold, with a grey pallor. Heartbeat? I'm not sure I've actually found it but I *know* what it is and enter that onto her card. Temperature? I won't even ask, I'm already noting it. Intuitive medicine? Subliminal medicine. What is going on? Trust your senses, Rob, save your time, let it pass. I get up, she's smiling at me warmly, nodding slowly. We *have* understood each other. I smile back. On to the next patient in the next shack and so forth, the same again. Later, the thoughts return. I'd be sitting at the chessboard with Geigy and the memory of that part of the day starts flickering in my mind, refusing to die down. This time I *can* feel the old woman's pulse as if I'm holding her right then and there. I look up, suddenly nervous. Dr Geigy starts to smile like he knows what is playing in my head and so I focus down at my pieces to contemplate my move. Nothing suggests itself, but I'm not really concentrating on the game any more. Instead there's a momentary panic that I'm trying to conceal: I have this notion that I'll never escape these people, they are now inside me, even when I leave Tarutz I'll take these people with me to Helensburgh or wherever I go.

Geigy leans forward, points to his rook, his bishop, and a diagonal running through my defence.

'Checkmate.'

A night of interruptions. First, an unknown visitor had knocked and then left without staying, leaving a small pot of meat casserole at the door. One mouthful was enough to kill any appetite, and I returned to the records strewn across the bed – I had been falling behind my self-imposed schedule of code transfers for a few days. An hour later, a guard appeared, gibbering about water or something. I didn't understand and sent him away. Fifteen minutes later he was back, accompanied by another, carrying between them the same rusty tub I had washed in just after my arrival. Luxury. My eyes savoured the sight of the steam rising from the water, and I ushered them in, thanking him profusely, trying to make up for my earlier impatience. Once they were out I raked through my belongings, searching for the soap I had brought with me from Berlin, gently perfumed, infinitely preferable to the blocks of carbolic at the wash-house, a gift from Joyce. And then I stripped and sank in. At last, a moment of private contemplation. I remember lathering up my limbs, looking down with detached interest at my changing body. Slimmer. My flat stomach had not been filled properly for almost a year, I must have dropped down to under ten stone. Taller; both of my pairs of trousers seemed to have become an inch or two too short. But what fascinated me most was the patch of hair that had spread across my chest – dark, dense, manly? My forearms were also somehow hairier and muscular, and it was difficult to work out how they might belong to me. Had I grown into some kind of werewolf? Who would notice the difference though, who could tell me if these were real or imagined changes and share my excitement – my mother, Joyce?

It was probably because of this moment's self-absorption that I failed to hear or notice Katryn coming in. The first I knew of her presence was the sound of the floorboards creaking as she knelt down behind me. How could she have entered so silently? Sometimes it was as if she could float, gliding like a swan. I was startled, but didn't move, what would be the point?

Since I had operated on her, Katryn had been to my hut about four times, presenting the wound for inspection. It had healed quickly, and there was now no real need for me to go on examining or dressing it.

I pointed to the towel at the end of the bed, would she bring it to me? Her face was close to mine. She smiled and shook her head, taking the soap from my hands, settling down on her knees behind me. I felt her hands begin to massage my shoulders, pushing me forwards so she could reach to the small of my back. A delicate touch. I struggled to relax and let myself enjoy it, to stop thinking about the door and what anyone would think if they came across us right then. I took a deep breath. They could think what they wanted, this was innocent enough; I hadn't invited the girl here, it was just a coincidence and she was simply showing gratitude for the attention I had given her. Anyway, I couldn't really tell her to stop because she never understood my words. It all made sense. Anyone would see.

The caressing stopped just as I succumbed to it. I opened my eyes, where had she gone? She had stood up and moved to my side. I watched her run her fingers through her hair and then bunch it all into a tail. She took a clasp of some sort from her mouth and fixed it to hold her hair together. Then she was unbuttoning her waistcoat and blouse, taking them off together before moving on to her skirt and underskirts which she let fall to the floor. She kicked off her boots last and stood naked in front of me, a vision I wanted to savour, not in a lascivious sense, but as a creation of beauty, a representation of a perfect form. I stood and stepped out of the bath, brushing past her as I turned to the bed. I had an erection, she couldn't have failed to notice it, but I felt no embarrassment.

I had stopped worrying about anyone disturbing us. I dried myself and sat on the bed, waiting for Katryn, watching her in profile. She was sniffing the soap, inhaling its scent, enthralled. The sight of her was itself equally captivating, I could have waited all night. She climbed out eventually and walked silently towards the towel I held open for her. She let me dry her, my hands carefully attending to every inch of skin as one might dry a child. And then, without saying a word, she eased herself onto me, sitting astride my lap, a hand disappearing to gently guide me into her, slowly and deliberately.

Katryn stayed until the early hours of the morning. We made love three times, although without any real notion of the stopping and starting that the phrase implies. No, more a continuous session, one endless attempt to satisfy the impossible craving I felt for her.

I was woken before dawn by Geigy himself.

'There is something you should see, Rob. Immediate –'

I struggled to come to. Something I should see, right now? Did I have to, it had only been an hour or so since Katryn had left and I was exhausted. Geigy cut a faintly comical image, dwarfed by an enormous coat and hat which had slipped down to cover his entire forehead, resting on the bridge of his beaky nose. He looked as if he had been drenched in flour and icing sugar, obviously there was some kind of blizzard out there.

'Of course. Please excuse me . . . I'll get dressed.'

There was a moment before Dr Geigy appeared to take in my request for him to leave. I could see him looking at the dishevelled state of the room: papers, notebooks, pens and instruments scattered around the floor. Perhaps he was annoyed that I'd let the hut degenerate to this after his help in clearing it.

'Uh? Yes . . . outside.'

I threw on trousers, shirt, the rest, and gathered a few items for my bag. Geigy was waiting outside with both of his orderlies when I emerged. It was obvious something was wrong, he had lost his usual polite charm, adopting a quizzical, almost confrontational tone from the start.

'Rob. Your programme. You examine every member of camp, yes?'

He was walking fast, my stiff legs struggled to keep up. We were heading for the ruin. What was this about?

'Yes. All of them.'

'How often? What is the last time you would have seen last patient?'

'Last patient? You mean yesterday?' Katryn, did he mean her?

'No. Most distant patient. What is the longest time any member of camp can have gone without examination?'

'Oh, I see. Eleven days. There's a continuous cycle . . .'

Geigy cut in before I could explain, 'Eleven days? You are sure?'

I wasn't. Originally it had been, but what with one distraction and another I had fallen behind. For some it must have been longer, at least two weeks.

'Why do you ask, has someone said –'

Again he cut me short. 'Inside. You see.'

We had arrived at the gate of the lower level chambers. This time, Geigy had his own key to unlock the main door, there was no sign of any guards. By this time my initial sense of fear had risen to a panic. Whatever was inside was my fault, I had let my system unravel and they had taken advantage. And Katryn, were they going to take her away from me? The familiar stench inside the dark passageway only made things worse, reminding me of other grim nights down here. I'd been a fool, so easily bought. Geigy's next words came as no surprise.

'Three, maybe four new cases. Progressing much faster than last time. Three men, one woman. Woman first.'

He motioned for me to follow him up the narrow hall and paused to fumble for the room key. I had been given a torch and went up close to offer some light. Instinctively, I forced the door. It was open and I pushed by the softly swearing Geigy to look inside.

Not as frightening as before, this time at least I knew what to expect. The figure of a middle-aged man lay on the hammock at the far end. Bloodied and tousled, he was obviously the victim of a particularly violent assault, with clothes torn open, stab wounds to his abdomen, and cuts and bruising to his face. I took his wrist for a pulse and found myself not so much feeling for a beating arterial line but concentrating on what my intuition told me the heart-rate might be, almost as if tuning in to a frequency. Geigy's hovering presence next to me, however, meant that

I couldn't read the signs the way I had grown accustomed to. I felt a rising anger, partly guilt over my own recent failings, partly frustration at not being able to connect in the normal way, and outrage that this torture had begun again.

'You see the wounds?'

Of course I did. I ignored the question.

'. . . and the surrounding tissue . . . necrotic . . . advanced . . . we don't understand.'

I shone the torch back onto the abdominal contusion. It was difficult to make out with such poor illumination, yet it seemed that Dr Geigy might be right. I reached into my bag for my magnifying glass and stooped down for a closer look, a movement I had cause to regret immediately, feeling a force rise up and strike me with considerable power on the bridge of my nose.

Gas gangrene. Any medical student will tell you how the smell hits you before you have caught its scent. This is not simply a matter of pungency, it's the way it attacks the senses. I remembered how my father would take visitors on a tour of the distillery and invite them to stick their heads over the oast where the barley fermented, laughing when they reeled backwards as the carbon dioxide struck them. Gas gangrene, the same only worse – would my father be laughing now?

'Let me see the others.'

Geigy pulled out his keys once more and we made our way next door. Waiting there – another macabre exhibit – the woman. Her injuries weren't as widespread as the previous case yet were gruesome enough – severe bruising around the neck, lacerations on her left ankle. The other two were back to the prior standard though, and by the time we had reached the last case I was almost indifferent to the horrors, and oblivious to Geigy's promptings.

'More necrosis, gangrenous tissue ... You see? This patient I examined myself less than two hours ago. Wounds were fresh then. I do not understand. And with the others, you say you inspected them eleven days ago ... then this would not be possible.'

He shrugged and looked pleadingly at me. What did he want me to say?

'What would not be possible, Dr Geigy? Your people seem capable of almost anything.'

He stared at me incredulously for what felt like an age. My heart was pounding, not knowing how he would react now I had inadvertently voiced my suspicions. The silence hung agonisingly but I wasn't going to back down now, too full of admiration of my own foolhardy courage. Eventually he spoke, the words slow and tinged with sadness.

'I thought you were more intelligent than that, Rob. You have not understood. These wounds, the things we have seen tonight, gangrene ... these are *old* wounds, untreated for weeks. *Old* sores, *advanced* infections ... older than eleven days. Can't you see now?'

Impetuous bloody fool. How had I missed this?

'Yes. Of course ... I'm sorry, I didn't mean –'

He let me flounder for a while longer, standing still as my blush threatened to light up the room.

'Alright. We talk again in the morning.'

'Yes! Yes, of course. I'll check my records. Do we have identification of these cases? If I knew their names and what part of the camp they were in I could confirm when I last examined them. Could even be less than eleven days.'

But it was now Geigy's turn to be deaf to my suggestions, sighing as he led the way out.

'Tomorrow, Rob, tomorrow.'

I spent three entire days poring over my set of records, three distraught days. I did not find those entries relating to the cases I saw that night at the ruin, or the four subsequent new cases after them. My system was in complete disarray and I almost drove myself mad in my efforts to unravel it.

As the cases progressed I would make the journey back up to the cells with increasing regularity until it seemed I was up there more often than down in the camp. My scanning programme had ground to a halt, and with it the fragile sense of order with which I had comforted myself since those first terrible days at Tarutz evaporated. Confidence gone, I had nothing to offer the investigation, except a lingering suspicion that this entire 'outbreak' situation was still being orchestrated somehow by Geigy and his devious comrades even though I had not one shred of proof.

Geigy would have me stand over another unfortunate victim, pointing, prodding, offering a commentary as he did so.

'Patient 11206. We looked at him an hour ago, remember? Leg ulceration, three inches in diameter, no gangrene. Look, now five inches diameter, advanced necrosis ... same patient, remember?'

I did, or thought I did. But then as I said, they all looked the same to me now, dressed the same, smelled the same, died the same death. Would it really be so hard for Geigy to be switching patients, bodies and corpses if his strategy was one of misinformation?

Forty-two cases. Twenty-seven deaths. The atmosphere in the camp one of total panic, rumours, fights and hysteria spreading daily. I decided I had to act.

I approached Geigy and asked for his help in sending a telegram back to Vesey in Berlin. The message? A simple one, a few lines.

'Tarutz inmates breaking out in trauma injuries stop. Request immediate assistance in medical back-up stop.'

'Breaking out in trauma injuries' – a contradiction in terms, a nonsense, yet one that would probably make it past Russian intelligence because of its innocuous medical language. What would they make of it at A.M.U. 4? Would they think I'd gone mad and immediately retrieve me? Or would they realise it was some sort of coded message to indicate the complicity of the Russians and therefore demand open access to the camp?

I couldn't see how my message could fail. Either way, help would have to arrive, and my nightmare would be over.

Wrong again, they sent Arthur Lee.

The Piper

IT IS ANOTHER IRONY of this history, although this time quite deliberate, that the figure with unquestionably the most direct responsibility for the horrors that brought about Hamelin's demise is the character about whom we know the least. Yet the very lack of detail and testimony regarding this individual and his role in the events about to be described offer an insight into his character and presence, for this was a man who took care to remove any incriminating evidence from the scene, who consciously sought to leave no footprint in the history he was making, and whose constant reinventions of his persona were so successful that all that remains of him is a name. This name, when judged on its own, is innocuous, a harmless conjunction of adjective and trade. However, it is a name which has come to represent the epitome of a sinister and uncontrollable power – the Pied Piper.

Any attempt to disengage the reality from the myth surrounding this character must take into account the atmosphere and culture of the times already outlined in this paper: the Thirty Years' War marked a period of unprecedented devastation in Europe and particularly the German lands. It also heralded the modern era of military technology and strategy as armies of a scale never witnessed before roamed the plains for three whole decades, causing massive disturbance in their wake. Inevitably, the steady displacement of peoples from the land and the ready availability of spoils thus accruing made Middle Europe an attractive prospect for those with little fear of battle and a talent for organisation, military entrepreneurs like Armando D'Ortez, as previously described in these pages. And there were other kinds of opportunists who travelled from far to join him. The large number of soldiers carrying both war booty and their own 'entertainment' needs, together with an ever-shifting population of peasants holding grievances gave these lands an appeal for those whose talent was the exchange of aspirations and desires, those like the Pied Piper, and it was to such a fervent environment teeming with possibilities that he was first drawn.

What can be deduced from the name? 'Pied' could conceivably be a corruption of the French 'à pied', meaning 'on foot', indicating that this man was by nature a traveller. It could also imply the style of clothing he wore, 'pied' meaning mottled or spotted, with the kind of bright and bold colour associated with a jester or clown. Finally, the word could be a corruption of his real name, particularly if this was Arabic in origin and therefore difficult for an uneducated German speaker to pronounce.

The issue of Arabic culture and its influence is an important one, and it is probable that the Piper was either himself of an Eastern background or had had access to its teachings. This was the age of magic, of alchemy, and it was mainly from the Orient that the sorcery of the times emanated; the East, home to the strange crops which could consume a man as he consumed them – hashish, opium.

On and off the battlefield an insatiable hunger for new ideas grew, yet, as virtually all records of the era show, innovations and inventions were feared. Within the army camps, rumours of strange new weapons would reduce ranks to an uncontrollable rabble, whilst in the peasant towns tales would spread of new diseases more deadly than the plague, and of men who had mastered the art of turning dust into gold. The craving for knowledge was widespread; warlords, their sponsors, and dispossessed peasants all sought the benefits it may bring, but it was guarded by those who held it. The motivations for shielding such intelligence were themselves part and parcel of the war-fevered atmosphere then prevalent, where learning would be hidden until such a time when an advantage might be gained from it – consider, from a slightly earlier age, the Spanish Conquistadors presenting themselves to the native American Incas and employing their superior understanding of astronomy to predict the eclipse and thereby appear to be controlling the very sun. In an age of magic, even meagre knowledge could wield enormous power; this is the first key to understanding the influence the Piper would eventually wield.

The second half of his name refers to the cover that provided the basis of his actions and movements – music. The Piper was, first and foremost, a minstrel who would attach himself and his troupe to whatever army it was fruitful and expedient to be with. At the height of the War, the larger armies would have had enormous retinues of such supporters in tow following their progress in the field. Their numbers would include blacksmiths, cooks, traders and whores, as well as the entertainers who would provide the backdrop for the revelry which greeted each victory (and, by definition, escape from death) on the battlefield. However, those who lasted the duration of several campaign seasons owed more to an inherent gift for survival than mere musicianship. Favour amongst brutalised soldiers was a fickle notion, anyone who was to profit from being with these men depended on an ability to sense the moment when to move on, the time to abandon a fading force about to lose, and selecting the best role to play at the next destination. In certain instances, it might be speculated, it would prove prudent to remodel one's name and appearance.

It is this paper's contention that the Piper was such a being; a chameleon capable of attuning himself to a particular surrounding and presenting himself as a harmless visitor. Someone whose very currency depended on an ability to intuitively reach for the sometimes powerful unconscious yearnings amongst his audience, and that in doing so he acted as the final catalyst in the tragedy of Hamelin. For the Piper was, as has been stated, a travelling player; yet his instrument of choice was not the mandolin or even the flute, but the soul.

'We must reach a solution soon, or the whole town will be driven insane. This is no way to live, gentlemen – God is mocking us!'

'You will restrain yourself from profanity, sir, or you will be ejected from this chamber!'

'But it is true! Even our own priest deserts us. How much longer can we go on ... what are we to eat if we cannot leave these damned walls ... what happens when the well is dry? ... And the rats! – the rats, gentlemen.'

Councillor Unger's words falter and then become audible only to himself as he buries his head in his hands, sobs breaking the silence at momentary intervals. Some councillors scratch their heads and try absently to pick out the vermin hiding there, others rub their bites in a vain bid to soothe them. Most are unable to stop themselves screwing up their faces at the stench which envelops the room and the town square. No one makes the effort to console him.

'Councillor, we will address the issues of food and water rationing later in this meeting. Can we return to the matter of D'Ortez' demands as it is perhaps more pressing?'

Mannau takes the sound of sighs and awkward shuffling as assent, and begins anew.

'Perhaps we should consider, I wonder, as no quantity of women was mentioned, how many does the Duke expect us to supply? Mayor, was any number actually referred to?'

The Mayor shakes his head. He has not said a word all meeting and continues to stare at the pathetic figure of Unger with noticeable distaste.

'Then perhaps we might be able to negotiate over that. Is that your impression, Mayor Ebber?'

Again, there is no immediate reply; the Mayor simply breaks his gaze from Unger and turns silently to Mannau. It is another who offers words to the questioner.

'The man has an army four hundred strong. You think we might send him one woman, even two, on the basis that he neglected to specify his desired quantity, and that he might then accept this and curse his own stupidity?'

Kunze's scorn hangs over Deputy Mannau, testing his new-found grace and statesmanship. He struggles to resist responding in kind and is grateful when Councillor Schmidt seems to speak up in support.

'Gentlemen, surely the way is to ask for volunteers?'

Mannau cannot contain his disbelief. 'Volunteers? For this? Are you out of your mind?'

'Whores . . . we would make sure they are well rewarded for their efforts . . . it may be that some would offer themselves if these rewards were high enough.'

Kunze's elderly features display the expression of a bemused man.

'Are there any whores in this town? I must confess it is some time since I sought their particular pleasures . . .'

The admission brings no equivalents from the other members. All eyes begin to focus on the younger ones in attendance, including the Mayor himself. However, his brooding presence makes such glances brief. Schmidt continues.

'Perhaps there are those who are, and whose activities are not known to the council. Perhaps there are those of a wanton nature who might be tempted if the rewards were desirable.'

'Are you suggesting we issue a proclamation asking these women to come forward?'

Schmidt pauses, inhaling deeply.

'Yes, once we have agreed what the rewards should be.'

Murmurs pass around the chamber immediately. All except the Mayor break into smaller groups to wrestle with the notion, even Unger, still drying his tears.

'But surely it is known that our treasury is empty?'

'Then we could offer privileges in water and grain, or promissory notes for when our coffers are full again.'

'What if there are no volunteers?'

'We could raise the level of reward.'

'And the husbands – what would they say?'

'They may be as keen as their wives to benefit.'

'But it may be that it is the town hags who offer themselves.'

'Then we could give greater reward to those who are in possession of the greater youth and beauty. We could even –'

'For God's sake, stop! Can't you hear yourselves?'

All eyes turn to the Mayor, such is the sudden and unrestrained power of his eruption. Schmidt toils to contain his fluster.

'Mayor, with all respect, these are desperate times.'

'Then I ask you a question, councillor. Say we issue our proclamation, we select the ones whom we decide to be best suited to the task and, no doubt, requisition those who prove more reluctant to come forward but whom we, in this room, judge suitable for this *delicate* mission. Perhaps those women we suspect to be of a wanton, or wayward nature . . . those fit to be sacrificed to a syphilitic army to –'

'With all due respect, Mayor –'

Mannau's attempt to halt Ebber's flow is only half-successful, for the Mayor cuts across him to continue, this time though adopting a superficially conciliatory tone.

'The question then, councillor, councillors of the chamber of Hamelin . . . these actions . . . this very discussion – what does this make us? What does this mean that we are?'

'Mayor, the survival of Hamelin demands –'

'Whoremasters? Is this now our duty – to procure the prostitutes for the soldiers who would raze our town?'

Ebber looks for an answer, casting a slow sweeping gaze around the table. No one returns his eye, not Wolfricht or even old Kunze. Mannau senses the time is right to speak.

'Mayor, with respect, all we are asking for is a few women to lift their skirts . . . to preserve our town.'

'So your answer is yes? We have been elected to select and serve whores to those who choose to threaten Hamelin.'

'Mayor, you begin to sound like the damned priest!'

Unger raises his handkerchief to his mouth, as shocked as the rest by what he has just said.

'And we know how *he* solved his problem of conscience . . .'

Mayor Ebber struggles momentarily; they are all turning against him. D'Ortez had never mentioned numbers or a deadline, perhaps he had known a vague threat was more capable of paralysing the council than a specific one. Yes, a formidable opponent. These people evidently felt troubled by the challenge he set, only now they obviously felt they could meet such a contest the better without the Mayor. Why protect them any more?

'With *respect*, councillors, I must inform you, and perhaps disappoint some of you, by revealing the truth about the absence of Father Seicle.'

Ebber takes a deep breath, aware of the hush now falling on the room.

'He did not desert us, nor did the errand boys who accompanied me on my visit to the D'Ortez camp. He died for us. I told the boys to take his body to Kulhun for burial and not to return.'

Unger's damp eyes glisten as he peers at the Mayor.

'Dead . . . how? I do not believe you.'

'Then I suggest you ask your colleague, the Deputy. He was with me when the Duke told us himself. Perhaps you would confirm this to the council, Deputy Mannau?'

Across the table, the nod of the head comes almost reluctantly.

'Then why was the council not informed, why did you keep this from us?'

'An error . . . on my behalf. I wanted to avoid any panic. I can only apologise for letting you think the worst about a man who loved this town. I can only hope his spirit will forgive me.'

'What do you mean, Mayor?'

Ebber closes his eyes and rocks forward as if leading them in prayer.

'When Father Seicle died he had been split from his throat to his ankles – cut by the same men we would now offer our women. Tortured, gentlemen, either for gain or for pleasure . . . and he knew that this was what awaited him.'

A fresh silence, and Ebber opens his eyes. Saying what he has just relayed has forced him to think back to that night, and think once more of his fallen friend. Somehow he feels the stronger for it. A familiar voice is calling from far away in his mind, pacifying him like the gentle breeze of a lost summer's day. He speaks again, his tone different, as if his audience now includes Seicle's ghost, whose approval he seeks.

'I feel that he did this so that we might learn, so that we might appreciate the danger we face. Gentlemen, this is not an enemy we can appease through gifts and generosity. This is an enemy we must vanquish.'

Ebber pauses, giving time for the vision in his mind to speak to him. Mannau cannot hide his resentment.

'You say that, Mayor, but how?'

'With truth . . .'

The murmurs start slowly but within moments a clamour grows to drown any hope of reasoned debate. Ebber knows that he has lost them, that they no longer understand, but he is reaching out to a higher authority than any of them can contemplate, and no longer cares. He gives himself to the sensation, retreating into the dream that is now beckoning him.

'See? He speaks in riddles – what use are these to us?'

'Order! Order!'

Mannau thumps the table with his fist but it is one of many now pounding the same surface, and though he shouts at the top of his voice he cannot make himself heard.

'He is – He is – *mocking* us . . . *mocking* us all!'

Unger is crying once more, words coming out in an interminable wail, a grating addition to the tumult around him. Mannau hits the table with renewed vigour, an angry rejection of the hopelessness he feels rising in his throat. Ten men, ten councillors, making the noise of a hundred. What is happening to them, what has possessed the Mayor, how can he lead the council if he can't control himself? He leans over towards the other man, stretching and grabbing his hands, squeezing them in desperation, look at me! But the Mayor does not seem capable of giving any response, his eyes closed, almost unconscious, oblivious to the shouts around him. The rest continue to screech and spray their venom at one another, attacking themselves with equal hate, scratching their sores until they bleed. Mannau watches Wolfricht glance furtively up his sleeve, does he think that no other is watching? He does. Wolfricht cannot remember how the rat had caught him; that recollection has been lost in the horror of seeing his arm swell up like a pig's bladder full of blood, so bloated the skin has begun to pull apart under the pressure, a noxious-smelling pus seeping out of the widening gap. There are tears in his eyes too.

'Order! Chancellor, I implore you, order!'

'Sir?'

The aldermaster had drawn close to Mannau, entering the room during the fray, now waiting hesitantly on the fringe of the chaos. Mannau feels a jolt to the heart; he had not realised he was there. What is it with this man, why does he intrude now? A wave of the arm, off with you! The aldermaster still lingers, he has not yet told what he has come to say and is plainly troubled at what he surveys. What is wrong with the Mayor? Mannau's intolerance rears its ugly head, a blow to the servant's side – you should not see us like this, off!

'But, Sir . . .'

Behind him, slowly entering, uninvited, the visitor whose arrival the aldermaster is trying to announce surveys the wretched scene. Although his head is still, there is nothing that escapes his eye; the jaundiced pallor of the men around the table, their unkempt hair and scruffy beards, the stained and dusty capes under which each man seems to scratch and fidget incessantly, working themselves into a frenzy. Each brandishes more contempt and fury than the next, all are too vexed to even notice him. The smell in the chamber would offend swine. It is hard to tell whether this comes from outside or is a result of the lack of washing of those inside.

And still they rage, clusters of contention pulling together then splitting amid further acrimony, like a colony of ants driven mad by a cloud of pepper, all of them choking on their outrage except the young man at the far end who gazes dreamily at the ceiling. Time to give the gift he had promised at the town gate earlier. A hand enters the leather satchel on his back, a thin hand, dark and bony, long fingers divided into segments by the white creases at joint and knuckle so as to appear to be those of a wooden mannequin, an illusion only broken when they reveal an impossible grace and fluidity, dancing along the holes atop his flute as he blows.

A gentle refrain slowly floats into the air, its soft echo returning from the panelled walls as the melody glides up and down, sharp and flat, and its notes begin to tease the ears of those in session.

First to notice is the one who had brought him here; the aldermaster takes a step back and thus reveals the source of the music to Mannau, now staring in astonishment at the apparition that has befallen the chamber. Next, Unger draws the soiled handkerchief from his temple to peer in confusion at the elfin form serenading them. Soon, the others start to follow the melody's strains and one by one lose interest in their squabbles until the only sound in the room is that of the stranger's flute, even Wolfricht managing to forget the pain of his distended arm as the airborne notes cast their mesmeric spell on him.

The final convert is the one who had been silent all along. The young man who had been lost in contemplation lowers his head and opens his eyes. A smile forms on his lips as he greets the guest, it is as if he knows this mysterious caller though no words are exchanged between them. Another flourish over the flues, and the song ends on a prolonged note that fades out into silence. The same hand tucks the flute back inside its pocket as the men wait. The buckle is fastened with a slow diligence. It is now the visitor's turn to smile, now that his music has charmed them.

'Good day, Sirs. I am the Piper – I have come to offer my services to Hamelin.'

When did the plan first take root in his mind? Was it then, as he entered the chamber, or could it have been earlier, when he had gained admittance into the town itself, passing through the gates and climbing up to the town hall square? Did the soft carpet of rat droppings under his feet, the empty bellies of the listless children, the scattered fires in the alleyways, themselves burning on wood stripped from the shutters of once proud buildings, all combine to tell him that here in Hamelin was a stage on which to conjure a new fantasy, one that could make him a richer man? A plague town? No, he had seen enough before to know that what he saw were symptoms of a different malaise, a more lingering affliction than the plague which could arrive and depart from a city so fast as to leave its cobbled pavement stones ringing with shock. It was clear that a different kind of illness had gripped this town.

Alas, with all Hamelin long destroyed, conclusive evidence will forever elude historians. What follows can only be conjecture, but who is to say that the notion did not occur still earlier, before he had entered the town, as the Piper sat impatiently awaiting his promised audience with the 'Duke' at D'Ortez' makeshift camp. The arrogance of the man would have affronted him, especially since it is likely he had little to be arrogant about. Waiting, two days of waiting and watching the strains ferment, until at last D'Ortez is ready.

The Piper is led from the main fire to a smoky den a short distance from it, a cave made up of ferns and hacked branches, a boar roasting on a spit immediately outside. The Spaniard ahead indicates with a wave of his knife that the rest of the troupe is to wait here, halfway between the two. The Piper curses inwardly, these companions are both his lifeblood and load, it is important that their secret is not uncovered by these heathens too soon. The concern is concealed as ever, he draws his lips, a thin smile; of course, sir, we have nothing to fear. Another wave of the knife, his knapsack must be left outside, take it off. The Piper slips it from his shoulder, pulling his flute from the side pocket as he lays it down. He lifts the instrument to his mouth and offers a brief shrill blow to prove it is no weapon. This time the blade is brandished to herd him inside, for the 'Duke' is waiting.

'*Hola, Señor.*'

The greeting is not immediately acknowledged by either of the shadowy figures inside, and it is difficult to judge from a mere silhouette which one is the leader he should be addressing.

The Piper hears the duo murmur before the nearer of the two strides forward to stand immediately before him, a small man like himself, perhaps only a few inches taller, black leather boots and strapped breastplate creaking as he stares into the other's face. Suddenly, eyes still fixed on the Piper's, his hand jerks forward and snaps his wrist to halt his playing.

'*Was ist das?*'

The grip is painfully tight, the Piper feels as if the blood is being wrung from his hand.

'*Flote*. . . is a flute.'

The squeeze on his arm intensifies for a brief second and is then released. The other man still stands close as the Piper gently flexes his numbed fingers, furtively bringing the instrument to his mouth and blowing a gasp into it, a merry scale played with comic gusto to indicate his foppish relief. The two others laugh and the Piper has achieved his aim; *yes*, laugh at me, I am but a simple fool. He waits for them to subside and offers a stooping bow. When he next speaks the words are in German; he has understood D'Ortez' resentment at the familiarity assumed by addressing him in his mother tongue.

'I come to offer my services, sir, to you and your fine army. Music to soothe the soul, music to stir the spirit, music of magic and charm – the choice is yours, sir . . .'

This time his offer fails to move them, he continues after a brief pause, still uncertain which man is D'Ortez.

'There may, of course, be other services I may be able to provide.'

The man directly in front of him gives a single nod to indicate he should stop. He then turns and indicates that his companion should leave, again with a brusque nod of his bearded chin. The silent command is instantly obeyed and the two are left alone.

'Speak'

'The town of Hamelin – your men say it is a plague town, yet in these times many things are not always as they seem.'

D'Ortez offers no encouragement for him to continue. The Piper's unease returns; only the dead and the insane could stare so impassively.

'It might be . . . that it could be . . . worthwhile for you to know for certain what condition the town is in.'

Outside, the fire crackles, spitting back the heavier snow-flakes that drift unknowingly to its heart. The Piper can hear shouting. Are the soldiers interfering with the troupe or has the revolt started already? He decides to press on.

'It could be that it is worthwhile . . . paying for such information . . . if there were someone who could gain admittance to the town and report back.'

The Spaniard seems never to blink, although it could be that a smile is forming on his face, the merest hint recognisable in the dimness as the Piper continues.

'How much might such information . . . be worth to a force like this?'

The Piper looks to D'Ortez for an answer and the smile is gone, eyes unyielding, cold. Was it ever truly there? No sooner has he heard the rustle of leather and iron breast-plate than the hand is upon him again, this time grasping his neck, snapping shut around it like a hunter's iron trap.

The effort of maintaining the grip is not apparent in the slow voice of the Spaniard.

'Hear this, player. What I need, I take, including *information*. The only things I receive are gifts. I will be pleased to receive your *gift* when you come back from the town. Your party will remain here until you return . . .'

The hand withdraws from the Piper's throat, and he rubs his skin instinctively.

'A gift?'

'One that may bring its own reward when we enter the town.'

'But I will need my band to enter Hamelin. They must travel with me.'

'They will be safer here. Besides, I may wish them to play for the men. A celebration when you bring back your news . . . Now leave. Do not speak to my men and do not return without your gift.'

Four hundred Thalers was the price agreed that day, the sum the council negotiated to rid itself of D'Ortez' army and, ultimately the notional sum Hamelin would die for. The Piper left with a down-payment of around fifty Thalers on his person. It is likely he would have been pleased with this deposit; he may not have ever imagined returning, demanding the balance and would have doubtless had to endure a round of awkward questioning on his proposed method to rid the town of the soldiers' menace. Whatever the challenge, he managed, thanks to a judicious use of musical repertoire, to remind the council of the chaos and despair that had greeted his arrival. Surely any chance was worth taking at this stage? The council, in its disarray, had agreed, and thus would vote itself into extinction.

Three miles the distance from the town gate to the soldiers on the edge of the forest. The Piper waited until dusk before commencing his journey back across the plain between. Even then he set off slowly, affecting a limp and asking to borrow a staff to aid his walk, his stumbling gait disguising the fact that he was veering to the left of D'Ortez camp ahead. It was not that he had lost the desperation to return to his troupe, anxious to see that they had not been interfered with by inquisitive hands; no, the detour was a necessary evil, it would be foolish to arrive back laden with money fresh from Hamelin's coffers – if it were discovered how could he hope to explain it, let alone retain it?

A hiding place, that was what was required, somewhere to keep the treasure safe until the situation resolved itself.

The reeds grew thicker, and the Piper had cause to be grateful he had asked for the staff, using it like a scythe to clear a path of sorts. This would once have been farming land, now overgrown through neglect, the wild and brittle harvest around him at shoulder height. Rye, fields of it left to rot whilst the town starved. Madness, although this crop was beyond rescue, another symptom of the strange lethargy strangling Hamelin, a town where even the rats were insane. What had happened to them all?

The Piper stops and reaches for a billowing stem. The light is fading and it is difficult to examine the plant in the way that he needs to. Rye, but not ordinary rye; he holds the grain pods close, sniffing the damp seeds he crushes in his fingertips. An unusual redolence, for a moment he can smell the sweetness of alcohol caught in the wind. This is a type he has not encountered before – could this be the mutation he has heard of in his travels, is this what they are storing inside the town walls? He slips the knapsack from his shoulder and places the grain inside, wrapping it inside a brightly-coloured kerchief. Daylight will reveal more. He will go ahead and bury his money but perhaps the rest of the plan should be amended, perhaps D'Ortez is right, there should be a celebration, a feast to end all feasts.

The riders came and took him when he was a mile from the camp, slinging him onto the back of a starved cavalry horse and riding recklessly and needlessly fast until pulling up on the edge of the wood. Once more he had to be seen to take it all in good humour, yet be suitably harassed by this treatment. He rolled comically as he dismounted, spinning from the saddle to lie flat in the snow, blowing the flute with a tune of pique. The soldiers laughed but the performance was cut short by the arrival of D'Ortez' aide coming to take possession of his 'gift' before he could share it with any others.

The Piper stalled for as long as he could, bowing to the jeers of the troops, turning to face each corner of the camp, sweeping low to each in succession whilst scanning anxiously for sight of his players – where were they?

A sharp tug on the strap of his satchel told him the patience of his guard was exhausted and he was led to the clearing that housed the Duke he had met two days earlier. This time the man himself stood outside his lair, and in the morning light the Piper had his first chance to examine him properly. There was nothing physically impressive about D'Ortez, he had the same diminutive frame, sharp features and weak chin as most of the Spaniards the Piper had encountered before. The threat was all in his bearing, from the way his hands caressed the sword at his side, the imperious scowl that adorned his face, the penetrating glare of his hazel eyes, dead as the leaves blowing around him. The Piper conjures a clown's smile to greet him, indignantly brushing the snow from his back. This will have to be as convincing a performance as he has ever mustered, failure will cost him dear.

'Where is the rest of my party?'

D'Ortez nods to the inside of his den; not here. The Piper steps reluctantly into the gloom and waits for the Spaniard to follow. Inside, the grey ashes of the night's fire and the blankets and bedding of the army's inner circle. The Piper steps round them and turns to the entrance. D'Ortez stands ahead, once more the Piper finds himself addressing a silhouette.

'What have you done with them?'

D'Ortez sighs impatiently. 'It is of no consequence, they are safe. A strange breed are they not, what are they?'

'Musicians.'

D'Ortez snorts with brief laughter. 'Musicians! What kind?'

'Whatever you want them to be.'

'Quite.'

The sneering tone of the Spaniard's reply worries the Piper and he curses inwardly – what does D'Ortez know? The success of the plan depends on the participation of the eunuchs, have they been discovered already?

'You have information for me?'

'I may.'

'Then speak.'

'Hamelin is in a state of disquiet but is not a plague town. There is nothing to stop you from exercising your right to shelter there.'

'Nothing?'

'The town is prepared for an onslaught but were you to wait another day it would not be defended. You would not have to fight to take it.'

D'Ortez seems sceptical at the news. He steps closer to the Piper.

'The Mayor agreed to this?'

'The Mayor has lost his mind, his voice is an irrelevance. The Deputy, Mannau, will grant your force admittance to the town.'

'And why would he do that?'

'I told him you would make him Mayor, that you were familiar with his name and reputation and would rely on him to restore order.'

D'Ortez snorts again. 'And if I do not honour this promise?'

'An irrelevance . . . you will already be inside the walls.'

'Quite. And did this "Deputy" mention the women I require?'

'He did not, sir. I am afraid I was unaware that I was to ask. They will, sir, supply materials for the celebration tonight – beer, bread and the like. As far as the rest of the council is concerned, your force will move north tomorrow to join the Saxons. This will be their farewell gift, one that you might choose to personally thank them for tomorrow on your way out . . .'

The details seem authentic enough to please him. 'Quite. My men are restless, they will fight the better for some carousing. See to it that they have what they want and I will consider your reward once we are inside the town. You may go.'

The Piper bows graciously.

'Thank you, sir. I will see that they have whatever they have dreamed of.'

The music carries over the distance with occasional ease, gusts of wind bringing whole portions of melody and dance across the plain and into the town, together with the shrieks and guffaws of the men enjoying it. Mannau peers into the darkness, trying to make sense of it all; it was he who had persuaded the council to part with the final gifts after the Piper's sudden reappearance. He could only hope the man was sincere and that this was not another grotesque joke being played on Hamelin.

Beside him in the bell-tower stands Kunze, hearing less acute than the Deputy's but no less envious of the carnival being enjoyed on the other side. Had he been a younger man he would have considered joining such an outfit; there was no doubt the degenerate life held appeal and he could understand why so many towns had lost their sons to it. The 'civil' life he and his colleagues had so virtuously promoted would always seem weak and insipid by comparison. Who was thanking them for their righteousness now?

'Listen!' Mannau waves his arm impatiently to indicate he should be still. 'There! More than one flute . . . an Arab tune.'

'Did he say he had men over there?'

'"Companions" he said, he was eager to return to them.'

'Well, there you are.'

'Listen! Sounds like a hundred flutes, how can they do that? And, can't you hear that . . . the shouting?'

'Trick of the wind. I don't understand what it is that troubles you.'

Mannau stares out to the trees, hands cupped behind his ears. He does not understand either, yet the sensation will not release its eerie grip on him and he has no choice but to listen. This is the look-out post in which Seicle used to spend hour after hour staring at the same view. Was the Mayor right? Had the Priest's ghost returned to guide and protect them?

The glow from the camp fire seems brighter, its flames at a peak. Mannau tries to remember its size when he first started watching. It is almost as if it has spread or spawned other fires, burning up the snow. A trick of the wind? Possibly, that and the way its image is split by the trees at its border. If only he could see more clearly. Then, the noise that travelled the miles between to shake him to the core; a yell, a scream of pure terror, one man, then two.

'Hear that? You must have! Listen!' Mannau closes his eyes to concentrate on the sound alone.

Kunze remains baffled, hearing nothing but Mannau's shuffling feet.

'There!'

Another salvo of shrieks reach the tower. Mannau tries to focus on the blaze behind the first trees, figures appear from behind them, darting out and tumbling headlong into

the drifts – men or animals? A new sound arrives, a cross
between thunder and a drumbeat. Even Kunze catches it.

'What on earth was that?'

Mannau ignores him, already scrambling down the lad-
ders leading to the top of the tower. He yells as he descends.
There are others below gathered in the church.

'Fetch the Mayor, and the rest of the council. They must
come . . . immediately! Something terrible is happening out
there – they are slaughtering each other!'

The supplies from the town were delivered an hour before
dusk as agreed, two carts making the same journey they
had made weeks earlier when carrying the Mayor and his
Priest. D'Ortez had displayed no suspicion when the Piper
had first told him of this parting 'gift' but he had surprised
his men by appearing and demanding that the Piper and
his mute crew, together with the unfortunate men who had
transported it, sample the goods provided for his soldiers to
feast on. The test was duly passed, the Hamelin men forced
to devour two phials of grape brandy before passing out
to the merriment of the observers. Left to lie in the snow,
the Piper knew they would be dead within the hour from
the chill yet he did nothing to help, his priorities at that
moment lay elsewhere.

If D'Ortez had known the exact nature of the Piper's
companions, he had not shared this knowledge with the
ranks who remained curious about these oddities amongst
them. The Piper had taken them to one side, whispering
in Turkish to their veiled and exotically swathed figures;
they were in danger, in the court of a cunning and devious
man, yet riches would be theirs if they could execute the

plan. The Piper would signal which tunes to play, when to drop the veil, to expose a breast. Everything depended on exploiting the factions within the camp, flirting with one group then another. These men had never seen eunuchs before and would be confused and excited in equal measure. Encourage them to drink, above all, encourage them to drink!

Interest in the fate of the visiting army had spread through the town like a fever. Mannau had wanted to ride out with as large a party as were willing to make the trip, it was Kunze who advised caution. If the scene was gruesome might it not frighten those who witnessed it, what if there were still enough soldiers to capture those venturing out and then mount an attack on the town?

So it was that the four of them had travelled: Mannau, Kunze, Mayor Ebber and Schmidt, their journey made uncomfortable by the prominence of the spine and ribs of their mounts. The foursome had grown steadily silent as they approached the remnants of the camp, Mannau feeling the same shiver he had the night before, daylight bringing different portents. Where only hours earlier there had been raucous mirth now there was unearthly silence, even the ravens had taken their leave of the camp. Yet any feeling of joy he might have felt at the deliverance that had been granted Hamelin was already waning as he felt himself already succumb to a sense of dread over the deal he had agreed with its perpetrator.

The first bodies lay less than half a mile from the forest. They had died making their path to the town that had shunned them, perhaps looking for safety rather than plunder. Some bore musket wounds, others none. All had the twisted and contorted form and expression that would be apparent on their fallen colleagues nearer the camp. Mannau stopped counting after fifty, it was obvious the survivors were few, too few now to trouble Hamelin's defences.

Around the embers of the main camp fire, the bodies lay four or five deep, scattered with abandon as if shed from the sky. More musket wounds, sword wounds and pike mutilations. The battle must have approached delirium, it was no wonder he had heard it from the tower.

Mannau steadies his horse. 'We should return. It is not right to stay here, there may still be danger. We can send a burial party in due course.'

He looks for approval from the rest, they are too engrossed in the bizarre abomination to hear him. Eventually, Schmidt speaks.

'Where is the Piper? Should we not seek out his body? What of D'Ortez, does he lie here?'

Mannau scans the ground immediately in view, his eye has almost become numb to the sight of the dead. Below, however, a new shock, the naked carcass of an ebony-skinned being: feminine and womanly from waist up, hideously deformed underneath. He retches.

'We must go. This is work of the Devil's hand. We must go and pray.'

Another horseman draws alongside, a comforting arm rests on his shoulder. Mayor Ebber smiles.

'Not the Devil, an *angel*. God has sent an angel to save Hamelin.'

ARTHUR APPEARED ten days before the letter informing us of his imminent arrival. I came back one afternoon from the ruin and there he was, lying on my bed, anything I had left lying on or near it dumped in a heap in the corner. A rusty-looking camp bed had been brought in and jammed alongside the other, a couple of inches lower and narrower. Arthur obviously didn't fancy it and had staked his claim for my bed, the same bed Katryn and I had made love in earlier that day. What justification would he have given himself for such a selfish act? That he was older, wiser, more important even if we were the same rank? I don't know, I never asked. There was a line you never crossed with Arthur and this was on the other side of it.

'Bugger of a journey, old fruit. Don't think the driver knew where he was going, seemed a bit of a dimwit. Completely fucked now . . . Any chance of a brew . . . tea, I mean, around here?'

Not once did he look up from the notes he pored over as he spoke. I took this as my cue to be similarly ignorant and turned my back on him to tidy up the pile of my things on the floor, sighing as I did so.

'Bugger all.'

'See . . . yes, I see. Bit of a shithouse this, what? Food good, bad, terrible?'

He appeared suspiciously jaunty and eager to chat, different from before. It was my turn to be the sullen one, where could I find for moments with Katryn?

'There,' he said, nodding briefly to a bundle of letters, 'latest dispatches . . . from that girl. Seems a bit of a dimwit, what are you doing with her?'

The handwriting on the envelopes matched those stacked by the window, gathering dust and condensation – Joyce's. I sighed again, he really had brought Gershalt with him, and somehow I felt the lonelier for it.

'I'm not "with" any . . .'

I gave up. He was still locked into his damned papers. Was he listening, did he care, did I really care about what he thought? This was a different Arthur; that bit greyer, thinner and more drawn, what was this kind of life doing to him?

We settled in silence, me trying to pull the hopeless mess of files into some kind of order, him horizontal, humming in apparent agreement with whatever he was reading.

After we had been like this for a while Geigy arrived, having come to see how we were settling in, tucking his head round the door and smiling like a zealous headmaster, checking if the new boys were behaving themselves in the dorm. Arthur was astonishingly rude.

'Hello again, Dr Lee. Good to find you comfortable.'

'Piss off.'

'I beg your par – ?'

'Piss off and leave me alone.'

Geigy hovered by the door for a second, I could see him wondering whether he had stumbled across some peculiar English humour that had failed to translate. I shrugged as if to say No, I don't get it either, and he left, mumbling something about coming back once Arthur was less tired. A retreat then, forced by the unprovoked attack by my roommate. I wondered how I would endure his presence, one minute chatty and upbeat, the next irascible. Whilst I told myself I didn't care about Geigy's hurt pride I realised that in the atmosphere of a camp like this I would be judged by Arthur's actions as much as he would. I let my gaze fall on him; he was still reading.

'Sanctimonious cunt. Freezing my balls off here, Robert. Isn't there something you can do?'

He blew on his hand to warm it, then stuffed it into his armpit. He still had his coat on. It would take him months to get used to the temperature drop, if he ever would.

'I'm going out.'

'Wait a mo . . . what time's grub?'

'Later.'

I shut the door behind me, careful to let in as much wintry draught as I could. Later. He could wait, everything later; another visit from Geigy, food of sorts, a trip to the chambers to view the live corpses. I hoped he'd enjoy it all, but now it was my turn to be selfish. In amongst all the agitation of the arrival I'd lost the sight of Katryn's face in my memory, and I now had to see her to get it back.

How was I ever capable of such passion, to hold some-one so preciously that to be unable to conjure up the vision of their face in your mind would be the source of such panic? Katryn dominated my thoughts for so long in a way that seems inconceivable to me now – was it part of the condition? Never more than one thought from the front of my mind during my waking hours, I would go under dreaming of her so she was with me in sleep as well. During the day I would concentrate so hard on her, on what it was that aroused me, that I'd lose grip on her image. Of course, as the weeks went by I could hold it longer, but never more than that, so I would be forced to seek her out, desperately hoping to reassure myself that she was as beautiful as my heart screamed she was, telling myself that it would be enough just to confirm this, but when I did find her I would be unable to resist exploring her all over again, every time as if a new experience.

I recall these emotions more readily than that face, I'm afraid. In the years that have passed I have lost it for ever, left with a shadow instead of the form, and an ache to remind me of the place in my heart where the love used to lie. What does it say about me that the only things I can remember are the faults, not the whole which moved me so?

My theory, ladies and gentlemen, is that we all possess an erotic code – a sequence of levers, needs and desires unique to every one of us. Once or twice in a lifetime we will meet someone carrying the combination to match the formulation we were born with and when we do, we are powerless to do anything other than follow the demands of the sexual machinery that clicks into gear. That then is the theory, my *scientific* theory. A flawed theory which implies an equal need for both parties to succumb to the process when such an occurrence takes place. Sometimes however, it is not like that, ladies and gentlemen, and this is the fault in the system I would fall victim to.

The case conference was my idea, originally devised to stir Arthur into some kind of action and to get him out of my hair. For ten days or more since arriving he'd hardly shifted from bed, and had shown no interest in anything other than his historical studies, an obsession which had grown even stronger since I had last seen him. Already we had guards and refugees turning up at our hut, all offering relics of dubious origin which Arthur was happy enough to trade for cigarettes and dollars. Then it was back to his papers which he would furiously add to and annotate by day and then endlessly review by night. There had to be some way of forcing him out of the cabin so I could return, however briefly, to the privacy of old. This would be my best attempt.

But there was another problem, that of my commitment to exposing the tortuous cause of the 'condition', which had not so much begun to waver as to evaporate, vanishing into the gaps being caused by the pulls of the disparate personalities and demands surrounding me. My loyalty should have been to my patients, yet I had tired of carrying their weight; how lighter the world was if one allowed oneself to believe Geigy, to believe that we were a team searching together for the medical roots of the suffering. A coward's way out, yes; although not a route chosen consciously. The instinct of youth is to preserve one's energy when facing a force that may drain you and I began to let myself look the other way, losing myself in the distractions of Katryn's body, Arthur's eccentricities and the abstract notions of medicinal diagnostics. The conference would provide a fresh harvest of the latter.

The suggestion was that Geigy, and then Arthur and I, would each propose a theory for the root cause of the 'Condition Six' outbreak, give a brief supporting talk, and then swap over the suppositions for each other to test. I told Arthur I already had a hypothesis worked out although I was still finalising the presentation. My suspicion was that his vanity would never allow him to let me speak on his behalf on medical matters and that this conceit would force him to begin his own investigations to contradict mine. To my surprise and frustration he showed no inclination to do so, remaining embedded in our cramped little quarters right up to the morning of our consultation summit. I wasn't to know he'd already been briefed before leaving Gershalt on the nature of the condition.

We met early on a crisp January morning, the previous night's freeze still keeping everything outdoors – walls and surfaces – powder dry, and bringing an artificial brightness to the camp huts as they glistened under a dull sun. I led Arthur to the hut which Geigy had set up in anticipation. He had laid on a special breakfast, chicory coffee and dry meal biscuits there in the centre of a table made up for four. The room had been tidied since I was last in it, the table itself new, and a blackboard stood at the foot of it lest any of us should feel the urge to chalk out our theories. We arrived just after Geigy had left to chase a new update on the patients at the ruin, leaving the pair of us with one of his assistants, another thin and wary-looking type with the yellowish pallor of the Slavs. He spoke no English and so we sat in awkward silence, me smiling politely and pretending to study my notes, Arthur testing the stability of the table – one leg was shorter than the others and the imbalance this caused seemed to particularly unsettle him, rocking it back and forward.

At last Geigy arrived back, short of breath but gushing in apparent enthusiasm.

'Rob! Dr Lee. Good! Very Good. Let us begin.'

He turned to say something in Russian to his cheerless colleague who began to pour the coffee. A cup was filled and pushed over at me; black, almost like tar. The cup was stained and chipped, and my eye focused on the greasy film spinning in the centre of it. I sipped anyway, grateful for the heat and distraction.

'Most impressed . . . I am impressed by your suggestion of conference, gentlemen. I think this must be the way to achieve progress, by working as team . . . can only help process. Dr Mussorgy here will take notes, Russian notes. Perhaps you take your own or I translate later. Rob, Dr Lee, you wish to begin?'

It was my automatic response to refuse. I was, after all, the product of an entire education system where it paid to be middle of the road; too eager and the tutors had you tagged as arrogant, too far down the field and they had you marked as slow. I looked to Arthur – no response, he was still playing with the table.

'Well, perhaps I begin by summarising?'

Geigy waited for encouragement. I nodded.

'Yes, please do. You have visited the isolation cells this morning?'

'Indeed. Two deaths overnight, nothing new to report other than usual symptoms. Twenty-seven deaths now in last two months, five cases currently held in isolation suffering from early stages . . . rate of infection in camp slowing down again, two new cases a week . . . was five cases a week earlier in month. Typical rate of progression from condition one to condition six is now steady, at a faster rate than initial cases at the start of quarantine camp eight months ago.'

Geigy stopped to offer the briefest of smiles, an incongruous gesture born more out of what he might have thought was polite than any ghoulish enjoyment at the detail of his own report. I wondered if I had got him wrong, maybe he was just an ordinary man and a product of his system like we were of ours. Maybe he just wanted to be home.

'I have brought death papers of all fatal cases, including last night. I will translate if there is any content you wish to know. Rob, please . . . I am interested in your theory . . . please.'

In my short medical career to date, I had been asked to express a professional opinion many times, mainly during clinical training when ten of you would crowd round a hospital bed to listen to some shy old crone outline her symptoms before offering a full gamut of potential causes for the suffering in question. This system was designed to intimidate of course, to test only the mettle of the medical students. Now, in this freezing shack with three others, one of whom would not understand my language anyway,

I found myself struggling to hide a similar anxiety. It had to be something to do with Arthur, a fear that he was about to expose my lack of perception in front of class for all to see. Damn him, why hadn't he thought up his own hypothesis, and why couldn't I at least count on his support if he had to be so idle?

I took another small mouthful and swilled it around my mouth.

'I would hesitate to be so bold as to describe what I have as a "theory", Dr Geigy, more something worthy of consideration.'

Geigy smiled, bowing in deference as if to acknowledge the point, eyebrows raised, he wanted me to go on. Arthur grunted and shifted in his seat, his arms were folded tightly, probably against the cold though I couldn't help thinking it was to help repel whatever words I was about to utter.

'There is a disease, a severely infectious disease which may be connected in some way to what we have seen here. A bacteriological infection characterised by ulcers at the site of infection, fever, and loss of weight. I am referring to tularaemia. If I am correct, we could treat cases with a variety of penicillin agents, and immunise camp residents against infection.'

I halted there, unwilling to proceed any further until the others passed first comment. It was a lightweight hypothesis, conjured up in desperation and it was unlikely its weaknesses would go unnoticed.

'Rob, I am afraid I am unaware of this affliction. Can you explain more?'

Geigy wanted to remain constructive, but it was telling that he hadn't yet translated any of this for his colleague on his right. I felt my face begin to flush as I tried to endow my words with some kind of conviction.

'Tularaemia, first observed in America forty years ago, named after Tulare County in California where it originated. Not always fatal, we would have to consider why it would be so here. Perhaps the camp inhabitants have compromised their immune systems in some way.'

'Animals,' Arthur interrupted without warning. I turned to him and he stared back aggressively.

'Sorry?'

'Animals, isn't it? Disease of animals, sometimes transmissible to man?'

'Yes.'

'So where are the animals here harbouring the source bacterium?'

He had me and knew it, but the situation dictated that I defend my theory.

'Well, obviously there is no . . . livestock . . . within the camp but the patients have access to the wild game that makes its way into –'

'Nonsense.'

'– the compound and those beasts that are trapped –'

'There's no beast that can make it inside.'

'And what do you think you've been eating since you arrived?'

'Not the same bloody codswallop as you obviously.'

'Gentlemen, please!'

It was an embarrassment that it took a Russian to curtail our juvenile squabble, even if I was the only one to feel it. Geigy waited for the silence to hold and then continued in a softer tone.

'Gentlemen, first a key, and then the solution. I am willing to consider Dr Rob's suggestion as a key. Please, we must work together or we do not progress at all.' He leaned forward to peer into the coffee pot, sniffing the dregs inside. Another exchange in Russian with his companion and the other left, presumably to order a fresh fill. Once he was gone, Geigy addressed us again.

'Rob, how can we proceed with your hypothesis, what can you ask us to test?'

Arthur snorted as I began to speak, stretching across to lift Geigy's file of death certificates. I tried to ignore his churlishness.

'I will try to obtain some more information, background, recent case studies and things from camp at Berlin. I'll also request the antibiotics you might want to run under trial. I'm sorry my idea was not more . . . developed.'

Geigy magnanimously waved down my apology. 'Wait until you hear our proposal,' he said.

It was false modesty. When Dr Mussorgy returned with another pot of uniquely disgusting brew, Arthur and I were treated to a full presentation of a more cogent examination of the facts. Geigy's contention was that we were dealing with a new form of faciitis, an opportunistic gangrenous infection that seemed to be inherent in the ulcers our patients first yielded to in the early stages of the condition. He was particularly concerned with understanding the peculiar form and evolution of the tumefaction seen amongst the cases, something my own effort had neglected to address. It took him over an hour to explain his lines of enquiry to us, pausing frequently to include contributions from his colleague which had to be translated into faltering English. Geigy had written a summary paper for us to take from the meeting; it was just as well, I had struggled to follow some sections, concentrating too hard on Arthur's incessant fidgeting, worried that he was about to erupt again. It had been Geigy's paperwork rather than his talk which had enjoyed his attention.

'So. You will take our findings and scrutinise them as we will examine yours?'

'Yes, we will.'

'And we shall meet again, when? Two days, three?'

I had no idea how long it might take to carry out the task outlined. Arthur offered no sign either, and I decided to try to prompt him.

'What do you think?'

'Hummn?' Arthur snorted again. He seemed determined to avoid both my eyes and Geigy's, screwing up his face with all the grace of a truculent adolescent, pointing to a section on the certificates he had pulled earlier from Geigy.

'That there . . . is that age?'

Geigy peered across to him, and asked Mussorgy to confirm.

'Yes, it is estimate of age at death.'

'No children?' Arthur's question emerged as he flicked through the reports once more.

'No, Dr Lee. No fatalities amongst children. But . . . no children in the camp.'

'What? No children at all? Isn't that extraordinary? What kind of refugees have no children? What have they done with them?'

It was a valid, though inconsequential point to make, typical of Arthur. I had only realised myself after two months in camp that the youngest inmates were of Katryn's age, and then assumed that any children were housed elsewhere.

'I do not know, Dr Lee. You think it may have significance in the propositions that have been made?'

Arthur didn't reply, instead waving his hand dismissively.

'You wish to investigate any link between age and infection?'

Geigy's attempts to consolidate some form of common ground between us were becoming more laboured, it was obvious his patience was beginning to wane.

'Oh, I don't know . . .' Arthur wrapped his arms in front of himself as if to control them, twitching with what seemed to be frustration. Was Geigy unwittingly straying over the line?

'Look, you two do what you like, I've been given my own little task to work on here.'

Lazy bastard. I was determined not to let him shirk his way out of this after the way he had humiliated me earlier.

'Really. And just what would that be?'

He pulled a new face, a kind of disdainful scowl. 'Thing is . . . I'm not supposed to say . . .'

I wasn't going to hide my anger, I'd had enough of his sneering.

'Oh, go on, Arthur. Obviously it will be more worthwhile than whatever I might try to address, surely you might enlighten me?'

'Well, I might . . . for what it's worth. If you insist.'

'I do.'

A deep breath. 'A.M.U. 4 – they want to know if this is related to cancer, rather a particular cancer, radiation sickness.'

It was a word I was barely familiar with.

'Radiation?'

'Think his lot,' he pointed to Geigy, 'have been up to something naughty, atomic bombs and the like, that they've tested one in Europe. Mind you, his lot will be thinking the same about us, which is why they let the two of us come here to watch what we get up to.'

He paused, satisfied that his words had pierced the air of normality the rest of us had tried so hard to maintain. Geigy and I sat quiet, Mussorgy opposite suddenly feeling left out, leaning towards his compatriot and whispering. What was this man saying now?

Arthur's expression completed its slow transition into a rueful smile. He shook his head.

'Yes, absurd, isn't it? Was it you? Was it us? Perhaps it was the Germans. Think they might have split the atom, Dr Geigy? After all, they destroyed just about everything else.'

I didn't know how one might set about testing for radiation sickness. This was January 1946, barely six months after Hiroshima. That is not to say that we were unaware that Arthur had introduced something dreadful into the equation, something that both Geigy and I, although for different reasons, were frightened to hear more of. Our ears were closed then, the meeting swiftly concluded. Geigy undertook to explore the mysteries of tularaemia, I to familiarise myself with his work on the necrotising faciitis his paper described – both entirely pointless exercises. Everything had changed.

Arthur's crime? He'd brought the outside world crashing in around us, shown us how that world would laugh at our efforts, how it was squaring up for its next fight with or without the truth we had been directed to find. You could choose to disregard whatever Arthur said as the product of a bitter mind, but the danger always remained that his words were half true. The challenge was discerning which half.

I closed the door shut.

'I can't believe you did that, Arthur . . . just cannot damn well believe it.'

He seemed to know he'd overstepped the mark, even if my outburst drew no immediate response. For once he hadn't flopped out on the bed when we made it inside, and was standing instead by the window, hands thrust deep in his pockets. His mood was now noticeably glum.

'You ever write back to that girl?'

His gaze had fixed itself on Joyce's letters. I didn't feel inclined to share the intricacies of the relationship with him.

'What did you hope to achieve by that? Don't you realise the danger you've put yourself in, *me* in?'

'Seems a bit of a shame really . . . she thought you were dead, always on at Vesey.'

'Arthur . . . why? Does Vesey really think that this is all the aftermath of some atom bomb?'

He was looking out beyond the letters on the ledge now, as if the horizon stretched away further than the latrines immediately in view.

'Vesey? What does it matter what he thinks, he's OSS, you know. He's got his orders.'

OSS? I took it to be another of Arthur's public school acronyms, an arrangement of letters implying something infantile like 'old silly sausage'. Once more I had chosen the wrong half; Arthur was serious, he meant the Office of Strategic Services, then in its final months before being reborn as the CIA. Should I have known this? I would wish that I had, the rest might have been avoidable.

Arthur took two steps backwards towards the bed and sat down on it, feeling his way like a blind man. He still had a faraway look to him, one I took to be part of the act meant to discourage my attack.

'And what were his orders to you? To tell the first English-speaking Russian you could find about the whole damn mission? What if we are denied access to the patients now because of this? What would we do then?'

He pursed his lips for a second, a slight hum preceding his words.

'Go home, I suppose.'

'Look, Arthur, is this . . . to do with atom bombs, is that what the condition is?'

'Could be, you never know . . . think there would be other signs though if they had been that naughty. I'll keep you posted if I spot them.'

I moved over and punched at the foot of the bed. 'Arthur, for God's sake be serious. What if the Russians interrogate us, try to get whatever they can out of us . . . about secret weapons?'

'Can't think why they'd do that, old fruit, I don't know anything about atom bombs, do you?'

'No.'

'Then they would be wasting their time, wouldn't they?'

'But they don't know that, Arthur.'

'They don't know that we don't know? Or maybe they don't know that we know they don't know that we know . . . nothing.'

His tone was deadpan and I realised I was chasing him in circles. Was he enjoying this, was this a deliberate effort to infuriate me following the case conference debacle? I gripped the metal base of the bed and shook it, Arthur's head jerking left and right as I did so. He didn't protest, remaining lifeless and slumped. I took a deep breath and stepped back to my own bed. My head was in my hands.

'Look, old fruit, I really wouldn't worry about it. They'll appreciate that we are fairly low-calibre staff unlikely to know anything useful. Even if they don't, their bosses will understand that A.M.U. 4 wouldn't have sent us unless we were a pair of nitwits.'

'Why will they think we're that?'

'Because they'll know A.M.U. 4 wouldn't have released anyone really important, in case . . .'

'In case what?'

'They decide not to give us back.'

'Keep us here forever?'

'Or kill us.'

I quickly drew myself up on my feet, snatching for my overcoat. Time to get out, and to clear this nonsense out of my mind. I had to convince myself that I wasn't scared, that this time neither half of what he was saying was true. Once more I'd lost the vision of Katryn's face.

* * *

I can't remember when she first said it, it might even have been before Arthur arrived. She seemed to whisper it into my ear just after I climaxed and lay on top of her in sweet exhaustion, 'Amore', it sounded like, and I'd thought she must have picked up some knowledge of Italian from somewhere. I would have smiled and rolled onto one side to savour the delicious and relaxed intimacy of the moment, now that the need had temporarily been satisfied. Gone the demand to rush; my fingers running through her hair, leaning forward to plant a delicate kiss on her forehead, thank you, gently laughing with relief.

Once Arthur arrived, of course, our lovemaking became by necessity a more hurried, almost brutal, affair. We would have to steal the time and seize whatever opportunities were open to us. I look back and think of frenzied couplings in Geigy's admin hut with a chair jammed up against the door, of trying to perform quietly behind the drawn curtain in Katryn's own quarters, and then of the charmless merits of the al fresco version, coat on, trousers down and skirts up. Amore.

But then Arthur grew more friendly with Geigy, sometimes taking my place at the chess table, and so we began to fall back into the old ways, risky though it was. And I would hear her whisper this word again, she is smiling, nodding, silently asking me to do the same. I fight my embarrassment. 'Amore,' I mutter. She shakes her head.

Sometimes she would be a passive lover, sometimes passionate, biting and scratching, writhing underneath. In the beginning I took my lead from her, responding with tenderness or gusto to whatever tone she set. As my confidence grew however, it would be me who would establish the pattern and agenda for our play, and I wonder if she was happier with this, that I, the 'man', was the dominant sexual force. Or was it all part of the plan?

Arthur leaves after supper, papers safely stacked away. He doesn't tell me where he's going or when he'll be back or even invite me along. No matter, the routine has been established, I know what to do. I reach for my coat and towel, the latter slung over my shoulder, this will be the flag that Katryn is hopefully looking out for. I take my time on the walk to the wash-house to give her time to see it. Once there I might even wash or pretend to urinate before turning back. An anxious wait follows, listening for a knock on the door. Eventually I hear the tapping and she's there, I beckon her in. A risk, all of it a stupid risk, Arthur could be back at any moment. I look into her eyes and I don't care any more, the code matches mine and the machinery has taken over.

Soon, always too soon, we are back at that moment. I am tired, I want to fall asleep with her in my arms, to take her with me to the other side, but she is restless and still playful. She puts her mouth to my nipple, giggling as I turn to take it away from her. Then her head disappears under the blankets to do the same to my drained manhood and this has turned into a new game as I draw my knees up and she tries to wrestle them down. I bend to grip hold of her to find she has the same idea, an arm lock on my neck and she pushes her mouth into my ear, laughing and saying it over and over, and only then do I realise she's saying something different, not 'Amore' but 'Amerika'. Amerika!

I can feel a shock bring me to my senses as if Arthur

and Geigy and the whole of A.M.U. 4 had just walked in the door. America, take me to America. She sees me as her ticket out of here and the whole miserable East. She thinks I will take her to America.

Geigy told me the equipment had arrived, two crates of it. It was waiting outside the administration hut, there wasn't enough room for all of it inside. Would Arthur and I help unload it and show which items were required first? I said of course, and that I would tell him immediately. I hoped I sounded convincing, I didn't know we had ordered any.

We were in the largest of the underground vaults at the ruin, the room that had become a makeshift morgue. Under the new system, Geigy and Mussorgy, I and – theoretically – Arthur would attend the post-mortem and final examinations of the condition's victims before the bodies were taken for incineration. Late January now, the corpses had lost their ability to frighten and shock, only the smell retained its initial vigour. The stench got to me every time. That aside, these ghastly inspections had become almost as much of a mundane fixture as the rest of camp life, like queuing up for morning breakfast. I would stand back and spectate as the others took samples from the various ulcer sites and gangrenous points, sometimes pretending to take my own notes, for this was by now an empty routine, the main purpose of which was merely to show willing and a continued interest in the investigation. Arthur's sour conclusion was unavoidable, why had A.M.U. 4 sent a pair of half-wits like us if they were truly interested in this affliction, and in locating its source?

Geigy periodically stops to point to another area of the

body, take some from here? I nod, careful to keep the handkerchief tight against my mouth.

'The brain. Perhaps we should take more brain samples . . . spinal cortex as well.'

Geigy does not directly acknowledge my remark but I can hear him say something to Mussorgy, who reaches for the saw. I look away as the sound of it cutting through the first layers of skull echoes around the chamber. I can feel a sudden clamminess, and shivers darting down and across my body.

'I think I had better tell Dr Lee that his materials have arrived. You will excuse me?'

It is Mussorgy who replies. '*Da*,' he says, snagging on a stubborn piece of bone. I nod sheepishly and escape.

I stopped as soon as I was out of the building, not only to take a deep breath and clear my head of the foul odours of downstairs, but also to try to re-establish just what was going on here and what my role in it was meant to be. So Arthur's 'equipment' had arrived. Did this mean he was at last going to start some kind of analysis into the condition, and if he did, would I now be able to stop acting and just let him get on with it? But would his enquiries be sincere or just an attempt like mine to make the right kind of noises? How much longer could this go on for before we were found out?

I scanned around for somewhere to sit, it was dry, bitterly cold, and I wanted to feel the wind blow around me. Two young soldiers stood by the door at the top of the front stair smoking. I watched one of them inhale and felt a strange craving for a cigarette, envying the shock of the smoke on his lungs. Perhaps he would give me one. I turned back and made my way up the steps. Halfway up the pair stopped talking and looked down to me. 'Cigarette ... please?' I mimed the smoker's action with my hand, wondering if he would understand the request. The face staring back at me belonged to someone around my age, an ignorant-looking type. I realised it was a bad idea as a pout took form on his thin lips. He gestured rudely and turned his back on me, cigarettes were obviously in short supply, thank you, comrade.

Too tired to build up any kind of anger, I drifted back down the path to the camp. I must have been preoccupied because for the first time I passed Katryn's area of the settlement without pausing for a glimpse or contemplating her, meandering instead towards the administration hut, hoping to find it empty so that I could close its door on the world. No such luck. I had forgotten Geigy's words, the equipment had arrived and there was Arthur fretting over it.

'Robert! Robert, where the hell have you been? Here, give me a hand.'

The scene around him was one of utter disarray, packages and packaging strewn all over the ground; test tubes, clamps, culture dishes and chemical phials. I couldn't begin to imagine how it might be used. Was this how radiation sickness was tested? Steam was rising from Arthur's shoulders, he was out without a coat or jacket, madness in these temperatures which rarely rose above freezing by day. Somehow though, he'd managed to work up a sweat, and was growing frustrated as he hunted through the cartons for whatever object it was that he hankered. I couldn't help noticing how skinny he had become, bones almost poking out of the singlet he wore, ginger hair thinner and straggly. He would have to get inside fast or he would be risking hypothermia, someone had to tell him, and I knew that had to be me.

'Aha! Got the bugger!' He held his trophy aloft, tearing the protective paper from it.

'Look at that. Brand spanking new. Only the best for the damn Yanks, eh? Still, all the better for us, what?'

The article in his hand certainly looked new, a piece of shiny brass that resembled a candlestick holder. Arthur rummaged again and pulled out a length of rubber tubing and then I realised that what he had was a Bunsen-burner, a scientific instrument more beloved of schoolboys than pathologists, surely?

'Arthur, how did you get all this stuff?'

'Hummn? Sent a telex to Vesey after I arrived. Surprised you hadn't done it already.'

'But . . . what's it for?'

He stopped for a moment and smiled, for once a natural smile with no malice hiding behind it. 'Patience, Robert, patience. Now, grab hold of that and follow me.'

He pointed to a large gas canister to his left; there were others scattered around, all far too big for one person to carry.

'Where are we taking it?'

'To our hut, dimwit, where do you think?'

'But I'll never –'

'Then just roll it along the ground, come on.'

I followed behind him, steering the thing on its rim. It took me a while to make the distance, and Arthur had excitedly passed me to make two trips back to pick up further bits of the delivery now destined for our quarters.

Once at the door, he helped me lug it up the steps and inside.

'Arthur, what's going on, we don't have the room in here to –'

'Matches. You got any? Need some . . . Think you could find any?'

Perhaps matches might be easier to get than cigarettes. I sighed and ventured out to find some. In the five minutes it took to locate them Arthur had been busy, weaving the rubber tubing into an arrangement of connections so that three burners could feed from one supply to the canister. I threw him the box and he turned the tap on its top. One, two, three, the flames spurted from the burners and he adjusted their individual flows.

'Bingo!' He beamed, as elated as I had ever seen him. Jubilant that not only had he found a source of heat to sustain us through the rest of the winter but that he had hoodwinked Vesey into supplying it. Only the best for the Yanks.

'Arthur, you didn't order all the stuff just for this, did you? What about the rest of it?'

He warmed his hands against the flame. 'Just added it to make the order look a bit more . . . legitimate . . . you know. No harm done, Robert, especially if it keeps the frostbite from our bollocks.'

The effect of the heat in the small room was immediate. I tugged off my coat.

'Look, Arthur, we are meant to be helping combat this disease. Dr Geigy knows all this stuff has arrived and thinks it's to do with your investigation. What's he going to say now?'

Arthur flattened his palms against the flames, closing his eyes and inhaling as if he could smell the warmth.

'Hummn? Good question . . . but frankly, old fruit, I couldn't give a shit.'

His words produced the spark of irritation that would normally be enough to send me fizzing from the hut, slamming the door in my wake. This time though, the impetus to leave just wasn't there, perhaps the burners generated some kind of magnetism as well as heat. I looked to my coat and left it hanging, making instead for my bed and lying face down on it. I thought of the mess outside, of Geigy and Mussorgy still cutting up the bodies, and of Katryn somewhere out there telling her friends the doctor was taking her to America. Much as I wanted to get away from Arthur, there was nowhere left to run.

There was a knock on the door the moment Arthur left – I thought it might be Katryn. I scrambled to pull my trousers back on, struggling to find space for my feet amongst the apparatus now messing up the floor. It would have been early evening, I hadn't expected to sleep so long but the close warm air must have knocked me out like an anaesthetic, leaving me with the same sensations of grogginess and faint nausea when I came round.

I opened the door with one hand, desperately flattening my hair with the other. For some ludicrous reason it was important that I presented Katryn with a vision of steadfast masculinity, rather than that of a tired and sleepy homesick Scot. I smiled manfully into the doorway. A bemused-looking Geigy stared back.

'Rob, I wonder . . . can we have a talk?'

'Dr Geigy. Of course. Please come in.'

He edged into the room, sprinkling tiny flakes of snow and ice from his coat as he did so. The gas canister was right by the entrance and I watched him move carefully around it, taking in the construction Arthur had established during the afternoon. His silence cried out for some words of explanation from me but I didn't have them, there was no point. The burners, the tubing, the ramshackle network of clamps and pots to heat and distil the water that Arthur had set up was damning evidence enough. We were guilty as charged and nothing I could say would mitigate the fraud.

I cleared Arthur's pyjamas from his bed and unfolded a blanket to cover it. Geigy perched himself on it but showed no inclination to make himself more comfortable. I hurriedly did the same to my own bed and turned to face him.

'Arthur wanted to experiment a bit . . . couldn't stop him.'

I shrugged as the words dried up. Geigy did not reply or even acknowledge that I had spoken, gazing instead at the mess of equipment. He seemed more resigned than angry. I knew how he felt.

'I wish to speak about Dr Lee, Rob. Is this possible?'

He looked me in the eye, serious and troubled.

'Yes.'

'I think he should go home, Rob . . . I think he should, *go home*.'

Geigy stared into my eyes with such grave intent that I couldn't stop myself from nodding, even if I was unsure as to what it was I was agreeing with. I let him continue.

'Is possible . . . that I do not understand, that my English is so poor that I . . . You must tell me, Rob, if I misunderstand?'

My nodding had become more vigorous; this seemed an easy part of the deal to keep.

'When I first meet Dr Lee, he tells me his wife and son are killed, dead in the war, from bombers. We all lost people in the war, Rob, myself . . . two brothers, my uncle, my parents, when the Germans took Kiev . . .' He was shaking his head, obviously struggling with the pain of the memory, again I wondered if I had got him terribly wrong. It was as if he were reaching out to me, but that I wasn't worthy of his trust. I felt ashamed that my sufferings of the war were not more substantial.

Geigy wiped a tear from his eye. 'We play chess, Dr Lee and I. He is a talented player, intelligent man. But he says the exercises – you know my love of chess exercises – he says he will send them to his son. He says his wife is *here* and that he sees her very soon. Am I wrong, Rob, is this English expression?'

'No, I have not heard of such an expression. I have not heard him talk of his wife and son either. When I first arrived in Berlin I –'

I halted. I was just about to mention how Arthur would cry himself to sleep in the evenings, a habit that he hadn't carried with him to Tarutz. Did this mean anything, or should I respect his privacy? Geigy was looking to me, dark eyes still slightly glazed with emotion. Was this some kind of performance, a trap? Geigy had never mentioned the radioactivity theory since the day Arthur had first raised it, could this be an opening gambit for more information, to position me and Geigy together as Arthur's helpers?

'I'm sorry, no, he has never mentioned his family to me.'

'I think that he should go home. I think Tarutz ... *disturbs* ... him, Rob.'

And then I thought it had to be a ploy, for Arthur had been barking mad long before he ever arrived in Tarutz, and probably before he arrived in Berlin.

'Alright.'

'Then you will try to help him, to have him sent home?'

'I will.'

'Good, Rob. Thank you. There is no more to be said.'

Geigy stood and moved to the door, pausing to shake hands as he left. I had no intention of doing what he asked, but once more would have to play the role the situation demanded.

He had been gone barely five minutes before I heard another sound at the door. This time it was Katryn.

Deputy Mannau

THERE IS A TEMPTATION when examining the past to consider disconcerting events in isolation, to categorise them swiftly as freak occurrences thrown onto history's infinite canvas by the laws of probability, and to judge their participants as completely different to ourselves. This is perhaps a result of our hindsight having too narrow a focus, or the effect of an unstated desire to distance previous barbarous acts from the moderate present.

In either case the results are the same, and incidents such as the rape of Hamelin are universally judged as 'extraordinary' (and unrepeatable) events in an 'ordinary' past rather than ordinary ones within extraordinary times.

The distinction is crucial; the participants in this tragedy were not aliens whose lives, needs and values we cannot hope to comprehend, but conventional men no different from the readers of this paper.

The soldiers now departed, Hamelin began its final descent into the abyss.

It would have taken five days to bury the bodies, a grisly exercise made none the easier by the reluctance of the frost-bound earth to open up and accept the numbers of corpses offered, nor by the limited number of men willing to leave the apparent safety of the town to cross the plain and bury them. Mannau's wary eye is cast over every body before it is covered for the last time. Although there are those who claim to have seen both D'Ortez and the Piper, the Deputy knows this to be hearsay; true, he has stood over the charred and cleaved body of the Spaniard and wondered how such a diminutive man had exuded so powerful an air of malevolence. How many had it taken to cut him down? The wounds were on both sides of his body, heavy blades hacking through the leather on his arms, whilst the musket ball had hit him to the front, piercing the thin armour plate on his chest. Mannau still felt as if the remains had the power to leap up and strike him; he had had to force himself not to cower despite the absurdity of it all, standing anxiously over the grave, the warrior laid to rest, reaping what he has sown.

Of the Piper there was no sign save for his mottled cape, torn and bloodied like the rest. Despite the excited claims of those chiselling at the hard granite soil, Mannau knew that he was somehow still at large, that the ingenuity he had brought to the town in a time of weakness and desperation would return to haunt them. Five days it took to work through the dead, but he sensed after the first that the one whose demise would have comforted him most would not be found.

On the third afternoon the process was halted as the party made its way back to the town for another burial, this time that of Wolfricht, the Chancellor, victim to another poisonous bite from the rats overrunning Hamelin. Mayor Ebber had conducted the service, in the church where he now spent so much of his time. The whole population had turned out for this, the first such gathering since the siege. The atmosphere was bizarre. Mannau sat silently, trying to think kindly of a man he knew had conspired with the Mayor to thwart his ambitions for nearly a decade. Now the Chancellor was dead and the Mayor wanted to be a priest there was nothing to stop him. Indeed, Hamelin cried out for the strong government he had yearned to deliver, yet this tawdry inheritance seemed so hollow. Crowds singing on the pews, bewildered, confused; they still carried their disbelief at the events which had seen D'Ortez' army fall upon its sword. It was this that stopped any outpouring of joy at the town's reprieve, or any show of sorrow at the death of one of its revered councillors. Ebber smiled benignly at the gathering. Would he lecture them on the 'angels' who had saved them as he had the council, on how Father Seicle had told him of all that had come to pass? Mannau could only hope not; someone had to govern, and even if the Mayor no longer had the taste for it, his words could rob the whole council of any credibility.

'God has chosen Hamelin. He has sent his servants to disempower those who would seek to harm us. He has taken our dear Chancellor to join our beloved Priest to help him in this task. We must pray forgiveness for ever doubting. We must pray with gratitude for this blessing.'

Ebber's eyes were closed but the serenity was still there. Three rats scurried by the foot of the altar upon which he stood, but nobody seemed to notice. 'This blessing –'

Mannau gave up his attempt at prayer, looking to the heads bowed around him. Stooping, listless, lice-ridden. 'This blessing –' How could anyone take these words seriously? Was he the only sane man left in Hamelin?

On the sixth day Mannau led a party out to inspect the fields; himself, old Kunze, Schmidt and three others persuaded to venture out and take the initial steps in planning for a new dawn. Late February, the frost still held its grip on the land but the thaw would arrive soon. Now was the time to prioritise, to think about how to begin again, to decide where to make the start. The trip was entirely his initiative, though once more it was an exercise with an air of the surreal about it, so few now left with any faith in the future, not one farmer amongst them. It was hard to believe the plains retained any capacity to nurture life, the ground underfoot grey and impenetrable, like marble, as miserable and wretched as the town it surrounded. In places the rye straws still stood tall, over seven feet, wild and free. In others the winds had flattened them, snapping the brittle stems. Unharvested grains lay everywhere, long past any use, rotting on the ground or in the ears that stayed aloft, covered in mildew and fungus, giving off a strange sweet smell. This was what the town had been living off for months now, the last reserves of stocks in the store would not last much longer. If only they could plant some alternative, Mannau wished, wheat or corn – he had never been able to take the black bread the rye produced. Yet the soil was too infertile to support any other crop, and it would be to this tenacious growth that they would be forced to return. As he tried to envisage a new season's yield Mannau would have realised the question of unpaid taxes was still unresolved, as was the war itself. Would a triumphant Catholic army appear once they had rebuilt Hamelin, demanding reparations, or would a defeated army appear sooner and take all they had? These issues were now as abstract and pointless as Mayor Ebber's prayers to the angels, and Mannau knew nobody would entertain them. Let all the armies come, they would say, we will do for them what we did for the Spaniard's.

It was when they were out that day that the Piper reappeared. A small crowd had gathered at his feet as he sat on the steps of the church, and Mannau's returning band had had to force their way through to see him. Kunze made it first, pushing forward to clasp the stranger's cold hand. 'Thank you, sir, for what you have done for Hamelin.' Mannau noticed the lack of grace and enthusiasm in the visitor's response, a wearisome grimace, a pulling back of his arm, the sour demeanour hardly that of a man who had conjured an angel. The Piper had not been playing, yet the crowd had assembled. Nor was he wearing the flamboyant costume that had captivated the moribund town when he had arrived before. Instead he wore two shirts under a filthy tunic, sackcloth leggings, a shawl draped around him to ward off the cold and the rats. Only the satchel remained. There was still a curious and compelling quality to his presence though, and it was this that had drawn the throng, despite his efforts to suppress it. Dark skin, sallow eyes, and a manner that always suggested he was capable of the extraordinary.

'Gentlemen, we must talk. There are things we should discuss. Our agreement . . .'

'You! Good sir, on behalf of Hamelin may I say –'

Schmidt was not to be allowed to progress with his tribute, the subject of his praise snapping with impatience.

'We will talk ... *here*. . . if need be, gentlemen ... is that what you want. We have an *agreement* . . .'

'One between the council and yourself, it is the council who shall discuss your situation when it next meets.'

The Piper turns a waspish stare to Mannau, it is as if he can read his mind, his fears, his efforts to stall.

'When?'

'Next week.'

The gaze lingers as the Piper shakes his head.

'Not soon enough, gentlemen, not nearly soon enough.'

He yawns and pulls himself up onto his feet, reaching into the satchel for the flute. A fresh musical agenda is issued, the demands of the whistled notes stirring the crowd into slothful motion. Mannau can see the instant effect the intonations have, the strange connection it seems to forge so effortlessly. After the melody has repeated itself twice, the Piper halts. There are groans of disappointment in the fading evening light. He shrugs and holds his hands aloft in a mime of apology.

'Let me tell you, friends, about the kind of men who command Hamelin, about the deal they made and then –'

'Tomorrow!'

Mannau shouts with such urgency he startles even himself, and the crowd fail to recognise the voice as his, searching amongst themselves for the culprit. For one man the single word is enough however, and he allows himself a smile as he packs away his flute.

'Tomorrow? Tomorrow then, gentlemen. Let us hope no one is late.'

What might the Mayor have done? He would have gathered the council in the chamber prior to the visitor's arrival, set out the position, and agreed the line for them to take. There was strength in unity, a strength they would need. Why could they not see this, why were they all suddenly so blind?

Mannau had asked for them all to arrive early, only to watch them drift to the chamber as if attending out of a passing interest. Ebber himself was one of the worst, reluctant to be distracted from his penance in the church, and providing only a distraction when he finally arrived. Mannau found it hard not to waste energy and anger on him, knowing that the resentment he felt should be self-directed; it was he who had over-estimated the pious Mayor for so long, as he had the Spaniard, fearing what he might do. In any case the manoeuvre would have been as futile as any of the others he had recently tried to organise; the Piper announcing his arrival with a morning call on his flute as the men had entered the chamber, a sound that echoed in Mannau's head as he greeted those first to arrive. A message in musical code to mock his efforts? It almost seemed that way, or was he turning as mad as the rest of them, for all his endeavours to resist?

The Piper had taken a seat at the table as if he were a sworn-in member of the chamber, smiling now, relaxed and cordial; an act, one Mannau could see through, betrayed by restless hands and tightly-drawn cheeks. Still, the others had made him welcome enough, and Mannau realised there would be no support for a motion to have him removed until they had debated amongst themselves. No, better to wait and see who calls the meeting to order, better to let these fools find their own way. To his left they still waited for their turn to thank the Piper, testing the stamina in his false bonhomie. Did he think they were stalling too, or was he now beginning to grasp the reality of the situation Hamelin had fallen into?

'Gentlemen. Gentlemen, please!'

It was the first time Mannau had seen the Piper struggle to bring any audience to heel, though what was making it difficult was the depth of adoration they afforded him.

'*Please*! I must *insist*!'

The voice grew more aggressive, yet still they fawned over him. A shrill, piercing whistle punctured the air. Silence followed, the flute had cowed them once more.

'Thank you. I do not mean to be rude but there is business we must attend to.' He paused and turned his attention to Mannau, nodding as if granting assent for the discussion to commence. Obviously, he wanted Mannau to make some opening remark. Mannau held still. Why had he been chosen, was his unease so apparent?

Moments passed by in silent veneration until the Piper could wait no longer.

'Gentlemen, I have come to thank you for the hospitality that has been my comfort in the fine town of Hamelin and to resolve the outstanding business agreed between us.'

Again a look to Mannau, a gauntlet for him to lift, one he ignores. Around him, the faces of his colleagues are gazing at the Piper in child-like wonder.

'Four hundred Thalers, gentlemen – the price we agreed

to rid the town of the Spaniard's army. You have seen that I have carried out my half of the bargain, now I would ask that you do yours.'

It is an expression of some puzzlement that Mannau sees appearing on the Mayor's face, does he think it unbecoming for an angel to return and demand payment in gold for a miracle?

'You seek reward? God will reward you. He too has seen what you have done for us. He will grant you riches.'

'Four hundred Thalers, gentlemen.'

'. . . greater than you can imagine . . . a blessing . . .'

'As agreed in this very room.'

'. . . in heaven, for eternity . . .'

'*Four hundred Thalers!*'

The ire in the Piper's voice stirs the room as if its occupants had just woken from a deep slumber only to find the vision they took for reverie staying with them into consciousness. Mannau is content to let the others speak for themselves, perhaps their torpor can be used against the Piper.

Schmidt carries an expression of pique. 'But the soldiers are gone now.'

The Piper looks at him with poorly concealed suspicion, is this a demonstration of naivety or treachery?

'I beg your pardon?'

Schmidt smiles indulgently, more sure of his ground.

'Why would we pay now that our enemies are vanquished?'

'Because that is a service I performed for the agreed sum.'

'God performed.'

An impetuous wave of the Piper's arm swats down the Mayor's aside as he continues:

'Agreed in this very room, gentlemen, it is only right that I should take possession of the monies mentioned. All I ask is for that which was agreed. I shall be glad to take my leave of you when it is given.'

The Piper waits for a response as glances are exchanged around the table, encouraged by the nods of endorsement which seem to be returned to the Mayor. Ebber turns to Mannau last, does he have any objections? Mannau is lost for an answer to the silent question. The Mayor begins regardless.

'My friend, we have no quarrel with you, please do not feel obliged to leave Hamelin.'

The Piper's face flushes with rage, are they being deliberately obtuse?

'*The money*! *What about my money?*'

The Mayor is bemused by the guest's sudden anger, shaking his head as he speaks, 'But everybody knows . . . we have no money.'

The heads at the table nod again in unison, as if agreeing the foolishness of the Piper in ever believing them.

'Then you have deceived me, gentlemen.'

Schmidt is eager to soothe any disagreement. 'Deceived? No! Our Chancellor is dead, our treasury is bare. We do not hide this . . . we have offered to share what we have left. You can stay and play your music. We would be glad.'

Schmidt continues with his unlikely mixture of outrage and offering despite the contempt with which the Piper returns his eye. Mannau contemplates the situation as the others join in.

'Stay with us.'

'Play us music for our souls.'

'Teach us to dance.'

'And our children to laugh.'

Is the Piper as impotent as he now seems, or merely dazed by the ferocity of the love being targeted at him? Mannau thinks back to the night before he listened to the soldiers' act of self-annihilation. The Piper had returned to the town that day after leaving to carry out the deed. What could he have taken, was his weapon still here within the walls, or was it always with him, the flute which blew curses?

'I wish to ask you about your method.'

'My method?'

'You say it was yourself who rid the town of the Spaniard's army. I saw this force with my own eyes, hundreds of them. How could it be that one man could smite them?'

The Piper's eyes are alight once more. What strategy could this be, why does this man not speak with the same amiable foolery as his colleagues?

Mannau finds himself under the stranger's intense scrutiny, struggling to contain his discomfort. He knows he cannot yield to the other's intimidation, there are answers he must have.

'My *method*. . . need not concern you . . . any of you . . . except that it is skilled, and performed the task that was agreed, and for that I shall be rewarded as agreed.'

The Piper purses his lips when finished, forming a point with the end of his sharp nose. Mannau finds himself studying the face of a weasel, one that has scented fresh blood.

'I believe there is no method.'

The weasel smiles, an invitation to continue.

'And that *you* have deceived *us*. You must have known there was a madness in the Spaniard's ranks, one that was about to devour them. Yet you sought to achieve payment for this, an act that you knew you would only witness, not cause or incite. You are a charlatan, sir, you cannot prove otherwise.'

Mannau is shaking as he closes. It is him against the Piper, and his opponent will now understand this. And yet after waiting so long for his judgement to dominate in this chamber he feels naked without the support of his colleagues.

The beast draws a breath and slowly bares his teeth.

'Yes, I witnessed it, I saw it all, gentlemen, every moment of the massacre. And it was I who contrived this end, and it is I who suffers because of it. I have lost my companions, endured hardships beyond your understanding, and reserved a place in hell for the service I provided this town. You doubt my method? How unfortunate, how can I demonstrate its existence? I ask for the last time, pay me or you will have your proof.'

True to their word, the good men of the council elected by majority to let the Piper stay. There was only one voice of dissent, Mannau finding himself in familiar territory, made to sound spiteful and ungenerous by the foolhardy charity of the others. He chose not to pursue his point, struggling to articulate the real sense of dread the Piper's threat roused in him. Not for the first time he had let it pass, in any case the ears of the others were open only to music. Mannau had instead tried to raise the more pertinent topic of the future; the very last of the town's grain was running out and there were no more dried meats to be found. How could they survive until the spring? Were they to boil the leather of their shoes? Shouldn't the council be encouraging its citizens out into the fields, hunting for game, harvesting what they could of the wild heath?

God will provide, he was told. God, looking down on Hamelin, was now taking these decisions for them. The meeting had thus adjourned in deference to this higher municipal authority. Perhaps God would see fit to pay their taxes too.

For those like Mannau with little faith in the Almighty the words were of small comfort, and he travelled home a weary man, so weakened by hunger that he staggered like a drunkard, the hovering dance tones of the flute ridiculing his uncertain steps. This music would seek him out for the next two days. Mannau would labour to convince himself that it was not aimed personally at himself, that the echoes finding their way into his home were coincidental, caught by reflections off the walls in the square and chased down the lane through his door. His house? One of the finest in Hamelin, a testament to his abilities and ambition even if nothing else was. Twenty years ago he and Lisbet had arrived in this unwelcoming town with nothing, and in a way he still waited for acceptance. She had been the neighbourly one, joining in at fairs, cooking biscuits and jams for the children. Did they ever thank her? When the plague had taken her eight years ago it was he, the withdrawn half of the partnership, that had been left to toil on alone with his lack of social graces.

Mannau rolled his tongue around the dry corners of his mouth. It seemed that his teeth were loosening though he did not test this impression with a pull on them with his fingers lest it be proved disastrously true. Would they ever cope with good food again? It had been three days since he had exhausted his own carefully rationed supply of meats and pickles, and he still could not bring himself to consume the same gritty rye gruel the others professed to enjoy. Although he had never enjoyed their oily loaves, the bakeries had long stopped making any bread, and all that was left in town was the dregs of grain itself, to be washed down in a powdery soup with salt and water. He poured the grain into the bowl and watched the brown droplets float to the surface; rat faeces, would they add to the flavour? Some were proud they could eat it all. At least when the grain was gone the rats might leave too. He pushed the bowl to one side.

Outside, screams of children. Mannau reached for his keys, time to venture out, something had to be done, even if the whole council was failing surely Kunze would see? He emerged into the bright daylight to see a group of four girls and boys tearing down the lane, squealing with excitement. A change of tone in the Piper's flute and they turned and ran back again, back toward the main square. The Piper's audience was all children now, only they retained the energy to respond to his musical codes. One scale to gather, one scale to disperse, a language without words, no need to explain.

Mannau made his way towards Kunze's house, thankfully only five doors along the steep terrace. The knock on the door is answered after a pause that proves the lethargy that has gripped the town has been swept this far down. Kunze recognised his visitor but did not invite him in.

'We must meet. The council cannot allow this town to die of neglect.'

Kunze waited for more scampering children to clear his doorstep.

'Die? I think you exaggerate. There is food enough in the fields. I think we must let the people decide when to venture out.'

'The town is starving.'

'It will be reborn soon enough, you will see.'

'Is that what the Mayor says?'

Kunze scowled at Mannau's sharp remark.

'Let the Mayor be. The death of his friends has affected him, but he will be the stronger for it eventually.'

Mannau looked unconvinced, Kunze sighed despondently.

'He thinks D'Ortez was the devil. You saw him, is it true?'

Devil? Mannau could hear the devil playing in the town square, was he himself as demented as the Mayor? Whose devil threatened Hamelin most?

He took a deep breath; neither. This was the curse that had inhibited him all his life, this fear of imagined enemies with powers so much greater than his; D'Ortez, Kunze, Wolfricht, Mayor Ebber – why did he always believe they had 'method'? Were they so formidable? Who was to blame for assuming they were? It was he himself. These were mortals, ordinary men.

'I want the Piper to leave. His presence is a disturbance.'

Kunze shrugged nonchalantly.

'You are the Deputy, you tell him to go.'
'Yes, I will.'

He had heard him playing from the first moment he was awake, and this day he had immediately felt like joining in with the infants scurrying around his feet, an impulse followed by a deep sense of alarm. What was happening, was the music growing in power? He knew then he had to resolve this detestable affair, and began to rehearse the confrontation in his mind.

A wave of children frothed around him as he approached him, snapping like tied dogs. He closed his ears to the noise and looked to his target, eyes narrowed and squinting as if peering at the sun.

'I must speak with you.'

The Piper continued his playing, louder.

'Now, damn you!'

A wistful smile forms on his lips as the flute is drawn away from them. Thin lips. The face of a rat.

'Deputy, of course. I knew you would come.'

Mannau is nonplussed. What had been so predictable?

'The only sane man left on the council.'

Mannau swallows. This man must be the real devil after all, how else would he have known this?

'You must leave.'

'Of course.'

Another manic, although knowing, leer forms on the minstrel's face. This is not the confrontation that had been prepared for, where was the provocation, the insolence this man had shown before?

'Will you?'

'Once I have my four hundred Thalers'

'You know that is not possible.'

The grin fades. The Piper shakes a rueful head.

'You were the one who could have saved Hamelin, Deputy. Yet you choose not to. You have a hard heart, sir, one which will do for these citizens.'

He lifts his flute; one shrill blow and the infant entourage is straining against gravity again.

'Hear this, little ones! The Deputy says I must leave Hamelin, that I am no longer welcome now my work is done.'

The olive-skinned face is downcast, a jester's parody of sadness. All around the children are wailing their rage, flashes of venom in young eyes are caught by the early light, together with a glistening blaze of its reflection on sharp teeth. Mannau steadies himself, he has not faced down the Spaniard's army to be terrified by juveniles, they cannot attack him.

The entertainer is now comforting his following,' Do not cry, little ones, there is time for one game ... the final game ... the best game of all. Come! Who will show me the way to the grain store?'

Mannau closed his eyes and lifted the spoon to his lips. Contrary to his misgivings it tasted of nothing at all though he still avoided inhaling through his nose to avoid the smell. He chewed slowly, the water had mushed some bits more than others so that the paste on his tongue contained both the sharp and the soft, grime and glass. He swallowed hard, forcing the revolting combination down before his gullet had a chance to register nausea, hating it all the same, hating himself for eating it, hating them all – the self-righteous Mayor Ebber, gluttonous Wolfricht, senile Kunze, feeble D'Ortez and the charlatan Piper. Yes, fine food, he thought, guzzling the noxious brew with increasing vigour, the greedy bastards had tried to deceive him again, not wanting him to know how good it was so they could keep more for themselves. Why should he do anything for them, why not admit it for once, he hated them all. He hated Hamelin.

When it happened the music was inescapable, as loud as it had ever been, echoes rearing up from every surface, lanes and alleyways alive with the sound of flutes, not one but a battery, unrelenting, waves of noise catching each other, inventing new songs as they rebounded into cacophony. A pause, then a new tune, one pipe, different, a puzzle. A scale played over and over; circular, rising steadily in pitch only to end a note lower than where it had started. Round and round, a different message, no longer hypnotic, now a melody that mocked the senses of the listener, an irritant. This the very sound of anarchy, no more code telling the children where to run, no message at all, only the insane cry of despair being played as an anthem; up is down, black is white, heaven is hell.

Mannau could not remember it starting, or what he had been doing when it had, it seemed that it had always been there. Dusk was falling, it had been noon when he had returned to his home, he had not slept but somehow the hours between were unaccountable, as if they had been stolen from him, and now he was hungry again. Mannau's legs were jerking in time to the sound, heels thumping against the wooden floor in uncontrollable spasms. He watched, a detached spectator, choosing not to fight against the rhythm but staring at his hand as it began to beat against the table top in sympathy. An ugly hand, thin and pale, nails long, sharp and rounded, a claw.

A whiff of food in the air, someone was hiding something, had they not told him there would be sustenance? He sniffed, nose in the air, sense of smell suddenly acute, snout twitching, sifting through the odours. On the ground, the scents he searched for, of course! He fell to his fours, hands and knees, shuffling to the door.

Outside, others of a similar mind crawling low, whiskers brushing against the cobblestones, heads colliding, seeking out corners, pressing against the ordure and the excrement, where is the food?

Schmidt, Kunze, all the whores of the council have joined the chase, nose to tail the procession snakes its way to the main square. And there before them the most delicious repast awaits, moist and tender. No need to cook, or drown in soup, the meat is already cured on young bones.

Mannau's saliva drips as he continues his haunched progress, why had he not realised before? Be quick! The rest will follow.

He pounces forward and grips the listless child, front paws pinning its head to the ground, bite fastening on an unguarded neck. Claws draw blood tearing at the covering rags yet the screams and scent combine to heighten the hunger.

The others have now collected, equally carnivorous, Schmidt tugging angrily as his jaw pulls the opposite arm, exposing a choice chest for other teeth to select their spot.

No good. Mannau's feast calls for privacy, a leisurely chew away from the horde; he pulls anew, the cracking snapping sinews ping as taut violin strings to the Piper's flute. He twists the arm against its socket, a full rotation and it is off, secure in his mouth as he turns to scamper homeward, bleeding hands adding to the scarlet streaks on the glistening pavement stones. Mannau's pain is lost to anticipation of the banquet to come and he stretches downhill against the tide, still aiming for the square. Jealous eyes catch sight of the choice game in his possession, a crowd on his tail and a sea of faces ahead. Can he make it? The path to his doorway is blocked, teeming, the Mayor amongst them, better to drop the meat and make his way back for fresh quarry. He lets it fall and pushes it behind him, back legs kicking it as claws rip his calves in frenzy. The sting of the wounds seeps into his body and he turns angrily to see the discarded limb set upon by the pack. But in an instant it is gone and the eyes are back on him as the crowd closes. Too late, he looks to himself, too covered in blood, young blood on old flesh, too beguiling a prospect for the herd to resist.

A flash of insight as he catches the wicked face of the Mayor; they mean to eat him!

The claws of the pack tear at his breeches and shirts, jaws snapping into his skin as the flesh is exposed. There can be no escape. All vision is suddenly lost as the talons of an unknown assailant sink deep behind his eyeballs. Mannau turns in a spasm of agony, writhing on his back. A final hope, as he offers his throat to the mob – that the end comes quickly.

S HE MUST HAVE had something worked out with the others who shared the shack, the crones who would normally hover, clucking like anxious hens between the boxes and the beds, fluttering between the laundry shawls hanging above. Perhaps they thought the deal was that they would get to America too if they showed me enough favour. Whatever the arrangement, they weren't there, and Katryn was playful and relaxed, obviously eager for me to share the mood, leading me by the hand down the rutted path that led to the heart of the hovel. I'd been uneasy when she had done this – would any onlooker deduce by the way she clasped my fingers in hers that we were lovers, or would the scene appear inno-cent enough, the young doctor being taken to his next examination? I was worried that what might give it away was the way these thoughts must have been written on my face, or could even have been spelled out in a giant bubble floating over my head for all the world to see like some character in a comic strip. Still, I hadn't pulled away from her, no. By then every touch was to be savoured, I didn't know how many more there would be.

Katryn, why did I feel such a need to be close to you? Was it because of the distance she kept between us? In my arms she was compliant, passionate and giving but always holding something back. I would run my fingers through her flaxen hair and ask about her family, where are you all from? Who are your friends? And the children, why no children, *der kinder*? All my questions received with a smile, she does not understand, or pretends not to, always happier to provide a distraction of a more sensual kind.

When we were inside she had sat me down on what passed for a bed, a flimsy stack of large cushions draped in a heavy blanket, itself patterned in a swirling mix of creams and scarlets. I seemed to sink right into it. She giggled as she pulled off my boots, then continued the frolicsome antics by peeling off my socks one at a time, stroking and kissing my toes as they were revealed, resting my instep against her delicate chest. Leaning forward the way she was, I couldn't see her face, only her forehead, the tops of her ears, her scalp. All impossibly beautiful, too pleasing. I have never experienced an infatuation as intense, never found myself looking at anyone with the same sense of anticipation of pleasures to come, the bound-less sensual possibilities to explore. I struggled not to believe that every piece of her had been designed with my satisfaction in mind, every inch an erogenous zone whose potential combinations with my own would never be exhausted. We could fit together in so many different ways that the quantification of permutations was beyond even the most advanced mathematics.

Today she controlled the calculation, seeking out my

hand again, taking it to her lips to plant the kiss then guiding it through the forest of buttons of waistcoats and blouse to stroke her breasts. She lets it linger then leads its retreat out, my hand feels a moment's exposure to the cold and then her eyes lock on mine, and it is led on another journey, under her skirts, along her thighs, another forest, another pair of lips. I hear her let out a sound as the first connection is made, my fingers probe for warmth again. It is a gentle sound, a feminine sound, a girlish intake of breath.

I do not linger on these details out of any lurid desire to impress, and I am not unaware that these words may hurt and offend those whom I have no desire to embarrass in any way – my wife, my daughter, my daughter in-law; I apologise if this is the case but I must linger at this scene because, ladies and gentlemen, it was *me* who was in that room, it was *me* who was captive of those sentiments and I have to understand how that could have been, understand the passion, and revisit the source.

She slowly takes my hand from inside her, and then it is led back to her breast, now exposed through the blouse that hangs open. My glistening fingers paint honey on her raised round nipple and I am pulled forward to suckle; a taste of something sweet, something forbidden, a poison to alter the senses, to make me want to eat her.

She sits astride me; the best times seemed to be when we did it like this, I cannot imagine why, the habit did not stay with me. So slight that I could almost lift her up and down unaided and support her arched back in one. She loses herself in the motion but it is her that has me. I will do anything she wants – make it faster, anything . . . faster still, anything . . . hold her in the air like an angel, anything anything anything.

We always seemed to laugh when it was over, again a practice that has not stayed with me – when was the last time I laughed after making love? The notion is strangely incongruous now. I remember stretching over to pick up her blouse, discarded at some forgotten point in the fury. It was another object of resonant beauty, embroidered by hand with red and gold motifs, shining like tacky jewels. I fed my arm into the sleeves and pulled it on, careful not to tear the fabric as I squeezed into the shoulders. She looked at me and laughed like a mad woman, tears in her eyes. I knew how ridiculous I must have appeared, and grimaced like a fool, almost sending her into hysterics. Why had I done it? To entertain her, the way lovers do, and also because it was there, bright and colourful against the drab khaki of my uniform. I didn't feel like a soldier, I never really had, and now I didn't feel like a doctor either. I was changing, but into what?

That was the irony, ladies and gentlemen, for all that our bodies had been joined as one; while she wanted to change everything she had for the trappings and opportunities she must have thought I possessed, I wanted to be like her, a peasant.

I heard a cough from inside my hut as I gingerly made my way back from the engagement with Katryn. Loud, extraordinarily loud, enough to rattle the corrugated walls in welcome. I was still in a dream, patting my tender groin, trying to stop my swollen organ from rubbing too much against the coarse plaid of my trousers. The cough was so

deep in tone it reminded me of Vesey; it didn't occur to
me that he might actually have come, so it was a shock
when I sauntered through the door to find him there, poring over Arthur's contraption of burners and pipes, by now
taking up over a third of the room.

'Hi, Rob. You OK?'

How he knew it was me I don't understand, he hadn't
even glanced up to greet my arrival. His voice was downbeat, unexcited, as if it were four minutes since I'd last
seen him, not four months.

'Yes . . . fine. Yourself?'

'Good.'

This was another sound I recognised, the way he blew
out the word in one long bass note. He made it as he stood
over Arthur's creation, totally absorbed in it, attempting
to follow the tortuous path of each piece of tubing from
flame to distil base to mixing phial to more heat to sample
point and on. I searched for something to say. I had grown
used to this insane construction's presence over the weeks
but now I suddenly saw it as Vesey would have done
coming in from the cold. I remembered Geigy's first reaction to it, now it had expanded it could only look worse.

Vesey bit his lower lip and let out a sigh, eyes almost
disappearing behind the horizontal slits that formed as he
screwed up his face in loathing. When he spoke, it was in
the same resigned manner as before.

'I'm sorry, Rob, I really didn't know it was this bad.
Should have guessed I suppose . . . I'm sorry.'

I watched him run his index finger along the top of one
of the shiny copper ducts, what should he have guessed?
'Sorry'? Was his apology genuine and if so what was it

for? Could he be cursing both of us or just Arthur? The silence was now my ally. I let him continue his contemplation in quiet.

'Know how many messages we received in Berlin from here?'

I shook my head.

'Three. Three in four and a half months. One was the request for this stuff. I'm surprised they let it through. Know how many we sent?'

I stayed mute.

'We sent over sixty, nearly one every damn day. How many did you get?'

'About the same. Three or four, I mean.'

He bit his lip again and shook his head ruefully, silver speckles in his cropped black hair catching the light as he did so. There were more of these since I had last been with him, aside from that though he had hardly changed, the girth and the bearing of the man absolutely unaltered. Yank food, as Arthur had said, you hit the jackpot when you landed at a base with Yank food. And hit the bottom if you ended up in with the Russians. Thank God Katryn's friends were still feeding me. Three messages. I was surprised, I had no idea they had tried to get so many more through. They had got three from us because we had sent three, never imagining that they were so keen on communication.

'Yeah . . . should have guessed. I think it's a damn disgrace you are reduced to putting this thing up in here. Couldn't they have found somewhere proper for you to use? They said you'd be working together dammit.'

'I think . . . Arthur wanted . . .'

His flash of temper cut me short, 'I know, I know. They will have their excuses, always have, very good at excuses. Well that's got to change. Yes, got to change fast, alright.'

I found myself nodding in agreement, mimicking, albeit sincerely, the gesture he was making. Four months apart and then so quickly back into the old ways.

'How often do they swap troops in the camp?'

The question came from nowhere, though the way it was said almost implied that this was a matter under my influence. What could be irritating him now?

'I don't know.' I paused, thinking of the faces I would see every day, had they changed? No, I knew each and every one of them, like one knows the face of every other pupil at school, youngest to oldest, without actually being able to match a name to individuals.

'Never. The camp's quarantined, no one has left since I arrived.'

'Quarantine was lifted by the Soviets last month, Rob. They told us they didn't need it any more, only infections had ever been amongst the refugees, that they could conclude that medical and security personnel weren't at risk or carriers. Didn't they tell you that?'

'Lifted? No.'

'Their decision. Thing is, they probably need those troops for elsewhere, like there's something else going down somewhere. You get any sense of that?'

I hadn't any sense of anything other than my own daily circle around the camp, whose orbit drew tighter with every passing day. Should I feel resentful that this news hadn't been passed on? I couldn't decide, there was by now a tacit agreement with Geigy that we wouldn't discuss the condition, that Arthur and I could while away the hours as we chose, and it would have been hypocritical to complain about not being kept informed. But what if there had been some kind of breakthrough in the investigation that Vesey knew about and we didn't, how would that make us look? I had to get to Arthur, warn him, agree some kind of story, get to Geigy too. Surely he would help me, tell me what was happening, or was he happy to watch us hang for our laziness?

'We . . . we were never encouraged to take too close an interest in the activities of the military.'

I thought back to the day I had asked for a cigarette from the youth on the steps of the ruin, and my very first day inside it, the officer shouting at me in a language he knew I couldn't understand.

'I've tried . . . but I think they've been warned off. None of them are in the least friendly.'

Vesey's eyes lingered on me for an uncomfortable moment before returning to the patchwork apparatus that dominated the floor of the room.

'Where's Lee – Arthur, now?'

'Out . . . I mean, probably with Geigy, playing chess. Goes there most nights.'

'What time you eat round here?'

I fumbled, trying to find my watch under my shirt and jacket sleeves. I had the feeling my face was pulsating with the full vibrancy of obvious guilt. The damn thing didn't seem to be there, had I left it at Katryn's? Was she about to reappear, dangling it coquettishly on her little finger? Vesey must have wondered why I was suddenly so relieved to see it.

'About six or so. The hut next door – oh, you've missed it.' The time on my wrist was showing seven-thirty; it had taken me an effort to work it out. Telling the time was not normally an effort that would tax me but my mind had begun to spin with the questions I could imagine Vesey must have been thinking. Why was Arthur playing chess every night with the Russians if they were so unfriendly, why had I not appeared to take my food, where else was I eating?

'Doesn't matter, guess I can wait until breakfast. Want to get Arthur, see if he can join us? I need a brief on what's been going on.'

'Now? I mean where are you going to stay?'

'Why not, we can worry about other stuff later.'

'But I'll need to find out about your billet . . . everything is so cramped here.'

The features on his square head were realigning their symmetry into an impatient scowl.

'Just get Arthur first, could you, Rob?'

Now, everything now. Things would happen faster with Vesey around.

The new sense of urgency wasn't to prove infectious, not immediately anyway. Arthur wasn't impressed with the news of the arrival, he wanted to finish his game with Mussorgy.

'Why can't the fool wait until tomorrow? Ask him why he doesn't want to do it properly.'

Did Arthur really expect me to run back and forth with his dispatches like this? I had no doubt Vesey wanted 'to do it properly'. The problem was that his and Arthur's

241

idea of what constituted the 'proper' way were never going to match.

I pulled up a chair close to Arthur's side. When he bent forward towards his pieces I tried to follow him as best the seating would allow.

'Arthur, we'll have to talk as well, *now*.'

'Hmmmn? What about?'

His voice was noticeably louder than my hushed tones, like he was making a point about having nothing to hide from either Mussorgy on the other side of the table from us, or from Geigy sitting behind, immersed in some inches-thick cyrillic tome.

'About what's been going on, what we're meant to be doing about the condition.'

My sense of awkwardness wasn't helped by catching Mussorgy's beady eye as I said this. I knew his English was almost non-existent, yet there was still an illogical fear that he was absorbing everything, retaining it for future use. It was me he studied rather than his agitated opponent. Arthur planted his elbows down and slapped two hands on his cheeks.

'What the hell is it with everyone tonight? Can't I get a bloody moment's peace?'

Arthur's complaint was addressed to the room in general although obviously aimed at Vesey and myself. I was enraged to see him mouthing an apology to Mussorgy for my interruption of the contest. Were apologies really in order? Mussorgy's face showed no more emotion or expression than those on the wooden chess pieces below him.

Looking back, Vesey's arrival was the worst thing that

could have happened to Arthur. It brought out all the very worst elements in his character – the jealousy and mean spiritedness against our erstwhile benefactor, the intellectual snobbery against all things American, and the infantile determination to act in a way contrary to whatever desire Vesey would express. Yes, a fanatical determination. Had I employed a more adroit psychological strategy that night and told Arthur that Vesey didn't want to hear of our progress in defining the condition until some months ahead, it would probably have been enough to have him eagerly preparing his case then and there, perhaps even chasing me for my contribution. This was a determination he would sometimes hold purely to be contrary, like this time because Arthur had, despite his affectations of indolence, been actively pursuing his own highly individual inquiry into the condition and formulated his own theory. A theory which, ladies and gentlemen, when finally presented, would astonish us all, and blow all my attempts to preserve our little facade wide open.

The second case conference, March 13th 1946.

It had been slowly warming up since half way through the previous month, and the signs of an imminent spring were there for those with the will to spot them: birdsong, longer afternoons, weeds beginning to flourish in the gutters of the camp huts. That day however, we were back into winter, the thaw's advance halted by an overnight snowfall and corresponding drop in temperature. So it was a return to watching your boots disappear into eight inches of crisp white powder as one made one's way to the steaming breakfast-serving hatch.

Vesey must have been well informed; there had to have been a general thinning down of troop numbers within the camp – the queue ahead of me had been noticeably smaller – and accommodation for the man himself had been found in one of the smaller barrack huts. He had the place on his own, larger bed, desk and washing basin and all. I saw it myself when I went to collect him in the morning.

It made sense, I suppose, there were fewer refugees, less than three hundred now that so many had died. Why have so many guarding them? Was this another example of our Soviet hosts' paranoia or had they spotted a growing malevolence amongst the captives that I had failed to notice? My impression was that the spirit of the refugees was essentially peaceful, a simple people looking to find their quiet way in the world. I was wrong. This was an impression I had chosen to find comfort in, but the reality was different; something evil was brewing, the end was nearer than I could have realised, and this before Arthur made his spectacular contribution.

I had taken over a cup of coffee to Vesey, a peace offering; I felt he might still be irked by my failure to deliver Arthur the night before. He was, or it may have been that he was just tired after a cold and restless night, because he kept me waiting on the step outside whilst he grunted and slurped his way to readiness for the day. Then, when he came out, he surprised me again by asking to be taken down to see the main settlement toward the ruin. What he expected to see I don't know, we walked in silence, me slightly wary of the reception I might be given and whether anything might happen that would make Vesey suspicious. Suspicious of what? Again, I don't know, but things were obviously very wrong: Arthur and I had failed to make any kind of progress in understanding what the condition was; I couldn't answer any of Vesey's questions about the military activities around camp whilst Geigy and Mussorgy had pressed on with their own enquiries that we knew nothing about. Not all my fault, but it may as well have been, and in a few moments I would have to repeat a tale of worthless nonsense about my theory on tularaemia. One consolation though, this early in the morning our patients were in muted form, bickering and banging pots, sullenly staring at scattered wood-fires, squatting before them like grasshoppers on stiff and frozen limbs. No sign of Katryn, and no special greeting for the 'special' doctor. Vesey turned without warning and we headed back down the slope.

'Strange people, these refugees. Do they talk much . . . about what's going on?'

'Well, they try to, no one can really understand . . . different language. I think they are still a bit bewildered by it all, sort of mass outbreak of shock, frightened it might be them next.'

'I mean outside, Rob, do they ever talk about what they've seen in other places, further east?'

It was the west they dreamed of, the United States. That was all I had ever heard mentioned, how could I explain that? Vesey ploughed on, following his own thought's progression.

'Think the Soviets have done something to them, told them to keep quiet? You thought some of them had been beaten, didn't you? "Outbreak of trauma injuries" – that what you were getting at?'

It was at the time; things had moved on, I'd given up on 'getting at' anything; another difficult one to explain.

'I thought it might – There's more to it all though. Can I tell you inside?'

Vesey shrugged and scanned around, probably thinking that I was worried that we might be overheard. He must have had enough paranoia to think it possible and he didn't say another word until we reached the meeting hut.

Arthur had already set up and was waiting for us. It had been his suggestion that we meet there 'if we wanted to do it properly'. He was pacing the floor, silently talking to himself when we entered, almost as if conducting an internal argument. I dreaded that he was going to use this occasion to score points directly off Vesey instead of through me, to denounce him for the absurdity of our mission here. We came in just as it started to snow once more, a bitter wind swirling the first isolated flecks into an airborne dance of a hundred miniature kites. The wind was inside the room as well, creeping in under the rafters. When Arthur sighed I could see his breath blown in the same way as the snow.

'Yes, about time.'

'Morning, Arthur, what you got for me? Want to tell me what that stuff in your room is all about?'

Vesey was trying to sound approachable and friendly, perhaps to draw a straightforward response from Arthur, perhaps to show that he wasn't riled despite the attempts otherwise.

'Later, please be seated . . .'

Arthur bowed with an absurd formal air, extending an arm in the direction of one of the chairs, the brilliant and

exuberant professor to our limited and diffident under-
graduates. 'We can discuss everything there is to discuss
later.'

Vesey wrapped his coat around him tight and moved
sideways along to the seat, perching on the very end of it.

'Just tell me straight, Arthur, are we talking radiation
here?'

Arthur stood in front of him, silent, raising his eyebrows
as if to acknowledge an interesting question. Vesey wanted
more than flattery.

'Well, what then? Can't you just –'

His voice had been rising when it suddenly halted, interrupted by the activity at the door: voices, foreign voices.
The door opened and Geigy and Mussorgy shuffled in,
kicking their boots free of snow against the step.

Glances were rapidly exchanged all round. Vesey either
didn't know or didn't want the Russian pair's presence
and I saw him look to Geigy to check he had not stumbled
in without knowing we were having a private meeting.
Geigy in turn had sought out Arthur who waved to a chair.
Geigy then offered a pained smile to the American; anyone
would have sensed the lack of welcome but he was trapped,
as we all were, by Arthur's impeccable show of manners.

'Thank you, gentlemen, shall we start?'

All I could think of was what a bastard. To repeat a
presentation of my excruciatingly weak tularaemia theory
in the room where it had been ridiculed months earlier
would be testing enough, but now with Geigy and his
sidekick here it would be even worse. What would they
think of me, that I was stupid, or just a plain liar?

Arthur waited patiently for everyone to settle down, the

only one with any recognisable enthusiasm for the meeting, the only one ready to answer his own question.

'Right!' he said, clapping hands together. 'Let me tell you about one of the most exciting discoveries in history, here in front of us in Tarutz.'

I wondered if I had misheard him; the others must have too. Vesey cleared his throat and leaned forward, Geigy whispering something to Mussorgy. What could Arthur mean?

'If we are honest with ourselves, as *professional* practitioners of medicine, as men of science, I am sure we would admit that our efforts in investigating the affliction centred on the inhabitants of this camp have been somewhat *flawed*.'

The last word had been aimed pointedly at Geigy, as 'professional' had been fired like an insult to Vesey. Both looked puzzled.

'Flawed in the sense that we have been too immersed in *specifics*, too concerned about individual cases, isolated wounds and infections. In short we have been guilty of paying too much attention to *symptoms* rather than *causes*.'

Arthur paused for us to catch up, as if we were taking notes at a seminar. There was also an implicit invitation to interrupt and raise questions, though no one displayed an inclination to do so. Arthur continued, growing in confidence.

'These unfortunates who harbour, exclusively, the condition – what do we know of them? Do we know exactly where it is they are from, their ancestry, their history? Surely the way must be to examine their culture, lifestyle, language. There must be something in there that could indicate why it is they would be susceptible to this disease, anything, the rye-based diet, lack of children, what are these things telling us? Three hundred years ago the German people began to move eastwards to escape the overcrowding, the squalor, the war that enveloped them and here we have the opposite journey by the same people ... for the same reason! What happened to those first emigrants? Did they suffer in the same strange way, is there evidence of these kind of outbreaks happening to them?'

Arthur stopped to turn around and lift the pile of notes stacked behind him, brandishing them to his bemused audience.

'There is! Here ... manuscripts, notes made from registers and records of the time of the Thirty Years' War. Here, gentlemen, the first signs.'

The first interruption; courtesy of Vesey, clearing his throat, the gargling of sputum sounding alarmingly akin to the roll of a bass drum.

'Arthur, maybe we can go into this later. I think what might be more appropriate is a general discussion on the medical cause of the condition. Dr Geigy, how long do you estimate it will take your team to diagnose ... whatever.'

If Vesey thought Arthur would give up the floor easily he was to be disappointed, the show had only just begun.

'With due respect, that's a pointless question. He's no nearer now than when he started. It's the people who are the answer, the *people*!'

There was a wildness about Arthur now, an obvious desperation to make his point and have it accepted. This was a new development; normally he was happy in isolation, comfortably aloof from those he judged academically inferior.

'I'll take Dr Geigy's view on whether the question is irrelevant or not if you don't mind; I've heard what you have to say. Dr Geigy?'

'How can you! I haven't started!'

'Then I suggest you start some other time.'

Vesey's curt riposte stung Arthur into temporary silence, his face showing the hurt of a smitten teenager's first taste of rejection.

'Thank you, Dr Lee. Right now I'm more interested in facts. Dr Geigy, would you be so kind as to give me your view?'

Arthur cast an imploring eye to Geigy, would his chess comrade at least support him, hear him out? Geigy squirmed visibly, was his English good enough to find the words that would bridge the gap between the two others?

'The background of the patients is very –'

'*Patients!*'

Even this was too much for Arthur. He had lifted his sheaf of notes and brandished them as if holding some unanswerable truth, a zealot with his bible.

'Am I the only one to see it? Who will admit to it? These are not patients, that is a *delusion* we have all clung to! Why should we be so afraid?'

By now Arthur was on the verge of hysteria, unable to stop haranguing us, shouting, or flailing his arms as the papers were swept up into the air. It was Geigy who tried to calm him, his inquiry the result more of concern than curiosity.

'*Arthur*. . . what do you mean, Arthur?'

'These aren't patients, these are ghosts, man, bloody *ghosts*!'

Arthur nodded vigorously, eyes glowing in brazen affirmation; yes, we had heard him, and yes, he had meant every word.

Vesey's large shoulders began to bounce with laughter as Mussorgy demanded an explanation from Geigy, the two locking heads to leave me alone, wondering how to react.

'Well?'

Arthur stared, daring me to deny him.

'Have you ever found a pulse on any one of them? Understood what they are saying? The language they speak, a form of High German – it's three centuries old!'

I *had* found a pulse on them, or thought I had once I let myself be taken into their midst. All the same I knew what Arthur was implying; there was something of the night about these people but I was not in any kind of position to articulate it. Katryn was no ghost. It was Vesey, rapidly composing himself and rubbing the grin from his face, who rescued me.

'Okay, Arthur, you've convinced me. Next problem, how do we treat ghosts – surgical spirit?'

He rocked in his chair, occasionally bending over as though his sides would split, the only one to appreciate the joke. His laughter was a deliberate show of scorn.

Arthur was less incensed than I might have feared, determined not to succumb to the taunt.

'I don't propose that we treat them, we should use our resources to investigate them. We need documentary and archaeological evidence to link us to their past, we can use them to ascertain the truth behind German legend. Church records, land registers, a search on the banks of the River Treuwe ... these people are victims of a history we *must* understand, these people can lead us to Hamelin. Gentlemen, we could be on the verge –'

'Okay, okay,' Vesey cut across Arthur, suddenly brusque and businesslike, the chairman bringing the room to order.

'That's what you propose? I'll tell you what I propose.'

He paused to make sure Arthur was paying attention, a cautions nod of the head given as proof.

'I say we search for all this stuff, papers, documents, records, archaeology. We get it together, just as *you* say, Arthur, with *your* guidance of course ... gather everything...' He fixed his gaze on the nodding Arthur. '... and we shove it right up your ass where it belongs.'

Arthur showed no immediate response, the only sound in the room was the wailing of the wind and the hushed mutterings of Geigy's now simultaneous translation for the incredulous Mussorgy.

Something in the smile from Vesey though, perhaps the baring of those tiny white teeth, was enough to make Arthur lift his cherished notes for a final time. He took them in both hands and threw them at Vesey, individual sheets and papers flying off on their own course and scattering on the floor. Arthur looked at the mess as he made for the door, building up speed as he neared it. The wind spread the disarray still further once the door itself was open. Arthur didn't stop to look or close it after him, striding instead out toward the ruin. I was too stunned to even move, it was Geigy who lifted Arthur's coat and sprinted after him. The meeting was at an end.

*   *   *

The time of Arthur's exit? Around ten o'clock. I didn't see him again that morning or afternoon. It was evening before Vesey began to show any concern and by then it was too late.

Given the way things had developed, I was happy enough to hide away for these hours in between, busying myself with a variety of tasks in the relative privacy of my hut – tidying up the mess of my and Arthur's notes, trying to separate mine from his to provide the evidence that not so long ago, I *had* been fully committed to the investigation into the condition. I even began to dismantle the furthest extremes of Arthur's construction.

Vesey came around at six, and we toiled with our miserable food together in silence. I think he must have been regretful of the way he had treated Arthur, or just the way it had gone since he came. There were more questions, about camp, its security, about Arthur, and about Geigy. I answered as best I could, but there was a minefield of compromise that I had somehow to steer him round. I think eventually he got tired of my evasive replies and gave up the chase. Perhaps he thought I would throw a tantrum as well if he pushed too hard. Anyway, eight o'clock came and he sent me to go and fetch Arthur. He wasn't to be found.

Mussorgy was on his own in the games hut, shrugging his shoulders in reply to everything. I thanked him for his help. Geigy wasn't in the admin cabin or his own barracks, and my visit to the latrines proved equally fruitless. That left the refugees' allotments and, of course, the ruin. Would they be likely to be in either? I really couldn't face another trip to the chambers again, my feet were cold and sodden through all the trudging in the slush, boots having given up, much like their owner. But I could picture the two of them there; Geigy, a calm and superficially soothing presence, absorbing the energy of Arthur's need to explain, providing through his tolerant listening the absolution that was craved. That's what all these notes and writing had been about, a means to communicate something he believed had a desperate importance and yet was also somehow desperately personal. Arthur had his audience at last, but what could be in this for Geigy?

Outside, the wind stung my ears, joined in its attack by the tiny bullets of rain being driven into each side of me. I pulled my coat collar up for protection but it was flattened every time. Shouts and anguished shrieks rang out, carried by the shifting gusts, crackling bursts of what sounded like gun-fire also hung in the air; it was impossible to tell where they were coming from. Through the bitter hail I could see others struggling in the opposite direction. Was the wind breaking up the refugees' camp? I wiped my eyes to be sure of what I thought I was seeing. Two soldiers dragged a lifeless body feet-first through the mud. To my astonishment I saw this was another soldier. A figure emerged to join them, blown by the same force pushing me back.

'Rob?'

It was a relief to see Geigy, such a relief my first thought was of being able to turn back, and not to wonder why he would be on his own.

'What's going on? What has happened to him?' I pointed to the body. 'Have you seen Arthur?'

Geigy took a step forward, face pressed close to mine. The earflaps on his hat were down, and the wind was carrying my voice way past him before it had a chance to register.

'Arthur?'

I shouted as loud as I could but he still stared blankly. I felt his glove grip the top of my arm and turn me. He waved towards the nearest hut and motioned for us to walk over. We could converse inside.

The hut was one of the smaller barracks. As we walked in, two startled weary guards grabbed for their rifles, barrels pointing at us until Geigy calmed them down and they could return to lounging on their beds. I had never been in one of these huts before and an ignorant curiosity had me scanning the room in one quick take – the usual mess of underwear, boots and kit that men make when apart from women. There didn't seem an abundance of subversive goings-on to report to Vesey.

I waited whilst Geigy undid the strap under his chin. Some typically nimble fingerwork meant the hat was soon free. Geigy's eyes were as keen as ever but his hair was lank and greasy, highlighted by the lamp hanging directly above. It also caught the contours of his face, the deep lines and shadows under his brow. He was not a healthy man, as thin as a rickshaw Chinaman.

'Who killed that soldier?'

Geigy drew a deep breath. 'Disturbance, Rob. They begin to fight amongst themselves. Elements who choose to kill one another, in the name of honour. Some have brought guns into camp ... our comrade soldier was caught trying to disarm a group. Others killed tonight, three or four peasants.'

'Have you seen Arthur?'

'Arthur is . . .' he said, halting in concentration as though his command of English had suddenly stalled, '. . . gone.'

'Gone where?'

'From camp, Rob.'

'When?'

The alarm in my voice must have been clear enough in any language, the two others had obviously tuned in. Geigy put his arm on my shoulder and turned me away from them.

'He left twelve noon. He has gone to investigate, gone south, towards border with Germany.'

'Why didn't you stop him?'

'He is not mine to stop.'

I had not meant Geigy personally, but 'you' in the plural sense, the Soviets. I couldn't believe Arthur had been allowed to walk out, though I didn't pursue the point, at least, not immediately.

'What about the quarantine?'

'Quarantine was lifted for medical staff in January, Rob.'

'But he couldn't have had travel authorization.'

Geigy hesitated, pursing his lips.

'He told us he has verbal authorization from Mr Vesey to collect materials, as discussed at the meeting, that we had all heard this . . . is true, isn't it, Rob?'

Of course it was, but only in the most literal sense, and surely Geigy knew it.

'I don't think your Commander Vesey was . . . *entirely* serious . . . when he said that Arthur could pursue his theory outside the camp. I think there has been a mistake.'

Geigy still had his arm around my shoulder, eyes vacant, a sure sign he wasn't listening to my words.

'Rob, I spoke to you before about Arthur, you promised to help. Did you manage anything?'

He seemed to know the question was rhetorical, drawing a deep breath to fuel his next contention.

'I had to get them to release him. Arthur is sick – you know this. He has just this one thing left in his life – he has to leave Tarutz to pursue this or he will become more sick. You saw him, you must agree. As a doctor, you must agree?'

And then it was there again, the invitation to join in collusion, 'as a *doctor*'. Somehow I was going to have to relay all this back to Vesey; that the Russians thought Arthur mad and a danger to the camp, that I had been warned before but had not acted, and now that he had been let loose I was still not sure just how mad or dangerous he was, or if this were all some form of entrapment.

Geigy was practically hugging me, eyes imploring me to concede his point and join with him on the firm ground of his judgement.

'I'm sorry, I'd better go. I know Colonel Vesey will be concerned to hear . . .'

The arm around me dropped, the embrace vanishing in an instant together with the warmth in Geigy's gaze, the first sign of contempt after all our talking. The go-between had shown who he wanted to side with and was free to carry the message home.

Vesey was less anxious than I might have supposed given the commotion raging outside. He was seated at the desk in his room, hands resting on top, a bottle of whisky and a glass between them. I was completely soaked when I arrived, vaguely jealous of him for enjoying the sparse comforts indoors, unheated and draughty though the hut was. The whisky smelled like honey, the first thing I noticed when I entered. I couldn't take my eyes off it, not because of any intense craving but because of the incongruity of its presence. How had Vesey smuggled it here?

'Want a drink?'

He must have noticed my preoccupation with the bottle, lifting his bulk from the chair to search for another glass amongst the baggage on the floor, pulling out the silver top of his hip flask and raising it to me for my approval.

'This do?'

Vesey had his coat on, American issue, generous brown cloth cut to cover his enormous backside. He had puffed laboriously when rummaging through his case, rolling his head from side to side like some enormous grizzly bear trapped in a tiny cage. He hit the chair and began to pour, the cup minuscule, like one from a doll's set, in his claw of a hand.

'Well, Rob, you're a Scot. Tell me, this one any good?'

He handed me the bottle. The label read 'Old Parr', a cheap blend.

'Yes. One of my father's.'

'No kidding? Your father makes whisky?'

'A blender, he mixed this.'

'In the Highlands?' Vesey took an appreciative slug.

'Not quite. Dumbarton, near Glasgow. The malts come from the Highlands but they are mixed near the bottling plant.'

'That's one job I'd sure love to have, making whisky. He gets paid for it?'

'It's a difficult job, scientific. There will be about thirty odd malts in any blend, together with the grain spirit. Their flavours change all the time so the blender has to alter the mix to make sure the overall taste is consistent, year after year.'

He was polite enough to feign interest, even though the voice couldn't carry the lie. 'Really? I didn't know that, Rob.'

Another sip, one he tried to hold on the lips.

'Think that's what we've got here, Rob, something where the individual parts change to make the bigger thing stay the same?'

It seemed a surprisingly intelligent point. I thought he meant the condition, and my mind immediately began to think through permutations of symptoms, fatalities and infections. For that brief moment I was excited about the investigation, wanting to rush back to study my original takings. What had been happening to me? I had not given the Condition a single thought for weeks now, almost preferring not to know what was going on around me. Was this lethargy due to the exploration of pleasure with Katryn or was I now victim of the same lethargy I had seen grip the camp from my earliest days? Vesey changed the subject though before I had much time to consider the notion.

'So you didn't find Arthur then?'

'He's . . . gone. Geigy let him out to pursue the theory he had, seems he conned his way out, saying he had authorization . . . and there is something else going on, did you hear the gunfire earlier? Geigy says there's been some sort of bloodletting between groups of refugees, over some feud. Says they've had to put it down, to disarm those involved. I know they've taken casualties in the process, I also suspect they didn't hold back once that happened. Geigy says that three or four have been killed, it's probably more.'

I took my first gulp to steel myself for the interrogation that was sure to follow. The power of the alcohol was a shock to my system, my first taste since the dance at Freiburg, the prompted memory of which brought visions of Joyce crashing into my consciousness.

'Yup, suppose that figures. Got their own means of discipline and I guess we have to let them get on with it. It's their camp, goes with the territory.'

To my surprise there were no follow-up questions, only a sad stillness as Vesey sighed in contemplation of the bottle in his hand, topping up his glass, mine too, although I had hardly drained its contents.

'Yes, sir, this is good stuff alright, you tell your father from me.'

He smiled gently and swilled his new mouthful in one, the awkward sincerity of the gesture would have been enough to make me blush had I not still been so cold. All I could do was flinch to acknowledge the compliment. Why was he so unconcerned about what might have been a major revolt, how was it that he already seemed to know about Arthur?

'I hear you've been screwing one of the girls here, a refugee. That true?'

The little cup in my hand lifted itself to my mouth as I desperately clutched for time to think of something to say.

'I . . . I fail to see how my private matters could be any of your business.'

I stammered out the words with what I hoped sounded like indignant conviction, though the whisky hadn't yet been given enough time to fully loosen my tongue in the required manner. Vesey was unimpressed, shaking his head, speaking with a low disgusted sigh.

'Shit. You mean you have.'

He reached for my cup again, this time the refill was required and I snatched at it with gratitude. Vesey closed his eyes and looked heavenward, as if to say grace for the nourishment in our glasses. I don't know if he was genuinely trying to control himself or if this was a pretence designed to intimidate. I toyed with my whisky, struggling to resist taking one huge gulp to get me out of it all.

'You're a bit of a dark horse, aren't you, Rob? First I get one of the matrons at Gershalt complaining that you got one of her nurses pregnant and now you find yourself a new playing partner here, in this dump, of all places. They all like you where you come from, can't you control yourself, for Christ's sake?'

I felt my eyes begin to sting, the arid shame before the streaming tears of humiliation to follow. Joyce was pregnant, what a louse I was, worse than that, and everybody at Gershalt knew. Katryn – what would they think of me, for abusing her innocence? And if Vesey knew, who else knew here – Geigy, Mussorgy, the soldiers? What would they do to her? There was mayhem going on outside and here I was safely drinking with Vesey when I should have been with her, protecting her. I was a louse, yes, lowest of the low. I gulped down a punishing swill, for once I would do the right thing.

'It's not like that . . . it's different . . . I'm going to marry her.'

'Really?' The eyes opened wide.

'Katryn . . . Yes. I'm going to marry her, I'm taking her with me when I leave.'

Vesey's face turned mirthful, the corners of his mouth arching upwards despite his attempts to suppress the smile.

'And she knows this, *your fiancée*, you've asked her? Only I thought nobody understood what they say?'

Another mouthful to help rise to the bully. 'Well ss-she understands *m-me* . . .'

'Language of love, I guess, huh?'

This time he couldn't hold it any longer, and the laughter mixed with coughs as the whisky caught on his throat. His whole body seemed to bounce on his chair. I felt like a fourteen-year-old, and I had to leave. Gravity had somehow grown heavier since the start of the conversation; it was an effort to rise on my feet and I had to use the table to steady myself.

'I think you'd better sit down, Rob.'

'I'll be alright.'

'SIDDOWN!'

Vesey shouted so loud it must have been heard by the entire camp. Drunk as I was, it took time for me to realise that the sudden aggression and hostility in the voice was meant for me, even though there were only the two of us in the room. What had I done to hurt him when he had been laughing at me seconds before?

'We got a whole lot of sorting out to do here, haven't we, Rob?'

If he said so, we must have. I lowered myself back into

the chair with as much poise as I could muster, staying silent. I felt wobbly in every sense, afraid that if I started to speak I would break down. He knew about Katryn, I couldn't believe it.

Vesey studied the bottle with a look of distaste. There was only an inch or so of the rust-coloured brew left. Now he stood, turning to rummage in his case. To my dismay, he conjured up another bottle from inside. I covered the top of my glass to show I'd had enough, but he tugged it away from underneath my hand and filled it to the brim. Drink it, his eyes seemed to say, drink it if you're any kind of man. I tried to make a start.

'I told you to watch out, for Chrissakes, didn't I, Rob? Told you not to give these people the opportunity. They are the enemy, Rob, don't you know that? Didn't it . . . *for one second* . . . occur to you that the girl might have been put up to it, Rob?'

Every time he used my name I felt a sinking in my heart. His tone now was mournful, reflective; the questions needing no answer, there more to remind me of how we were once partners, me under his guidance, and how I'd now betrayed him.

'We got scientists back home, Rob, mathematicians, statisticians, they put together a theory, probability study into the likelihood of a war between us and the Soviets . . . fed in all the factors – territory, history, ambitions. Know what the probability of war is within the next three years?'

I didn't, and waited to be told. He washed his drink round his mouth and let it down gently.

'Ninety-seven per cent, Rob, ninety-seven.'

I tried to take this news that there would be another war stoically, the whisky helping cope with the immediate shock, but I could only think of life for me in more camps, and more upheaval, and of my brother being kept out in Singapore and none of us being together again for Sunday Service and how my indiscretions with Katryn had somehow contributed to this, and making love to Joyce too. Perhaps if these had been fed into the formula the score would have been higher – ninety-eight, ninety-nine, one hundred.

Vesey reached out and put his hand on top of mine although I could hardly bear to face him. It's okay, the gesture said, though I knew it wasn't. He had trusted me, or tried to, and I had let him down, forgetting where my loyalties lay.

'I think you better tell me exactly what's been going on here, Rob, everything. Think you could do that?'

He wanted it all, and I owed it to him to give him it all. He proved a patient listener as I stumbled my way through it all for the next hour. I told him how I had always harboured doubts as to the 'medical' nature of the condition, how what I had witnessed had seemed clear enough torture although I could not reconcile this with Geigy's relentless earnestness. I told him how Arthur may indeed have been right; that the answer was in the people. Could they be ghosts, no; but I'd known what he meant, the broken spirit, the listlessness, the fearfulness of the women. What could possibly have happened to them? I told him of the pressure Geigy put me under from the start, the bond he had tried to build, the flattery, calling me a 'doctor' when Arthur said he would have known we were low-level dimwits sent because we were expendable. By the same logic it was obvious that Arthur had never thought the condition was related to radiation, since if it was, the Russians would never let any western observers near the evidence. Besides, Arthur had said there would be other signs of the aftermath of an atomic weapon's use. As I spoke, I pleaded. I had never meant any harm by what I . . .

'It was a test, Rob, a test.'

Vesey stared at me, glum again. He seemed hardly drunk at all, not my whisky brother. His voice sounded deeper than ever.

'. . . to see how we would react, how seriously we would take it if we thought that they had used a bomb. Of course, they probably wanted to know what tests we would use to figure out if they had. These things, the other signs Arthur talked about, he ever tell you what they were?'

I could only shake my head.

'Think he might have let them slip to the Soviets?'

Again, I didn't know. Arthur had been let loose out there now, and the point wasn't lost on Vesey. He took a breath and let out a groan, irksome and fittingly huge, a snoring buffalo.

'Guess we got a real screw up here then, Rob, guess I've got no choice but to head back and hand responsibility for you two back to the British. Have to tell them you're both a security risk, Rob, for different reasons, of course, but both unfit for service.'

So that was it, I was a security risk – what did it mean? Dishonourable discharge, court martial, jail? The disgrace, I would never get over it, the end of my career, and my life was right there in front of me as Vesey fingered his glass. I looked to the walls over his shoulder, bulging in with each burst of wind. All my schooling, my training, to end here, what had been the point of it all? Then, the miracle, the thin light shining ahead, a way out. Vesey groaned again.

'There is . . . one way. I could keep this all quiet, Rob . . . if we could get Arthur back here before he says anything too bad.'

'Arthur won't come back. He hates Tarutz, hates A.M.U. 4, hates Americans, you.' I stammered through the list, suddenly aware that I had more in common with Arthur than I had with the supposed ally before me. Something dreadful was stirring in Tarutz, and Geigy's earlier words reverberated afresh in my mind – 'I think he should go home, Rob'. What if he was right, and Arthur was sick, how would the atmosphere affect him? But it wasn't all about just Arthur, all of us should go home.

'Then *you'll* have to go and bring him back Rob.'

'I don't understand. How?'

'I guess you'll have to think of a way, won't you?'

Vesey put the cap back on the second bottle. There wasn't much of it left.

Abstract

THE PEOPLE OF HAMELIN turned into rats and devoured first their children, then each other, the magic they had unwittingly employed turned against them to horrific effect.

This is the terrible truth about Hamelin, the truth history chose to ignore, to bury under layers of legend and lore. A truth too horrible to contemplate, too 'extraordinary' to be real.

It has suited the purpose of the historian, and the method of the weaker historian seeking easy acceptance, to blame such an outrage on an individual rather than a people. And so a solitary culprit was required, a guilty party to fit the villainous specification, someone to carry the blame for the disappearance of Hamelin's young.

The culprit was, of course, the Piper, the Pied Piper. His motive? A demonic repayment of the scorn bestowed upon him by a treacherous town council, unappreciative of the service he had provided in ridding Hamelin of its rats. The rats, could it not be argued that these are the true enigma of the tale? The weakness of the classic version of this story is the stated behaviour of these verminous animals and the change the music of the Pied Piper's flute brought about in them: first savage and ravenous, then cowed and obedient, strangely charmed. The reasons for this altered second state are never explained, yet its acceptance is crucial to the overall credibility of this interpretation of events, an acceptance that defies reason. No one man was responsible for taming such devilish creatures, nor for tempting the children to take a step out of the world, for the devilish creatures were the citizens of Hamelin and they were all guilty of this heinous crime.

Nevertheless, this paper has described a sinister mutation of man to rat; can this be offered in all seriousness as a more tenable representation of the truth, the 'ordinary' happenings that marked the termination of life within Hamelin? Could this transformation have really occurred? The answer is yes. By deed and actions, definitely; by appearance, that is to say perceived resemblance, most definitely; but by actual physical appearance, no. The transformation in question was only made real via a systematic altering of the senses for the good people of Hamelin, sharing in their final moments nightmarish hallucinations of hunger and the ultimate depravities, no longer able to maintain a grip on their sanity. The Piper, the Pied Piper, had poisoned them.

It is pertinent to return to the scene in the forest clearing outside Hamelin as the soldiers of D'Ortez' army prepare for their final feast. A scene of considerable activity; muskets and cannons greased and primed, brass rubbed down and oiled, swords flexed and polished. Although the Spaniard has not yet announced to his men that the town is to be stormed once dawn breaks, speculation has been enough to trigger the process of preparing weapons and armour for battle. It is not that it is expected that this will be a particularly testing encounter; no, the battle-hardened foot-soldiers can comfort themselves with the knowledge that Hamelin's men would offer only limited resistance.

Nevertheless, it is inevitable that some will fall during the course of the day, that some will not make it through the town walls and will be sacrificed so that their fellows pass through inside. The men that will survive, and have survived the war's previous engagements, do so through a combination of luck and applied concentration. It is the latter that adds an urgency to the men's labour as the blades are sharpened.

The Piper is also amongst them. He and his aides have busied themselves with the preparation of the feast – cured hides of pork have simmered in pots of wheat-beer stew as the afternoon light fades, vegetable roots chopped and added to the meaty broth. The odours that have roused the bellies of the fighting men include smells new to them; the mysterious Piper has added ingredients that have travelled with him from the east – saffron, cumin and cardamom seeds that have given an exotic colour to the otherwise staple European fare.

However, as the Piper moves to stir one pot after the other, he ensures that one flavour will dominate all. Tonight, all dishes will share one common ingredient – rye, a special kind of rye.

Rye has declined in importance as a crop over the centuries, particularly in western Europe where today its main uses are as animal feedstock or in the production of certain alcohols. It is only in the poorer east where it retains some of its former significance. Rye, *Secale cereale* in its basic form, was of fundamental significance in the development of the European agricultural economy from the Middle Ages onwards, treasured for its ability to thrive on the most unpromising and infertile of soils and to withstand the harshest winters the Northern Steppes could inflict upon it; the harvest of the peasant. Although the exact progenitor of this vegetation is not known, it is widely recognised that this is likely to be *Secale fragile*, itself first cultivated in western Asia. However, no traces of cultivated rye have ever been found in early Egyptian monuments and likewise ancient writings do not refer to it, a sign that perhaps the famed mystics of those times intuitively knew that here was a harvest of the angry gods and had it banned from the Pharoah's lands. With its winterhardiness this crop found its true home when it first travelled north, where it was welcomed without question or suspicion, spreading like a virus until its name occurred in all European languages, assimilating itself by stealth into the land-based culture of our ancestors.

In comparison to other cereals, rye has several extraordinary botanical characteristics. It has seven chromosomes in the *haploid* stage, and there is no evidence of a *polypoid* series which is an attribute of wheat and other small-grained flora. Because of the height attained by its stems in the course of a summer (seven to eight feet), harvesting of the yield takes place with difficulty and has always involved hard labour. Yet left to grow wild, rye has a tendency to mutate into other sub-species of the parent growth (*Dakold, Raritan, Aland, Rosen* and *Imperial* are just some of the types common to the fields of Russia), not all of which will produce an edible gathering. In addition, and most dangerous of all, rye can be prone to certain fungal infections of the ovary stem, a condition which can lead to disastrous consequences for those with the misfortune to consume the contaminated grains.

The process of infection is known as ergot, and can occur before and after harvesting, particularly in damp, closed environments. In this situation the grain kernel is attacked by the fungus *Claviceps purpurea* and produces a bluish-brown body called a sclerotium. Ergot sclerotia contains pharmaceutical compounds such as *ergosterol, ergotoxin, ergotamine, ergokim* and *ergosterine*, and the balance and composition of these toxins is itself dependent on the strain of rye which is housing the primary infection. It is known that these compounds can alter the brain's delicate neuro-chemical balance once in the bloodstream, and can effect powerful hallucinogenic properties within the mind of the afflicted, or in layman's terms, unhinge the senses. Whilst there are other substances which are noted for their similar potential – lysergic acids, ethyl-aspartomine-rich organic growths such as certain mushrooms and moulds, the body of evidence against ergotism suggests that it is capable of invoking hallucinations of a uniquely vivid and virulent nature. It is this paper's contention that ergotism is the connecting factor behind the 'mysteries' which have previously been explored in these pages; and those of deserted vessels in medieval marine folklore, that of the apparent self-destruction of mercenary armies

271

in the plague years, and that of the bewitching legend of the Pied Piper and the town of Hamelin.

If ergotism was the root of the phantoms which came to haunt those ill-fated sailors, soldiers and good citizens of Hamelin described earlier in these pages, how can it be claimed that it was also the cause of these victims sharing the *same* illusion at the time of their demise? Why, for example, would Hamelin's last inhabitants *all* dream of rats simultaneously? Can hysteria ever be claimed to behave in such a uniform fashion?

The answers to these questions are to be found in the nature of the times these incidents occurred, extraordinary times. Consider a crew aboard their medieval ship, stacked high atop one another on a leaky craft amid an endless expanse of ocean. For them, the longer the voyage lasted the more their thoughts would come to be dominated by the pressing concerns of their immediate surroundings; fears for their safety, petty jealousies over rations and privileges, the significance of the omens assailing the ship. Memories of land would be left further behind, the culture they were prisoners to would prove a fertile breeding ground for paranoia even before the poisons breeding below set to work on their minds. Whilst the enclosed physical environment would in some ways limit the canvas of their imaginations, the tales swapped between them as night fell would grow more important and ever more dangerous, for once planted in their sub-conscious these stories can never be exorcised. They will wait, like the rye below, for the moment to come when they can make themselves real, a prophesy that can only be fulfilled.

* * *

Meanwhile the fires crackle at D'Ortez' camp as the Piper plays in celebration. His army is a powder keg, waiting for a single spark to explode, struggling to contain the devils within. The Piper dances round each blaze, leading the eunuchs in a trail behind him, the notes from his instrument gaining in urgency and volume as the dance becomes more charged. His steps bring him closer to the group surrounding D'Ortez. He pretends not to notice that here they have shown little appetite for their banquet, gravy and beer left half-touched.

'Be away with you!' D'Ortez snaps, trying to raise himself to within punching distance of the infuriating minstrel. He does not make it, falling instead on his backside to the open amusement of some. The rage in him is growing; what is wrong with me? D'Ortez looks to his glass, he is losing control of his limbs as if drunk, yet he knows he has imbibed little of the sour brew. He looks to his men, many of whom have joined the Piper's tail, forming a snaking procession through camp. What is this, why do they move so strangely? The revelry is growing ever more possessed.

The music gains a discordant, reedy timbre as the manic twists and jerks of the chain dance against it. D'Ortez watches his legs twitch in reluctant obedience to its demands. Is it being played now to taunt them? The taste of the vile stew rises up in his throat as he retches, spitting onto his hands. The Piper is watching, the men have formed one long circle filing round and round him. When the two exchange glances the understanding is instant.

D'Ortez tries to rise again, to warn his men, but is losing control of his mind as well as body. He blinks disbelievingly; the Piper's head is transforming itself into that of a serpent, he has become a devil. D'Ortez claws his eyes in frustration.

'POISON! Seize him, he has poisoned us!'

But the men are too volatile to pause to consider him, hearing only the word 'poison' as the fury erupts. Poisoned, we are poisoned! Shots ring out, screams and roars, explosions as the cannon fuses burn to their ends and their cargo rips through the crowd. The division of the force which has been threatened for so long becomes immediate. Men throw themselves onto fires believing they are drowning, others slit their own throats in their thirst for blood. The devils have taken over, the devils from within.

And then there are the lost souls of Hamelin, with their rats, real and imagined, and their taste of the Piper's poison.

This paper calls for a full investigation into the core theory presented here – that ergotism was the cause of the self-slaughter that took the town. This paper must plead that the academic world, east and west, unites and makes this task a priority. *This theory must be proved*, governments must be made to understand. The materials and evidence is with us now, in the land, in the people. They must be found and examined with *great urgency*. This is *too important a task to be ignored*, now that the truth behind the fall of Hamelin is known we must satisfy ourselves that ergotism was the agent of its destruction. For if no catalyst can be found then those ordinary men *did* turn into rats and those rats *are still inside us*, and will always betray us. Waiting inside us all.

T HE MEMORIES of the final happenings of it all are the ones which are also the most distant. My mind's storage system has overruled the chronological order of events for its own purposes so that the recollection of leaving Tarutz is harder to evoke, as if it is further back in time than that of actually arriving. I remember being passed through the gates quickly, almost ejected from camp, no one showing the customary interest in the minutiae of my authorization papers. A truck was waiting, engine revving biliously, belching out clouds of ash-ridden fumes as it chewed on the lumpy petrol, a digestion forced by the driver's heavy boot's periodic flattening of the accelerator. I was pushed into the driver's cabin and we took off immediately, lurching over the cattle grid that formed the last ring of defence at the Tarutz complex. This was it, after almost six months I was out, even if I couldn't quite take it all in.

Somewhere down the line I would have to negotiate another lift going west. Vesey had assured me that the traffic flow to Berlin would be plentiful and that my papers granted me the authority to commandeer any appropriate transport – fine in principle if I could make myself understood by the Russian military rabble whose duty it would be to carry me. These difficulties were ahead though, this first lift would take me due south, to Olesnica, a drive on these broken roads of over seven hours. I could worry about the next stage once we got there. Of course Arthur lay at the end of the whole journey, I would save my anxieties about that until last.

Too uncomfortable ever to sleep, too tired and hungover ever to concentrate, the countryside soon merged into the same endless conveyor belt of fields and charred buildings, the procession occasionally punctuated by a flashing sight of some ruined country hamlet, each complete with its assortment of men and women scrambling amongst the debris. I thought of Katryn and wondered if she was missing me, had she feared the worst when I had suddenly vanished? There was no need for her to feel abandoned, I thought back to what I had said to Vesey and how he had derided me. Then I would see the head of a woman approaching, wrapped in a headscarf like hers and my heart would rise in hope that it *was* her and fall in disappointment and relief that it wasn't. I realised that I couldn't live without her, I'd meant every word. I had to get back, and I willed the roadside to pass by faster.

Only one colour had been added to the palette since my first trip out all those months ago – brown, or rather a sepia – a tint of brown that could mean either mud or blood sitting on the icy grey landscape of the previous winter. Spring's advance was tentative. The peasants still wore black and the soldiers were everywhere, especially in these initial stages of the trip. Would the new war be fought here, was that why they were amassing? If it was then I realised I would have to desert, this land couldn't be worth fighting for.

My travel documentation had been organised by Vesey, who didn't go through Geigy but through some contact he had with the military command at Tarutz, one he never explained. Could the same individual or office have been the source of his information on my activities with Katryn? The thought turned over in my mind, I couldn't imagine who it would have been. As the journey grew longer it became clear to me that this didn't really matter; Vesey had deliberately shown the strength of his hand, I now knew the score and the game plan I was tied into. It seemed right then that the simplicity and understanding I had craved had been delivered, albeit from an unlikely source. I had transgressed and had the opportunity to atone for that by fetching Arthur. Once he was back, and with Tarutz being run down, we would probably both be transferred back to British command, leaving someone else to solve the mystery of the condition. Our usefulness had obviously expired, and soon I could put the whole sorry episode behind me. That at least was what the pragmatist in me was urging. I have to say, ladies and gentlemen, that young as I was there was another voice crying to be heard, that of the hero, still troubled by the sufferings of those afflicted by the condition who had fed me and taken me to their hearts, still imagining that I was their champion, and still infatuated with Katryn. I sat throughout the journey, twenty-two hours in its various stages, the two voices in constant conflict, unaware that events would prove both voices naive and hopelessly irrelevant.

When Arthur had left, it had been with Geigy's consent, and it was he who had set up Arthur's trip along the same route and method, no car having been issued. All that was known was that Arthur had been heading south-east, back towards Lower Saxony, in search of the River Treuwe he had mentioned in his impassioned speech. What he planned to do once he had arrived was a mystery, as was how he planned to survive. Although Arthur was a wealthy man, and had paid cash for the artefacts and documents he had bought in Berlin, that stock of money had to be finite and he would not have been able to replenish it at Gershalt and certainly not at Tarutz. However, it was unlikely he would view this as a problem, this was a concept for logical minds when his was fixated, frayed. I suspected part of the urgency behind my retrieval mission was to find him before he starved or died of exposure, either of which could have led to embarrassing questions for A.M.U. 4. The 'River Treuwe' was where I was headed then, back into Germany but still in the Russian zone.

Finding Arthur out there turned out to be almost easier than finding him within camp. He had been arrested.

It had been after my third gruelling transition from one carrier to another, somewhere around the nominal Polish-German border, that our paths crossed. A checkpoint on the Breslaw-Dresden road, itself choked with the last slow dregs of the refugee tide to the west; the scene of tearful mothers, crying children and pleading grandmothers the permanent backdrop to a blighted tract. Early afternoon and the Red Army guard scrutinises my pass, ignoring the voices crowding around us.

'*Amerikan?*'

Does it matter that I am British, should I point out this subtle difference or is its relevance limited in this hole in time and geography? We are standing outside what seemed to be an old-fashioned hostel or staging post, a nondescript block with boarded windows by the side of the road.

'*Amerikan?*' he repeats, pointing to some section of the document. I nod. Yes, American, will this help me be on my way? My papers were in Russian and should have explained the nature of my mission. Arthur's name was in there too. Normally, I would have to wait as verification was sought via radio or telephone contact that this was approved at the appropriate levels, a process that had taken three hours at the last stop. My admission saw me led inside the command post, and I presumed it would be to sit out the same pained confirmation procedure. Instead, my hosts took me to a room on the upper storey. It was locked and bolted although it had no guard duty outside.

Arthur might have been aggrieved to learn his captors thought him an American, it crossed my mind to tell him on the way back. But as the light followed us into the room it became apparent that he was in no state to appreciate any kind of joke. He sat on the floor in a corner, arms wrapped tightly around his knees, face hidden underneath. There was a bed and a chair to the wall, both ignored, as were we when we entered. The Russian to my side seemed eager that I move forward and introduce myself, my impression was that Arthur was being held not because of any suspicion that he had been endeavouring some great mischief, but because they simply didn't know what to do with him. The door behind was left open and the relief felt now someone had arrived to take the mysterious 'American' away was almost tangible.

'Arthur? Arthur, are you asleep?'

My recollection is that it took some time for Arthur to respond, so deep was his withdrawal into himself. He was unshaven, hair unkempt, thinning ever more rapidly. When had he last eaten? I motioned a scooping movement to the mouth at the soldier. He shrugged and disappeared behind me and I went over to settle beside Arthur.

'I'm not going back.'

I'm not sure if these were the exact words with which he broke the silence, if not, they were to this effect. He still kept his head covered, still shut out the world that would hurt him, behind his own makeshift filter.

'It will be alright, Arthur, I promise. No one is going to . . .'

I couldn't think how to continue, 'No one is going to' what, laugh? Vesey probably would. Discipline him? I couldn't be sure. Stop his investigation into the 'ghosts' at the camp? They almost certainly would. I didn't know any of the plans for Arthur once I delivered him. I let the moment drift and rested my hand on his shoulder, a gesture of support that didn't promise anything.

'Did you see them all outside?' he asked, I didn't know who he meant.

'See who?'

'The rats . . . thousands of them.'

I took him literally, I hadn't seen any and looked for

evidence on the floor. Arthur must have sensed my lack of insight and continued.

'I came to look for the Pied Piper and all I found was the rats. Rats in all of us ... taking over, following the food trail ... It's always been the same, Robert ... there is no hope.'

None of this made any sense, yet when he had addressed me personally he had finally looked up, his choice of words sending a chill through to my heart which I can still feel to this day. Again, I was lost for anything to say, then the food arrived and I busied myself with efforts to get him to eat – stale bread and cold soup. Arthur showed no interest.

'We have to go back, Arthur.'

'When people – any people – have lost everything, all that is left is instinct. That's why we become rats. I had a home, a family ... and now there is nothing. People outside, what have they seen? The end of their countries, homes, bloodlines disappear, their lives left completely without purpose. Can you imagine what it is like to lose everything?'

'Arthur, we have to go back.'

He shook his head. 'Why?'

'To sort it all out.'

His pale face was expressionless. 'Sort out what? They've started, haven't they?'

'Who, Arthur? Started what?'

'Killing each other. I thought they needed a catalyst but I was wrong. That's all this experiment shows; it doesn't take an agent to turn us into rats, it's there all the time, we are waiting to fight amongst ourselves all the time.'

Arthur continued to spill out his words with lessening energy until they became inaudible. None made particular sense to me, but then I was concentrating solely on humouring him and trying to bring him to his feet.

'And is this part of the condition, Arthur?'

I hadn't meant the question as anything other than a further attempt to keep him talking before he withdrew again into his shell. I wasn't even looking at him when I said it and was startled when he grabbed my arm.

'Yes! Yes, you *do* understand, don't you, Robert! Part of the condition, the *final* part of the condition . . . turning on ourselves . . . the inevitable last stage . . . the slaughter!'

He covered me in spittle as he pulled me closer. I tried not to show it but he was frightening me. I had never seen anyone break down like this and didn't know how to react, part of me wanting to act like a medic, the rest cringing at the unseemliness of his behaviour.

And yet Arthur was once more displaying his uncanny talent; however much I tried to shut myself off from it I knew that there might be an appalling substance in this, a terrible truth amongst the ravings. I wondered how much of the disturbance at Tarutz he had witnessed on the day he had left. Surely it had begun after he had gone? I thought of the refugees, my refugees, were they capable of slaughter? I struggled to picture Katryn's face in my mind but could only think of that first occasion when I had found her, how they had gathered around her, ready to cleanse themselves of her infected presence. Where might it have ended if I had not arrived then? Panic seized my heart.

'Arthur, I've got to get back . . . immediately. I think one of my patients is in danger.'

He did not respond other than to nod as if he already knew this. I had to make him move and so I tried a different tactic, this time rooted in desperation.

'Please, Arthur. I'll be in trouble if I don't bring you back.'

'Do you mean you are in trouble?'

I thought about a response to suit the situation and in that instant it all seemed to catch up with me; the absurdity of it all, the fatigue I felt as a result of travel and trying to make myself understood in every language I could employ, and the poison in Vesey's whisky. I tried to speak but the words hung impotently in my throat. My turn to crack up, to hide my streaming eyes in shame. Now I felt Arthur's hand on my shoulder and heard his voice replace my own.

'Then we'll go, Robert. Then we shall go.'

Back through the gates for a second and final time. We had made the return trip in just over twenty-four hours via just two stop-off points, picking up a lift at the latter from a Russian truck whose driver was under instruction to take us all the way to Tarutz and sign us off to the care of the military HQ inside. Thus it was that Arthur and I were taken right through the gates and up to the ruin itself, not exactly handcuffed like criminals, but chaperoned all the same until we were given permission to depart from there to the huts, presumably once a runner had been sent to Vesey. I have to suspect that my whole excursion had been orchestrated under the watchful eye of the Russian secret service. There had to have been some magic ingredient in the pass papers I had been issued with upon leaving, some powerful concession that Vesey had extracted, for every Soviet officer who read them reacted with blushing politeness and an urgent desire to remove myself and Arthur from their patch with a haste and expediency that left one breathless.

Arthur had kept quiet during the journey, refusing any offer of food, occasionally sipping water, declining to go to the toilet. This thin man had the endurance of a camel. We walked through the fading light back toward the familiar cabins that had housed us during winter, Arthur slow and weary, stiff from the cramped journey. My thought was to get him back to our cabin and settle him there for the night, to put off any attempt by Vesey to interrogate until the morning, it was the least I could do for Arthur. It wasn't to be enough.

There was no one in our hut, the fear that it might have been reallocated had come to me as I began to notice the rate of change within camp – a much more obvious military presence, guns pointed and permanently at the ready, the number of soldiers out on duty, clearings emerging in the refugee allotments – and realised that we had been away for almost five days. Still, our lodgings remained unaltered, even down to the gas burners that had been set up all those months ago. I kept up a chatty commentary to Arthur, as I had done since finding him, and explained that I was off to tell Vesey and Geigy we were back. I left him sitting on the end of the bed, staring into space. It was hard not to be irritated by the lack of response and I began to yearn for a return of the old Arthur. I didn't say goodbye.

I remember being tired, desperately tired. I must have been, the sense of disorientation that now overcame me was acute, and I found myself toiling to find my way through the small network of huts to Vesey's shelter. My feet led me to the cabin where I thought I had been before, but I could hear voices inside, laughing, cajoling, guffawing; soldiers' voices surely. I loitered outside, trying to get a register of the language. It was initially impenetrable, had to be Russian. Then my ear grew more accustomed to the sound and I recognised it as English, heavily-accented, American voices. I knocked and entered.

There were three of them inside, only one of whom I recognised. The mood was obviously relaxed, Vesey holding court, standing over his companions. I don't know how dishevelled I must have appeared after all my travels, but I could almost feel Vesey's good humour evaporate as he looked to me with some kind of unease.

'Rob, welcome back. Let me introduce you to the guys.'

I instantly regretted going in, what had I been trying to achieve? I was so drained I could hardly keep my eyes open and now I would have to think up some chat or small talk, justify my existence to these strangers.

'Rob – Morris Brewer, David Greenbaum. Arrived just after you left. Morris is a medic like yourself, University of Minnesota, Dave is a statistician, medical statistician. This is Robert Watt, guys, whose notes you've been using.'

Notes? What had they been using my notes for, a testimony of my incompetence? Again, I cursed myself for going inside, I didn't have the strength for another defence.

Brewer was a chunky, sandy-haired chap who wore rimless glasses. A few inches shorter than Vesey, maybe about thirty-five. His grin had the same set of perfect teeth that seemed to be standard issue for all Americans. Greenbaum was thinner, had a darker complexion and jet black hair but with a bald, almost polished-looking, strip on top. He smoked a pipe and was the cooler of the two, perhaps because he was younger, late twenties, closer to me in age. I shook hands with both. Brewer offered me his chair.

'You must be whacked. I hear you would have had quite a journey.' I nodded and sat. The paranoia in my mind was raging; so Vesey had told them about my trip. How had he explained its necessity, how much did these two know?

'Rob, the boys here have been working on a new theory on the condition. Pretty exciting – want to hear about it?'

Vesey gestured for the others to take over. Brewer spoke first.

'We had to look at the population, Rob, the universe of source carriers and the infected. Obviously they are in a discrete group about which nobody knows too much. The hunch was, and it was Dave's hunch, that before they came to be here this was a fairly isolated bunch of people – the language and culture they have is a demonstration of this. So if the population is discrete and isolated, Dave guessed that there would be a fair amount of inter-breeding within family groups, that possibly what we might have is a hereditary condition, or at least part of the problem might be inherited through bloodlines, making some individuals more susceptible to the faciitis invasion.'

And then the other one took over, morose and monotone, explaining how my notes with their recording of family groups had helped. Thanks to my work Brewer had calculated that those in certain clans were eight to nine times more likely to succumb to the condition. He beamed as he relayed this, genuinely excited, what a case study this would make. What we had of course, said Greenbaum, was a genetic disorder. There would be other reasons why it was now occurring on such a large scale, but perhaps the family trees he and his colleague were constructing would highlight another related factor in this regard.

A genetic disorder, of course; congratulations, case solved. My paranoia and exhaustion wouldn't permit me to display any more enthusiasm. I noticed Vesey avoided my eye.

'And have you informed Dr Geigy of this development? What does he say?'

The two arrivals could not answer, I don't think they even knew who I was referring to. Vesey gave a dismissive wave of his hand.

'Look, why don't you go get some rest, Rob? Things have been a little different here since you've been away, a little rough, tell you and Arthur about it tomorrow. You should really get your head down until it's light, might get lively out there tonight.'

'Lively?'

'Dangerous. Our refugees are getting a little stir-crazy, having a go at each other. Russians been hard-put keeping a lid on it. Had ten of these sonofabitches killed in two days, stabbed, by their own kind, like they didn't have enough to worry about.'

'And what will we do about it?'

'Us? It's the Russians' call, Rob. No point in us getting involved.'

Vesey looked at me with a hint of suppressed pain, as if my naive questioning was causing a bigger problem than mere embarrassment. Was this lack of concern a front necessitated by the presence of the new arrivals? How could they discuss the refugees' welfare with such interest when it related to the condition and then have such a shocking indifference when they were dying by other means?

'You're tired, Rob, have some sleep. We'll talk in the morning.'

He had walked over and practically lifted me out of my chair, a hardly subtle hint for me to leave, one that I took. Perhaps he was worried that I would mention Katryn. From where I stood outside Vesey's cabin her own shack was five minutes' walk. The shame and disgrace I had felt when Vesey's knowledge of the affair was revealed was still fresh inside, but once more my feet led me away from the sensible path and back toward the refugee sector. I had to see her, it had been days and I had to show her she had not been deserted. I wanted to rest for a moment in her arms, to hear her breathing, smell her hair. I wanted, ladies and gentlemen, to propose to her.

It was dark and the only light was that given by the evening fires that I assumed were cooking that night's dinners. This should also have been a route I was familiar with yet it wasn't somehow. I blamed my fatigue. Yet things were undeniably different; so many more fires than previously, but nobody about to tend them. Spaces appeared between settlements where once they had been on top of each other, burned out, what had been going on? The shouting had begun, I could hear a growing com- motion by the eastern perimeter. A shrill wail reached my ears, this was a new sound, the whistles of charging

Russian soldiers, storming into the heart of the ramshackle hub of tents over there. I would have to find Katryn and take her back to my hut; Vesey was right, it wasn't safe out here. Where was everyone, why was no one in this section of camp? And then, sickeningly, right in front of me, a flat patch of mud and animal carcasses where Katryn should have been waiting. My God, I thought, she's died. They have made her pay, pay for her beauty, pay for her gift of love.

A burst of gunfire rang out, accompanied by hysterical shouting and screaming. The view to the east now had an orange glow as a new set of flames began to dance in the wind. This was no isolated case of inmates going 'stir-crazy'; the entire camp was falling into anarchy.

I staggered across to the other side, heavy-going through the mud underfoot. Over by the bushes, a crowd of peasants was being herded together by the guards, encouraged by a heavy boot or rifle butt whenever appropriate, which seemed to be most of the time. I yearned for the courage to intervene; the victims were unarmed and offered no resistance, hands held over their heads in surrender. Another gun-shot rang out as I contemplated the situation, and a soldier was suddenly dragged out from the compound by two colleagues. He was obviously seriously wounded. I found myself moving to him, but my attempt to administer instant treatment did not progress far, his colleagues practically fighting me back.

'Doctor!' I shouted, but they still pushed me away, and made to carry their comrade up the path to the ruin.

'*Docktor*! *Docktor*!' My words were being mimicked by the crowd under guard. I looked and saw for the first time that many of these were bloodstained too, leaning forward to offer their wounds despite the brutal attentions of the soldiers ringing them. I scanned through the sea of faces in the dark.

'Katryn? Katryn?'

There was no sign of her. I moved closer, trying to peer through the gathering.

'*Katryn, Ja. Ja, Katryn, Docktor*!' An elderly woman pushed her way toward me, holding out a bloodied stump of a hand. It had probably been stamped on, brittle bones in the fingers snapped like twigs under a Russian or refugee boot. The pain had made her voice feeble.

'Katryn, *wer*?' Where is she?

She nodded back, the hand raised imploringly to my face. '*Katryn, ja.*'

'*Wer*?'

'*Amerika, ja.*'

A nonsense answer from the hag. I turned in disappointment. More wounded were being helped to the ruin, which I realised was being used as an emergency medical centre. Could Katryn be in there, as prisoner or patient? Had she been taken somewhere because of me? Geigy would know, it was him I would have to see.

I sped up the path, overtaking the growing trail of casualties in transit. At the ruin, queues had formed on the steps, separated into soldiers and refugees. There were about thirty in all, with the former the apparent priority. Inside, a makeshift operating theatre had been thrown together in the main administration room, the ceiling lights looking down onto a bizarre scene of injured patients waiting for attention, lying on desk-tops. Dr Mussorgy stood in the midst of it all, bloodied white coat and stethoscope, a knife in each hand. He ignored me as I entered, absorbed in the damage to his patient's gut, rummaging in the unfortunate man's bowel as his assistant clutched an ether-soaked cloth to his mouth and held him down. Why were these two working alone, where was Geigy?

'Dr Geigy? *Wer?* Igor?'

I had to walk right up to him to gain his attention. I had assumed he would be pleased to see me, happy at the prospect of help from another medic. Mussorgy, however, scarcely acknowledged my presence. He looked over my shoulder as if to check my voice hadn't been thrown by someone else behind me and I was merely a ventriloquist's dummy. He stared at me with an intense disgust I found puzzling. What had I done to offend him? Was it this interruption, or did his grievance date back to earlier encounters? Perhaps he was thinking of my tularaemia theory. I realised I didn't care, I had other problems more worthy of consideration. Why couldn't he just tell me?

'Dr Geigy?' I repeated

'Gone,' he replied.

'Gone? Where?'

I had never heard Mussorgy speak English and wondered if I had misheard; had he coughed, or said something in Russian which sounded similar?

He saw my surprise and still glowered.

'Gone away, you little bastard. Gulag, prison camp. What does it matter to you?'

I blinked, was this really Mussorgy speaking or had I begun to hallucinate?

'I'm sorry, I don't understand.'

'KGB took him. Someone said he was too friendly with the British – *too friendly*. You wonder why I choose not to speak your language? You think I stupid as you? I warn Igor, never trust the British. He says he can, and then you betray him. Get out.'

He pointed at me with a bloody scalpel, cutting the air between us and motioning to the door. Was this really happening? Yes, this was no dream, Mussorgy's words drifted in and out in terms of clarity but I knew what I was hearing, and what the accusation was. The shock made me reel, I felt ready to faint.

'No . . . not me . . . I didn't . . .'

Two orderlies stepped in behind me. I stopped, half expecting them to join the debate, revealing a previously hidden command of my language. When I turned back Mussorgy's head was down over the patient again. The communication was over, he wouldn't speak English again with other witnesses in the room, no matter how much I pleaded my innocence. I wanted to tell him I had never discussed Geigy with anyone, not even Arthur. Then I suddenly remembered that night with Vesey, my confession, and I wanted the earth to rise up and swallow me.

I cannot remember how long it took me to reach Vesey's hut from the ruin. I know I would have been in a rush but fatigue and confusion would have slowed me, together with the traffic heading in the opposite direction. There was still no sign of Katryn.

It must have been the early hours of the morning by then but the lights in the cabin were still on. I didn't knock, walking in unannounced, too preoccupied to observe the usual niceties. Vesey stood over a trunk, his two new arrivals hurriedly sorting report papers into different piles.

'Rob, back again! Good, I was going to have to get you and Arthur. A soldier wake you up?'

'Geigy's gone. Did you have anything to do with it?'

Vesey's expression quickly turned to a familiar one of frustration, eyes closing in defence, his lower lids rising up like parts of a drawbridge.

'This is not the time, Rob, we got one hour to clear out of here. Russians are closing the camp, some mighty shit going on tonight. Looks like the whole place is going up. Listen, we'll have to take what's important, work fast –'

'I think it is the time to ask, I'd like to know if I can save him.'

He screwed his face tight and took a deep breath, wanting to show the mighty depth of his restraint. 'Boys, do you think you could . . .'

He didn't need to continue; Brewer and Greenbaum were already on their way out. He shrugged apologetically. They left in silence, Brewer actually waved to me.

Vesey watched the door close, then a growling sigh. 'So you want to *save* him. Well, that's admirable, Rob. That your British sense of fair play? What were you doing looking for him this time of night anyway?'

'I . . .' I paused. What should I say to this? I decided I had nothing to feel guilty for, my motives had been pure. 'I was looking for Katryn. I thought he might have been treating her . . . or known where she was.'

'Kathleen?'

'Katryn . . . the . . . the girl.'

He actually smiled, the same smile he had used against Arthur at the calamitous briefing. 'The girl . . . of course.

Well, I can save you the trouble of another search . . . she's gone too, Rob, went three days ago.'

'What have you done to her!'

He shook his head at my histrionics. 'I didn't . . . do . . . anything to her. I gave her a pass to leave here and apply for entry to the United States. Her and her husband. Seemed glad to get it . . .'

I was lost for something to say, wanting to believe it wasn't true but knowing just from the way he had said it that it was, just like Mussorgy those minutes before.

'You are a bastard.'

My mumbled insult was never likely to wound. Vesey was neither apologetic nor angry. 'Listen, Rob, I did you the biggest favour anyone's going to do for you in your entire damn life.'

'Where is she?'

'The *second* time I've done you a favour.'

'*Where is she?*'

I screamed out the words. Vesey waited for the quiet to return, arms folded. 'Take what's important, so that we can work on this on the other side, otherwise we'll let these bastards off the hook. Now get packing, Rob, for Chrissake!'

I couldn't bear the thought of leaving until I found her, yet I'd already covered most of the camp. One hour, what else could I do?

It had started to rain and I wondered where she was at that moment, was she under cover, warm and secure? Could she really be married? I would go back and ask the old woman who had known she had left for America, try and discover her surname – I would need that in any future search. I would have to move fast. After so many days and nights killing time there now suddenly wasn't enough. And then another thought – before I could set off I would have to warn Arthur that we were on the move again. I hoped he would be compliant and not waste precious moments with more obtuse questions.

Arthur had left the door open, an inch or two ajar. It was unusual for him to be able to sleep with the draught, or the noise that had enveloped the camp that night. I thought how he must have been tired; it was still only three hours or so since we had arrived back. I climbed the steps and went in, closing the door quietly behind me. He wasn't in his bed.

I will always remember looking up to his head first; one might think the eye would be drawn to the dangling feet, like in a film, where the camera lingers and then pans upward. No, I looked to his head, limp but at a taut angle to the cord tying the neck to the rafters in the ceiling. Arthur, is this what I brought you back for?

Oh Arthur, Jesus Christ, no.

I suppose Arthur was just doing what he'd told Geigy he'd do; he went to meet his wife and child.

I had minutes to clear out our belongings. His manuscript had been worked on that night and had been left with my name on it. It was the only thing I took.

I would later pass it on to his brother in a box marked for England. I couldn't read it, not then, although Vesey did, furious that I had not lifted something of more 'importance'. How wrong he was.

The manuscript still had my name on it after all those

years and that was how it finally caught up with me again.

Reading it, I find myself wondering which of the Hamelin characters he portrayed he identified with the most. Was it Mayor Ebber with his lofty aspirations for his fellow citizens, or the Priest Seicle, sacrificing himself in a desperate attempt to regain his faith? Might it have been Deputy Mannau with his need to be loved by those who did not understand him? The answer is, of course, all of them. Even D'Ortez and the Piper – creations, and prisoners, of their times. I think that Arthur recognised they were all in him, together with the rats; an inescapable part of the condition.

We left Poland two days after the body was taken down and then, after three months of doing nothing in particular in Berlin, I was back home in Scotland, ready to complete my registration and look for my first job. My hope was to leave all of this behind, but I took it with me, and have carried it for the rest of my life.

I became a GP, but never the doctor I could have been, or indeed the man I wanted to be. Is it pathetic to blame these events for that? I married within seven months of returning; once one has known intimacy with a woman it is hard to surrender to a life without it, a selfish reason to marry, I know. The loveless state of my marriage has been my fault and I take full blame, it is I who imposed this situation on those who deserved better from me.

There are other faults I cannot forgive myself for, now so painfully clear in hindsight. Arthur was sick, suffering a profound depression, he needed help. How was I to know? I was only a doctor. Geigy knew, an honest man who did his best to find a way past my ignorance and appeal to my better judgement. Thanks to my ineptitude and cowardice he found himself deported, victim of a needless purge, ending his days in the same Gulag as the refugees whose revolt booked them a journey back east and caused a premature end to the investigation. Sometimes his death hurts the worst.

Joyce? Poor Joyce, I hid myself from her with the same passion that I chased Katryn. And where is Katryn now? Perhaps she did make it to the United States, perhaps she was more shrewd than I would have taken her for, perhaps I was, after all, her ticket to America. And over there, somewhere, is Vesey if he is still alive. I tried to trace him. What I was looking to gain I do not know – absolution? The trail proved cold, the CIA are not in the habit of passing on details of former operatives. Fifteen years ago I tried contacting Morris Brewer, through the University of Minnesota. He had died though, cancer, 1971. There is no one left to try.

My speech must conclude then, I have already taken up too much of your time and I must apologise for leaving so much unresolved. The 'condition'? My thoughts on this mystery have changed so many times over the years. Sometimes I was sure that it was indeed the inherited genetic disorder that Vesey's Americans had diagnosed, sometimes that it was the test Vesey thought the Russians had set the Allied medical and intelligence bodies and sometimes I have returned to my very first thoughts, those of systematic torture and abuse of the wretched Tarutz inhabitants. But I understand now that we see what we *expect* to see, what we have been *prepared* to see. I was a cold, lonely and frightened young man when I was led into those cells and it affected what I saw as much as Vesey's Cold War obsessions affected what *he* saw. We see what we want to see. I think of Arthur finding traces of Hamelin in every relic and manuscript he could buy, fake or otherwise.

Yes, the answer was and is in the people, yet no-one was equipped in any way objectively to consider and define something of the complexity we faced. 'Condition Six' was more profound than any except Arthur realised, and he killed himself once he recognised its poison. The poison in all of us.